PRAISE FOR

THE
CAVE

more . . .

THE CAVE

ANNE MCLEAN MATTHEWS

WARNER BOOKS

A Time Warner Company

WARNER BOOKS EDITION

Copyright © 1997 by Walker & Collier, Inc.
All rights reserved.

Cover design and art by Tony Greco

Warner Books, Inc.
1271 Avenue of the Americas
New York, NY 10020

Visit our Web site at
http://warnerbooks.com

W A Time Warner Company

Printed in the United States of America

Originally published in hardcover by Warner Books.
First Printed in Paperback: April, 1998

10 9 8 7 6 5 4 3 2 1

My Prayer

My cave, O God, your gift thank you.

I remember each one you give me as a delicate meat.

I am become as Job my heart is so sore.

Lift my burden God.

This is My Prayer.

THE
CAVE

CHAPTER ONE

Mother Death

Helen Myrer's heels rattling on the floor reminded her of guns in battle. As she hurried along, she found herself almost sickened by the stale, wax-tainted air of the Capitol building, aware that she was late, aware that everything she did on this day mattered. Once she entered that committee room, even the slightest error would be disastrous.

Today she might well see the destruction of all that she had worked for, all that she cared about. The Subcommittee on Health Services was considering the worst cuts in mental health support in the history of New York State. If they passed, she would be converted from the head of one of the world's great mental health systems into a demolition expert. But she would not go gentle. The report in her briefcase—the last of ten she had presented to these twelve increasingly unresponsive and hostile politicians—showed the devastating cruelty of the planned cuts, demonstrated their brutal consequences.

A lifetime of work with the mentally ill, first as a clinical psychologist and more recently in administration, had sensitized her to the overwhelming need and helplessness of the patients. She believed in the ability of her department to relieve suffering; she believed in the value of the work.

No matter what she did here, today the Omnibus Health and Welfare Bill would be sent to the floor of the state legislature, where it was sure to pass. The question was, would her budget be gutted or just trimmed? A ten-million-dollar fiasco or a two-million-dollar problem?

She wished to God now that she'd never taken this appointment. She had been brought in to downsize the department. But not to kill it, not to be a murderer like this!

Her husband Al's friendship with the governor had gotten her the position, a job that traditionally had been held by a psychiatrist. She was not an M.D., only a Ph.D. psychologist. If the budget was gutted, she would be in the position of relieving over fifty psychiatrists of their positions, in addition to all the other carnage. The mental health community in this state would remember Helen Myrer for a hundred years.

The committee was only passing sentence today; she was the one who would have to do the actual killing.

Maybe—just maybe—this last cannonball would do the job the others hadn't. It was full of pictures, highly quotable—the kind of thing that might get her the press coverage that she had been missing all along.

As she circled the senate chamber, she could see the doors of the committee room looming up ahead. Senator G. G. Joiner could be heard over on the floor, droning to an empty chamber about riparian rights. Farther along the hall, a maintenance man ran a floor waxer. In the distance a siren rose and fell, and sunlight shone down from the high arched windows that surrounded the dome.

She had once loved this old building full of marble glory, loved the way it glowed in the light of the sun, loved its history. She loved the state itself, its wonderful, open people and its rolling, verdant land, its history and that fabulous city to the south also called New York. She had an apartment in Manhattan, where she had become a subscriber to the Philharmonic and the Metropolitan Opera and an enthusiastic supporter of the New York Film Festival.

She loved being alive, if the truth be told, despite the hollow place at the center of her world, the emptiness that Al had left behind him. In a sense, though, it was a good emptiness. Their marriage had been happy and long, and it was right that she grieve and right that Al's place in her heart remain empty. It's not really empty, Al, she said within herself, you're still here, my love.

The day she had taken her oath from the governor, just weeks after Al's death, had been one of the saddest and most beautiful days of her life, a sublime moment dedicated to the great and gentle man who had been at her side for twenty years.

She reached the committee room, found herself pausing before the closed doors. If they made the big cuts, maybe the thing to do would be to resign. How could she retire Dr. William Walker, who had been chief of the Department of Psychiatry for thirty years and was one of the leading psychiatrists in the world? She couldn't do that to a man of such stature—and he was only one of many.

Not to mention the patients, the poor patients! How could they hurt the autistic children like this and the helpless schizophrenics and paranoids—how could they put all those people into the dingy, understaffed, dangerous facilities that awaited or even out onto the street?

Her last report was called "Passing Sentence on the Mentally Ill, the 1997 Budget and Its Consequences." It was only ten pages long, ten pages of brutal statistics and one-line explanations, of horrendous pictures of mentally ill people in need.

It was a last cry for help to anybody who would listen.

A long, rolling laugh came through the closed door. She continued standing there, trying to make her heart stop thundering, trying to make her jaw work properly. She'd gotten TMJ from the stress of the job and had to wear a prosthetic insert to keep her left meniscus from tearing itself apart.

All right, take a deep breath, put the facial muscles into neutral. Al, she said to his place in her heart, here we go.

She put her hands on both knobs and threw open the doors. There was a brief hush, then a swell of whispered conversation as she came in—not exactly a sweeping entrance, but an effort in that direction.

Mal Camber's camera clicked. Tom Woolsley of the *Times* raised his eyes from a page of what looked like fascinating doodles, and Senator Warner gave her a sharp little smile. "M'lady enters," he said.

"Traffic, Tom," she said, vaguely referring to the fact that she was late. She took her seat at the witness table alone. She had not brought any of her assistants, not for this last battle. Let her do it alone, let her take the loss herself, if there was to be a loss. Her people had been through all nine grueling sessions, some of them chief psychiatrists made to explain the number of towels and lightbulbs their facilities used.

She looked up at Warner, a sharp-faced, gray-eyed young man of thirty-two, handsome and tanned from his recent skiing expedition to Vail. With his tan and his Savile Row suit, he looked every bit as wealthy as he was.

He was not a bad man. In fact, he had many wonderfully innovative ideas about budgets. But he also had a fundamental lack of belief in the very idea of mental health.

This was not his only blind spot. As far as Helen was concerned, there was something decivilized about him. Except on paper, he was not well educated. She had once confused him merely by mentioning the *DSM-IV*, the diagnostic bible of the American Psychiatric Association. She'd learned early in the hearings that she had to avoid professional phraseology or he'd feel threatened and start needling. In a sense, this sweet-tempered young man was really a sort of savage. For him the only justice was retribution. The idea that some people, criminals included, might be insane and thus helpless to control themselves only angered him.

By contrast, the therapeutic promise was the foundation not only of her career, but of her meaning as a person. The mad could be helped and even cured; that was basic.

"I'm ready, Senators," she said as she heaped copies of the report on the witness table. A secretary began handing them out to the committee and the press.

They told a brutal truth: the proposed cuts would leave state mental health with only one basic mission—to confine the criminally insane.

"We've gotten all this stuff before," Senator Warner said.

She must not let him go to a vote, not just yet. She leaned in to her mike. "I just wanted it charted. So the stats are clear."

"Well, it's nothing new."

He was in a hurry, and that was bad. She needed a little more time. She plunged in. "You must face the reality that these cuts create, and I don't think you've done that. You will see every outpatient facility in the state reduced to part-time or occasional operation."

"You were brought into your job to downsize the division," Warner said mildly.

Good, he was talking instead of racing toward that damn vote. "Downsizing and destroying are two different things. Public mental health will be destroyed as a state function after this. I want to put a question to all of you: Have you considered this from the standpoint of the human suffering involved? Have you personalized it?" She looked from face to face—and saw that the truth was that they had. They were suffering with her, even Warner.

A silence fell, filled only by the humming of the fans that moved warm air through the room. There was a stir in the back, and Helen saw that her daughter, Selena, had arrived. She gave her a wink. The response was a thumbs-up. Good Selena, loyal Selena.

She briefly enjoyed contemplating Selena's success as a young businesswoman, and her son Mike's brilliant beginning with his law firm. Your kids will give you their support, she thought. Selena would take her to lunch, Mike would have dinner with her. Under pressure, this family circled wagons. This family had a secret weapon, which was its love and its loyalty.

Then, very suddenly, the vote was called. She started to protest, but it was too late. They'd spoken softly among themselves, using her moment of inattention as a sort of doorway.

They're doing it like thieves, she thought as Warner murmured a few words and there was a show of hands.

It was over. The Omnibus Health and Welfare Bill would go to the floor, with the cuts, and would be passed, she knew, by a landslide. She would try for a veto, but she knew that the governor wouldn't do it. He'd been elected on a "stop taxing us to death" platform, and he wasn't about to defy his own mandate, not even when it went too far.

People were getting up, people were speaking together to confirm lunch dates and discuss afternoon appointments. She was part of the committee's past now, left to her department and her disaster.

It had all been so brief and so pointless. She thought, Barbarians don't care about reports, followed by, I don't have to be nice to Tom Warner anymore. She champed down on her oral appliance; her jaw cracked and pain shot through her left temple.

Without speaking, she closed her briefcase and walked out, Selena behind her. She wished that Mike had come, but he would have had to take an early-morning flight and rush right back. They would have dinner at eight, after his day was over.

Still, she wanted him, she wanted them both with her and with the secret Al within her. She was being selfish, she knew, but she really needed her kids right now, because it was a very hard thing to be undone like this, to see a lifetime of work swept away in a strange budgetary tide that she did not fully understand, and suddenly to find that the last place you were needed was . . . well . . . gone.

"I'm gonna be an executioner, looks like," she said as Selena caught up with her.

"You're double-timing, Mom, slow down."

"I can't, I'm too mad." She went even faster, did it on purpose. Let them see her anger.

Distantly she heard Tom Warner call after her, but her eyes were now getting damp and she was damned if she was going to let him see that.

"Lunch," she said to Selena. It wasn't a question, but an assumption. She had been planning to eat at the Capitol Restaurant, but not now. Now she would eat at Cristal, the best place in Albany and the only one that approached Manhattan-level excellence. She was even tempted to use her state credit card, but she knew that she wouldn't.

"Mom, it's just so wrong."

She regarded Selena. "I want to go to Cristal. I can't face the Cap today, not with all those happy faces waiting for me to keel over."

"Cristal—Mom, that would be great. But—I know this is awful—I have to get back by one, and I just don't have the time."

She stopped. "You're gonna let me cry in my beer all alone?"

"Sorry, Mom."

Helen stood on the steps of the building, looking down the wide esplanade with its view off into the southern tier of the state.

Selena's hand came into hers. "I really love you, you know."

"Dinner? Mike's flying up."

"I'm finalizing my first proposal. It's an all nighter for sure."

Helen would be strong now. This was the time to be an understanding mother. Kids had their lives, and that had to be respected. "Look, thanks for coming. Thanks from the bottom of my heart."

She watched her daughter leave, the sun shining on her long, swaying hair, on her pale arms, this beautiful young woman who was the outcome of her love for Al, who mixed his exotic eyes with her regular features and managed to come out just wonderful.

She watched her and yearned after her and felt as she went toward the visitors' parking lot an anguish of soul that was much, much stronger than she had expected.

Then she went off to her Taurus, her shoulders back, her head high beneath the white clouds of summer. She tried to tell herself that she had done the best that could have been done, that Selena was genuinely busy. At least Mike would come, and they could have a long, serious talk about her political future. Should she even continue? Maybe resignation was the best next step— make a statement with her career.

She got in the stiflingly hot car and leaned her head against the steering wheel and would have bawled, but she simply was not the type.

After a few moments she sat up straight and started the engine. When the air-conditioning was roaring, she headed off to Cristal. She had driven about three blocks when she began to think how it would look to be sitting there at a table alone after a debacle like this. Warner went to Cristal occasionally. What if he was there today? After all, he had something to celebrate.

She turned toward her apartment building instead. There was some bread and lunch meat in the fridge. She would make a sandwich and maybe listen to a little music before going back to the office.

In a few more minutes she was pulling into the garage. She stopped the car and got out. Hoping that she wouldn't have to face the garage attendant, she hurried toward the elevator. "Hi, Benny," she said as he came out of his cubicle.

"Hello, Doctor," he replied. "Hope you done some good."

"Not a lot," she said.

"I'm sorry to hear that."

He had a sister in mental health maintenance at a local outpatient facility, the very sort of place that Helen would be closing down. She found herself hugging Benny, much to the surprise of both of them.

Thank God nobody was in the elevator this time of day. Ascending to the twenty-second floor, she felt tears trickling through her makeup. Deeper she went into her privacy and herself, and deeper into her failure as the whisper-quiet elevator took her to her very silent apartment.

Like all of her places, it was decorated in shades of blue. She'd brought her collection of Mexican masks and *Days of the Dead* sculptures here, because they were such a contrast to life in Albany, New York. She had gone through a period of being fascinated with the unique Mexican view of death as a celebration of life. She'd even written a paper on it, "Death as Enterprise and Celebration in the Nahuatl Cultures of Northern Mexico," which had been published in *Psychological Anthropology* in 1984.

"The dead," she said, lifting a dancing skeleton from its black base. The skeleton wore a flowered bonnet and had a cigar in its mouth. *Madre Morte,* she was called. Mother Death. She went to the broad living room window, which on this clear summer day had a view all the way to the Berkshires.

She turned away from the view outward and the long canyon down to the street. The refrigerator came on, filling the silence with its soft humming. She didn't want food. She couldn't think of food.

Then she noticed that the light on the answering machine was flashing. She almost didn't want to push the button, but on this machine it had to be either the family or the office, as the number was private.

"Hi, Mom, it's me and guess what, I can't manage it tonight. What I want to do is try brunch on Sunday, say you come down to old Trollhattan and we meet at the Palm Court? Love ya, darling."

She slammed her thumb into the erase button. Wow, but this was really painful. This made her chest ache with loss, tears choke her throat.

Maybe it was Al's charisma that had kept the kids close. Now, at her moment of crisis, it turned out that they just didn't feel the same kind of concern they would have had for their father. She had to face this.

"Don't be ridiculous," she said. "You're just feeling sorry for yourself."

True or not, something broke in her at that moment, as if some hope or essential part of her had come loose and floated off down the river. She threw herself on the couch and sobbed. It went on for some little time. In the end, though, it faded into silence. She stared around her at an apartment that seemed to belong to a stranger.

The phone rang, then rang again. Each time it rang she lurched toward the receiver. But she did not pick it up. She listened instead as the machine clicked on and her announcement played, her own voice droning. She hoped that it would be Mike with a change of plans, or even Selena, but it was Victor at the office. "Just trying to track you down, boss. The gov's called to cry, all the supers are calling to beg. As if you didn't know. Am keeping hatches battened. When do I get my pinkie?"

She would not put V out to pasture, never, which she told him.

After they hung up, she found herself gazing at a particularly droll skeleton that was cavorting with a pretty young thing in the back of a black plastic car. "Why in the world did we collect this stuff?" she said to Al. It probably wasn't good to talk to Al like this, but she had to talk to somebody. "At least I have your attention."

Maybe she ought to go to Mexico, to Mazatlán for fishing, or maybe to one of the big resorts. Then she thought of the couples vacationing in those glittering places and found her eyes tearing again. Lonely in a crowd was a very bad place to be. What she wanted to do was go on a nice trip with Al.

"Al," she said as she stared into nowhere and the past, "let's you and I go to the Old Secret."

She got up and went into the study. Would that guy's name be on the computer? Surely not, not after—how long? Twelve years? No, she'd lost all that.

The Old Secret was a cabin, a very special and wonderful cabin on a lovely New Hampshire lake. When last there, she had been a mother with two preadolescent kids and the handsomest, smartest, strongest, sweetest lawyer husband in the entire Northeast.

The most recent address on the laptop she kept here was three years old. Now, what town had the cabin been in? It had been owned by a little man in . . . was it Carlton?

She picked up the phone and tried to get an area code, but there was no Carlton, New Hampshire. Suddenly she wanted to return to the Old Secret very badly, to be there with her memories, to talk to Al and let the night wind bring his answer.

Most of their belongings were in the Manhattan apartment or in storage, but she knew that there was one thing of Al's, a shoebox in the top of the closet, that contained the correspondence he'd been working on the week he died. She'd kept it against possible requests from clients but had never opened it. His personal address book, the one he carried in his pocket, was in there. She'd dropped it in with his keys.

The letters, written on fine legal bond, were still white. She saw one on the Allied Chemical case, another about the new desk he would never sit behind, a third from the executor of the Trammell estate, transmitting a fee check. Another to her: "Hey, lady, I am sitting in my room at the Stanhope wishing that you were here and we had the drapes drawn and the TV on and an obscene pizza and a whole night just to explore it."

She took it out and pressed it to her face. It was one of his small, delightful habits to send off these notes when he was traveling. She had saved them all; there were hundreds of them in boxes in her storage space in Manhattan. But this one was here, and maybe it even smelled a little bit like him, of sunburn and bay rum.

Then she found the ancient alligator-skin address book. Holding it in her hands, she paged along. Restaurants, friends she hadn't seen in years, his tennis partner, Gower Chambers, golfers, his poker and bridge buddies. It was what he'd called his "guy" book.

She groaned, told herself, "You're being stupid. Five years is enough time to accept a death."

Had a patient come in grieving like this after so long a time, Helen would have treated it as mild pathology, an anxiety disorder.

Then she found it. Meticulous Al had listed it under the name of the owner of the cabin, Henry Matthias. Along with the listing was written, "Good cabin, hick area, bring wine."

Taking the book with her, Helen dropped onto the bed, then rolled across to the phone. She hadn't been far off about the name of the town, she reflected as she dialed. Tarleton Corners. She recalled a tidy little collection of clapboard cottages with black shingle roofs.

The Old Secret itself had green shutters and wonderful views of the lake and a very squeaky bed. She remembered that they had sat together on the deck in the quiet of the night after the kids were in bed. They had grilled a fish Al had said was a lake bass and eaten it with a very fresh white wine. After the sun went down they'd watched bats fluttering in the afterglow of the day and had kissed like teenagers, side by side in the wonderful Adirondack chairs that stood on the deck.

Her problem was not that she was inconsolable, but that she had too many good memories to ever really consign him to the land of the dead. Despite the opportunities that had offered themselves, she hadn't even considered another man. When Al had died she'd bought a double stone, and there was no question in her mind that it would be used.

She almost hesitated to make the call. Matthias had been old twelve years ago. He'd be dead, too, surely, and with him another beautiful part of her life. The cabin would be burned or sold to strangers or just plain abandoned. The past was abandoned.

"Matthias Realty."

Dear God, it was impossible. "Mr. Matthias, please," she said, hoping that she wasn't asking for a corpse.

"This is Henry."

Ten minutes later she'd taken the cabin for the next two weeks, for the amazing rental of three hundred dollars a week. She'd been assured that it was in good condition, that there was even a new telephone. It hadn't had one at all twelve years ago.

"The Old Secret," she said, and her heart touched lost and sunny days.

CHAPTER TWO

The Old Secret

She called V and told him to tell the governor she was fine and she was off to the deep woods for two weeks. She knew that he would let her lick her wounds. In any case, there wouldn't be anything more to do until the full session started and she could put on her begging uniform and go from "no" vote to "no" vote with a great big grin on her face.

If you didn't mind small planes, the flight to Concord, New Hampshire, was lovely, a silvery gliding passage among magical clouds. She arrived in the evening and stayed at the Airport Quality Inn for the night. She watched AMC and ate pizza until she felt like hell. She called Selena and Mike both a number of times, finally contenting herself with leaving messages on their machines. It was good that they were busy. They were happy. She and Al had been busy, too. They had been happy.

She decided not to cry anymore, not even when *The Snake Pit* came on and she heard that fabulous Brahms symphony swelling behind Olivia De Havilland's moving plea for more humane treatment of the insane.

The only flight to Tarleton Corners was at nine-fifteen the next morning, in an even smaller plane. It took but half an hour and involved a steep turn above Lake Glory, which lay gleaming gold in the sun, vast and bright and—she knew—full of fish that you could actually catch and eat.

Henry Matthias met her at the airport. She did not take him up on his offer of a ride, because the Old Secret was quite isolated and she had reserved a car. Hands gripping the steering wheel of the big Mercury much too hard, she followed Henry into town, reflecting on how little he had aged. Small-town life seemed to be good for him, but her experience of patients from little places was that everybody tended to look at everybody else too carefully. You got a lot of paranoia out of little towns, a lot of panic attacks.

Realizing where her mind was going, she said, "No." She took a deep breath, tried to relax her stranglehold on the wheel. "You're not here to diagnose," she told herself.

She and Al had meant to come back here the next year and every year. Their fantasy was that nobody ever rented the Old Secret but them, that nobody knew about its green shutters and wonderful broad deck overlooking the lake from atop that seventy-foot cliff, and that nobody else had ever eaten fresh-caught fish there and drunk pale gold wine while the sun went down.

She pulled into a space beside Mr. Matthias's and got out of her car. He unfolded himself, smiled suddenly, and stood as if staring out into the middle distance of the world. He clapped his hands. "Look over there, Dr. Myrer," he said, pointing.

She looked across the quiet street, toward a hedge of flowers and a prim clapboard drugstore. "Yes?"

He lowered his head. "The birds," he said in a soft voice.

Two small birds were mating in the road. When she realized it, she laughed, and her bark seemed incredibly harsh in the air of morning, in this soft old town.

He chuckled. "The mating season."

"Are they . . . finches?"

"Trash birds. Sparrows." He pronounced it "sparrer," and she decided that he was a bit of a funny old man behind the exterior. Why would he point out mating birds to a strange woman? What was in his mind, what was driving his unconscious? "Come on up, Doc, let's do the deed."

She followed him up an outside stairway to an office with gold lettering on the frosted-glass door: "H. Matthias, Real Estate."

She'd expected to see others here, but instead the office was empty. In a city there would have been air-conditioning and secretaries, agents on phones. Here there was only a manicured desk and birdsong coming through the open window.

Now that he was inside his space, Mr. Matthias bustled, subtly self-important, clearly contented. Once behind the desk, he officiated, sitting down and spreading his long arms. She sat down opposite, gazing into his eyes. Then he looked down, his lips pursed, and cleared his throat importantly. "The file." He lifted a yellow folder from the center of the blotter.

She took it, opened it. "You're kidding."

At this moment another man entered, rattling the door. He began looking for something in an oak filing cabinet as tall as his five squat feet. "We need supplies, Henry," he said testily.

"Well, Kevin, you know what you need."

They were like a couple of married people, nattering at each other.

The forms were absurd. "All this for a two-week rental? I don't think so." She tossed the file back.

His gesture, narrow hands raised, palms out, seemed to ward it off. "I have to ask you."

"Henry?"

Matthias glanced sharply toward his assistant. "Yes!"

"I just thought—the doctor—surely . . ." The small man smiled nervously. Helen looked up at his gray Munchkin's face. He gave her a grin so big that she could not help but smile back.

"It's the state. Meddlesome fools." Henry Matthias did not look happy. "They could confiscate the property if you turned out to be a drug dealer."

Kevin clucked. "They'd love the Old Secret, they would."

She realized she had to give up and do the forms. She jotted her name, her address in the city, then all the other information—job title, place of employment, years there. The last time they'd leased this cabin it had been a matter of cash, keys, and have a nice time. The presence of this elaborate form in this simple, old-time place saddened her. It made the twelve years since that dear, lost summer seem an awfully long time.

Al, she said inside, isn't this nuts? She wanted silence, not forms; she wanted the company of her ghosts.

In deference to their liability problems, however, she filled out the paper completely, moving meticulously from point to point. When she finished she gave it to Matthias. He looked down at it, nodding, making small sounds of assent in his throat as he read.

She signed the form, gave Matthias six hundred dollars cash, and stood up. He smiled so widely that she was rather shocked. People did not smile like that, not in her guarded political world. "Thank you," she said, trying hard to be friendly. She was just so darned washed out.

Birdsong and the grinding of gears came in the window with the shouts of little boys. As he rose, Henry Matthias closed the folder. "Now, that's all right," he said. "Sure am sorry about all this bother."

"Don't be."

"We need a new government. Top to bottom, ream 'er out. So, okay, Kevin McCallum here'll lead you. Them roads ain't got signs."

She prevented herself from uttering a sound of dismay, did not prevent her hand from coming up to her cheek, communicating all too clearly her horror at not being left to her own devices. "I know the way."

Kevin laughed, his chortles mingling with the sharp, true laughter of the boys in the street. "Oh, you don't need to worry! I won't bother you. I'm out that way anyway. My house is ten minutes up the ridge from your cabin." He, also, smiled one of those big country smiles. "Best to know that, lady. Where safety lies."

"Thank you," she said again. "I'll just get groceries and head out. If I can't find it, I'll come back."

"Well, good luck," Matthias said. He'd put her money in a metal box. "That's just fine." They gave her keys and a photocopied map.

Alone again, and very happy for it, she left the office and moved slowly off down the sidewalk, taking a better look at the town. Tarleton Corners, as it turned out, had addressed the years in much the same way that Grover's Corners addressed time in *Our Town*.

There were wide hickories and oaks overspreading the streets, with golden sunlight filtering to green in the leaves. The noises of the town were soft and intimate—children still calling, a radio playing in the grocery store, doves and robins in the trees. It all melded together into a message that she needed to hear, that the world abided, and no matter the cares of men.

The predominant colors were green and white: the white of clapboard, pronounced in New England "clabbered," and the sanctifying green of the trees.

She went up the three wooden steps and pushed through the swinging screen door into the grocery store. The smell reminded her so powerfully of childhood that she almost sobbed aloud. Here the fruits and vegetables were kept not in coolers, but in the old way, in uncooled bins. Their rich fragrance combined with a thousand other odors to produce this ancient, glorious smell. She wanted to buy everything, she wanted to buy the store, and she thought: You want to recapture the past, you want to go back to the days when the world seemed new. Have the skies in general gotten more gray, she wondered, or is it that good pasts are always sunny?

She went through the store, buying various little needs—milk, cereal, a lovely local melon that felt soft with the promise of interior richness. Then she happened to see some fishing tackle, a small rod and reel that could be had for thirty dollars. There were lures, too, and she recalled how they had fished from the boat that had been at the bottom of the cliff . . . and wondered if it was still there.

They'd grilled the fish on the deck overlooking the lake. She remembered well that evening of fresh fish and fresh fruit and wine as cool and hard as the stars of night.

She toyed with the tackle, wondered about the condition of the boat. Then she saw Kevin in the stationery section, getting office supplies. "Hi there," she said, trying to be more friendly.

He was staring down at a spiral binder.

"Excuse me, Kevin?"

He threw her a smile, and she found herself pitying the untended yellow of his teeth.

"I was deciding on these," he said. He held up some of the binders.

"I wonder if you could tell me about the fishing situation."

"The fishing situation is that you'd have to fight to keep 'em off your line, out along the rocks out there. You take that boat along the rocky headland—"

"I remember the headland. What about the boat?"

He looked up and to one side. "I'll tell you what. I'll get our handyman, Slim Goode, to go out and give her a caulk-up. You don't want to sink. There's currents in there."

"That's for sure." She wasn't a brilliant swimmer.

"You can live on the Lake Glory fish. Some do. Here, choose."

For a moment she did not understand the change of subject. Then she saw that she was meant to decide among the binders, one green, one black, one dull red. "Oh, I'd take the green. Green's a peaceful color. Ideal in an office."

"A shrink's office, maybe. What about a plain old practical office?"

Had that been bitterness in his voice? Anger, even? She decided to ignore it. "I'm going to buy some tackle. Lures. Can you recommend lures?"

"Not me, I'm a fisherman of a different sort. Live bait."

"It's better?"

"Living things eat living things. Even a fish can usually tell a plastic worm. Choose my binder. It's good luck if a stranger chooses it."

"That I never heard."

"Probably because I just made it up."

"The red, then." She headed for the tackle.

"Don't."

She stopped. Was that warning? What was in his voice? She turned around, concerned. "Don't what?"

"Don't buy the tackle. There's plenty up at the cabin. Bait's right in the ground. Just dig worms in the dawn. Simple things work best, Dr. Myrer."

"Thank you, wise sir." Now that was a little less stiff, a little more natural and easy.

"Wise sir," he said, "wise sir."

She was soon at the checkout, then out the door and walking down the brick sidewalk to her car in front of the Lowry Building. Al had liked the symmetry of the Lowry Building, had reveled in its elaborate cornices and arched windows. Al had liked . . . Al had seen . . . Al had remembered.

She unlocked her car and got in.

Following a slow pickup, she fiddled with the knob on the radio, trying to find an NPR station. Soon she heard the familiar tones of Karl Haas's voice and settled in for the drive with a musical lecture about compositions for carillons. She turned off the air conditioner and rolled down all the windows, and the music of the bells filled the morning air.

She hummed with the clanging of the carillon, stopped to giggle at her own tunelessness, then hummed some more.

Trees lined the road, the hollows misty and dark.

CHAPTER THREE

Noon Shadow

Helen edged her car down the narrow road to the cabin. She gritted her teeth every time she scraped a tree, which was often. She really should have rented a smaller vehicle.

She reminded herself that it was a minor problem. Her insurance company could pay Hertz for a new paint job if it came to that.

The old blue pickup she'd followed out of town until it pulled away ahead of her had turned up again, now parked back on the last switchback. She almost had to knock down trees to get around it. It must mean that Slim was already here fixing the boat, which made these guys the fastest workers in central New Hampshire.

The tires actually skidded a bit on the last, steep downhill.

She came to the end of the road and there was the Old Secret tucked into the side of the bluff. It looked just exactly as it had twelve years ago, with its dressing of sunlit flowers, its green shutters, and steep alpine roof. For a moment she sat listening to the hissing of the breeze and hearing also the voices of her children and Al's laughter within.

The Mercury's tires spun more as she parked, maneuvering inexpertly into the rutted space in front of the steps that led down to the cabin door. Part of the fun of the place was the way it was perched on the side of a forested bluff: everything was up and down, and the lake views were superb.

She got out and gathered up the handles of her two bags of groceries and small suitcase. As she descended the rickety wooden steps, her skirt brushed the masses of marigolds that crowded alongside them.

There was some difficulty with the key—until she realized that the door was already unlocked.

"Slim?" she called.

The only answer was the lazy buzzing of whatever bugs buzzed in central New Hampshire.

She peered into the cabin, then entered, moving quickly across the large living room with its cathedral ceiling and broad deck overlooking the view of the lake. After hanging a few things up in the bedroom closet, he approached the well-remembered and still very old-fashioned kitchen. The refrigerator actually had a compressor on top that made a sort of pottering sound when it was on. The stove was called a Royal Rose and took lighting with a match. The water that gurgled out of the tap tasted as though it had bubbled up from the morning of the world.

As she unloaded her groceries, she glanced toward the lake. At the moment there were two sailboats out there, both heeled far over, both with all sails full. She was pulling a box of Raisin Bran out of a bag when she noticed that the boat was not being caulked by Slim after all. It was still tied up down below, a graceful green toy tethered to a fairy's tiny dock. Slim must be engaging in the Tarleton Corners version of cooping, what cops did after they got their doughnuts.

Well, let him coop; it didn't matter, not on this soft and lovely forenoon.

Carrying the Raisin Bran and a box of sugar cubes, she stepped into the pantry. It was a long closet, with a hatch at the far end that led to the basement. Even twelve years ago she had not cared for this little room. She could remember Al saying, "I'll bet they've got actual root veggies in that root cellar. Nothing like a ten-year-old potato." She and Alfred, in this very pantry . . . how he had frightened her, nuzzling her in the dark like that, coming up on her without a sound. She chuckled, nestling the Raisin Bran on the shelf before her.

As she did so, something made her hesitate—not a specific sound or movement, nothing so overt. More, it was a sense of tighter enclosure, as if the space were not as large, or not as empty, as it should be.

She became conscious that there was a figure pressing itself against the far wall. She glanced, making sure it wasn't a shadow. No. Terror pumped her heart. She'd seen that it was darkly bundled and had an unfocused face that suggested a stocking mask. Its fist was clasped against its chest and in it pointing downward was a huge, breathtakingly lethal knife.

Long years as a clinician enabled her to stifle her panic enough to organize her retreat. Like an aircraft that had been shattered but still followed its old trajectory, she finished putting the sugar on the shelf, then turned and left the pantry. There was no question in her mind about what she'd seen. A man was hiding right there and he had one terrible knife and he was in disguise. Was he tall? Short? She didn't know. Twelve years ago Slim had been tall and angular—a shy man who grinned. How did she know Slim even had a blue truck? No, this man was muscular and solid—not Slim.

Her reflex was always to become extremely calm when a patient became violent, but that impulse did not help her now, and in her haste she almost crashed into the wall. In the course of her career she'd interviewed men in prisons for the criminally insane, and she had no illusions about what was waiting for her in that pantry.

She left the house. This enabled her to regain her presence of mind, and she moved quietly but quickly, even managing to cover her retreat by whistling a few casual bars as she stepped out the door. She hoped he'd think that she was just going back for the rest of the groceries. She concealed the fact that she was thrusting in her purse for the car keys.

She reached the car and got in with her blood racing so fast she feared she would faint—and then found that she had her house keys from New York. They were clutched in a bloody palm.

She rummaged, pushing aside lipstick, neatly folded tissues, compact, wallet—but there were no car keys.

She stared out the windshield, thinking. The blood-freezing truth was that they were lying on the drainboard in the kitchen.

You have some choices, a voice said within her, a calm voice, a clinician's voice. She could go back into the house and get them. Or she could try to escape.

She inventoried. One alternative might be to go around the house and down the bluff steps and get in the boat and row out. But if he realized what she was doing—as he would—would he not simply overtake her on those steep steps? And the boat wasn't properly caulked, it might sink.

Kevin was up the slope, but it was terribly steep and she didn't know the path.

Maybe the thing to do was to get out of this car right now and start running up the road. But how far would she get in the minute or so before he understood? Somewhere between here and the Tarleton High Road, the chase would end.

There came from between her lips a small sound, completely involuntary. It was in the secret language of victims, this dry, trembling sigh, and it spoke of her mind's inability to cope with helplessness this sudden and this absolute.

She was trapped just as certainly as if he had her on a leash, as if he had her already tied. She leaned her head back against the seat, pressed her foot against the gas pedal until the floor creaked.

The windows of the cabin were dark behind their

shutters with the hearts carved in them. The marigolds bobbed in the sun, a warbler raised song in the oak that overspread the mossy roof.

Could this be a former patient? No, she hadn't treated many of the violent, certainly no rapists or—God forbid—compulsive murderers. None of the killers she'd interviewed in the prison setting was ever going to be released.

Perhaps the best course of action would be simply to go back into the house and get the keys and return all in seeming innocence. As far as he knew, she needed them to open the trunk. Perfectly believable.

The point was not to give off even the faintest signal of distress. So she'd keep moving briskly but calmly, giving no indication by her body language of how she actually felt. Loosen the shoulders, slack the jaw, return the gaze to the vacationer's easy focus. Above all, do not step too hard, do not hurry.

She put her hand on the car door but found that she was literally too weak with fear to pull the handle. Amazed at herself, she stared down at the long fingers, the taper of her forearm. She was called beautiful, and although her forty-something years were perfectly apparent and she made no effort to hide them, nature had been kind to these hands, to these smooth arms, even to the face she knew was now shimmering with sweat.

She had seen the destructions wrought by the mad upon the bodies of women. She knew, also, that these cases were so intractable that the fringe in her profession had even made arguments for euthanasia. But her professional commitment was clear: all personalities, no matter how dysfunctional, were available to therapy. So, profile him, you've profiled half a dozen ultraviolent men.

Her breath started coming quickly, her heart pattering. The world began to retreat from her grasp.

Panic attack, don't let it develop, profile him! Okay, the knife is being used right now as a shield. His problem is concealed behind it. Will the knife ever become a weapon? Yes, but only if he's triggered.

All right, calm down. *If* he's triggered. If.

Presence obviously wasn't enough—she'd been right there in the pantry and he hadn't moved. So what would trigger him? What must she in all circumstances avoid doing?

Maybe the interviews could help her here. Had any of the compulsive murderers spoken of being triggered and being helpless to move until the trigger was engaged? Guy Cobb—that creature with his fingernails bitten to the quick and seven mutilation killings on his record— he'd used a knife and made it his modus operandi to hide in closets.

But he hadn't waited, certainly not. If Guy Cobb had been in that pantry, she'd be dead already.

She needed time, time to think this out. But she couldn't wait, she had to act. If he came to a window of the cabin, he'd see her sitting in here and know that this had not been an ordinary return to the car. He must have watched her arrival, after all. He'd seen the groceries and hoped to trap her in the pantry when the moment was right. For whatever reason, it hadn't been right a minute ago. If she was lucky, it would never be right, not before she got out of here.

God, he'd come out here just before she had; he'd been the driver of the pickup she'd followed. She fought to remember—had she seen him, maybe getting in? No. The truck had been on the street before she'd pulled out.

This was no accident. The man had been stalking her. He was somebody who knew about this cabin. A local. In a way that was good, because no known compulsive murderers were operating in this area. So maybe he was planning to rape or rob her.

Her jaw cracked; she touched her appliance with her tongue. She sniffled and realized that she was crying. Her cheeks were wet with tears. Would he enjoy that? Would he enjoy making more?

Carefully she dried them. Then she sucked in air and compelled strength and pulled the door handle. She pushed open the door and stepped out.

How quiet this place was, and so damned isolated. Now that she really looked at it, she saw that the road was as athletic a climb as she had feared, and the forest that pressed its shoulder was not only very dense, but also ran up its own precipitous bluff. Kevin had said that it was ten minutes to his place, which had to mean that the woods weren't too deep. The ridge frowned down at her. If only she could see the path!

She regarded the cabin. The sun was shining at the worst possible angle right now, and she could see nothing beyond the windows.

She had to take the risk. She went down the steps to the front door and yanked it open. She could not stop, she had to sweep right along, she had to pretend to have forgotten something and be returning for it, tapping across the living room, creaking the wide floorboards in the hall.

As she passed the pantry she saw a small sign of his presence: the pantry door had been adjusted to an inch-wide crack; surely she'd left it hanging fully open. Now she was deep in the house, now entering the kitchen. The compressor pottered, the sun shone on the drainboard. The lake was empty, the boats had sailed on.

Her eyes fixed on the drainboard, looking for the yellow Hertz key ring. But the keys were not beside the bag that was left.

The whole kitchen lurched, she had to grab the edge of the counter to avoid collapsing, because they didn't appear to be anywhere.

Okay, then they're under the bag. She steadied herself, lifted it.

He knew what a trap this place was, oh yes, which is why they were now in his pocket.

She dropped her hand to her side, rested her fingers on the handle of one of the drawers. Inside was a pitiful collection of aged cutlery. Memory would not serve, but she wouldn't have been surprised to know that these were the same three knives, the same corkscrew, the same fish scaler, that had been here twelve years ago. A hammer, then, even an icepick? But where? The more she rummaged, the more likely he was to take action.

Using one of these knives would do no more than enrage him. You do not come at unbalanced people with weapons unless you are absolutely certain that you will win.

All right, the telephone. She could dial 911, the county had 911. Moving quickly past the pantry, she went down the two steps into the large room. Across the rag rug beside the Morris chair stood the three-legged telephone table and an incongruously bright red Princess phone.

She crossed the room, her shoes quiet on the rug. She didn't even have proper sneakers to run in or hiking boots to negotiate the woods, just these walking shoes, pleasant enough on concrete but no good for a hell-bent run down fifty winding, damp stairs to a dock or up a road that was cut into a virtual cliff, let alone the trek to Kevin's.

Beside the phone table, she stopped. This had to be done with extreme care. It would take the sheriff twenty minutes to get here from Tarleton Corners, so she couldn't come right out with it, she had to talk in some sort of code that he would comprehend. Say she needed her heart medicine, act as if she'd already instructed him on the matter. She'd say to bring it at once, that it was a matter of life and death, then pray he'd figure out that a call like that was an even more desperate emergency.

She reached for the handset—but stopped. What if he'd cut the line? If she picked it up and found it dead, then she would certainly also find him coming down on her like an avalanche. Unless he was disorganized, in which case the phone would be working. Was he a dis-organized criminal? The opportunistic place of conceal-ment suggested yes, but the taking of the car keys said the opposite. So it had to be assumed that he'd cut the phone line on his way in.

Concealing it as an effort to get a magazine, she managed to tumble the phone to the floor. Casually, easily, she replaced it. She was ninety percent sure that there had been no dial tone, and it was so frightening that she nearly became sick.

The phone swam in sunlight, a red blur. Maybe she should sit down beside it, maybe pick up that copy of the *Reader's Digest* circa April 1989 and wait him out. No, that would simply be delaying and probably not for long. Even so, she sat. She couldn't simply stand here.

Any other way to communicate with the authorities? A radio? No. Nothing. No cellular this far out in the middle of nowhere.

It must have been a little like this for Al when Dr. Sykes had told him, this ghastly sense of helplessness. Awful, lethal world. Al pacing, Al crying in the night, Al checking into Sloan-Kettering, Al at the last clutching a Bible. God, must they both die horrible deaths? Poor Selena and poor Michael; they would blame themselves, to have abandoned Mother to the forest in favor of their busy lives.

Act, woman, do not delay. The only hope left is obviously that terrible stairway to the dock and an escape in a leaky rowboat. Unless he had a gun, of course.

Hadn't there been a gun here, back in the old days? No, that had been a BB gun left by other guests, left twelve years ago and certainly gone by now. Still, she glanced into the corner where it had been. Gone, long gone. What use would it be, anyway—a spring-loaded toy against a knife two feet long? She sucked in air, thinking of how thoroughly such a thing could eviscerate.

The trip to the dock—make it as casual as possible for as long as possible. He was still waiting, after all. So he must not know that he'd been seen.

There were so damn many steps out there! Well, be careful, don't let the panic trip you, get ready now, go out and go down.

In a single, swift movement that recalled her girlhood ballet lessons, she rose from the chair, swept across the room, pulled back the sliding door, and went out onto the deck. The sun was warm, the air sweet. She mounted the stairs and hurried in an agony of suppressed urgency down to the first landing—and found that the second section of steps was simply not there.

Unable to stop her flight, she reeled and skidded. Only at the last instant did she manage to grab the loosely nailed remains of one of the rails. Hanging on, feeling it give, listening to its creak, she swung helplessly out over the abyss.

Her feet angled against the rough edge of the landing. Both hands grasping the unstable rail, she began to try to get back. Breath held, jaw set like stone, she pulled herself on trembling, insufficient arm muscles, making it back onto the landing, but only barely. Gasping, she clung to the safety of the moment.

Looking down, she could see broken lumber scattered on the land end of the dock and more of it floating in the reedy shallows. Thus the question was answered: he was organized. So the phone had certainly been dead, too. And now what would he do, now that he was sure that she was aware of his presence?

She looked up the short flight of steps. From here she

could see only the top half of the door onto the deck.
Then she turned and peered down. Could she jump, perhaps find purchase somewhere?

No doubt other people could. But she knew that to try
to climb down that bluff would for her mean death.

The calm voice spoke again, and it asked a question:
*What is better, hours of violation and torment or thirty
seconds in the sweet, deadly air?*

At that instant she discovered something in herself
that she had never before been aware of: she discovered
that she did not feel any sense of finishing or comple-
tion. On the contrary, she felt herself to be in the peak
middle of her life, just on the point of making her greatest contributions and doing her greatest good—although
maybe not in the state of New York.

"Al," she said, and it was almost as if she could taste
his taste and smell the dear smell of him. She decided
that she could not go back up those steps. Any further
movement would have to be compelled.

No, no, and no! There *had* to be a way! Had to be.
Sorry, Wrong Number, Wait until Dark, Rear Window:
there was always a way, something clever seized upon
with the brilliance of the desperate. Oh, hell, this was
not like that. No magnificently simple alternative was
going to be handed to her. This was the sort of thing that
all the blood-drained and whipped and burned and laid-
open corpses had been through prior to their destruction.
Doubtless, many—perhaps most—had been made brilliant by their need.

She could make a club out of a banister. She could
make a spike out of one of the nail ends that protruded

where he'd torn off the stairs. Torn them off . . . dear God, she would be in the hands of a testosterone-soaked, muscle-bound monstrosity. Overdeveloped muscles concealed sexual fears. You saw the sadness of such men in their eyes.

She got to her feet, deciding to at least face him standing up. Shaking, her legs almost numb from terror, she stood with her back against the undamaged banister. Now, though, she found that she could see more of the deck, and unless he was crouched or lying down, he was not there.

Step by step she mounted the cracked board stairs. Now she could see into the living room, into the kitchen windows. On this side of the house, the sun helped her. She saw an empty house. He might be back in the bedroom or still in the pantry or even in the root cellar. But he was not in the visible part of the house; that much was certain.

So he was toying with her, playing. She knew, then, something more about him: his fantasy was likely to include torture. As he continued it would build on its own extremes: the slap would become the scratch; the first, hesitant cut would develop into a knife blade sliding under red skin.

There had been William K. Harrelson, who had cut off his victims' faces. That one she'd never interviewed, thank God, but she'd read that study of his psychometrics in the *Journal of Abnormal Psychology*. He had been so unconscious of his crimes that it had taken four years of psychotherapy before he was integrated enough to remember them.

A sharp pain stabbed up from her right palm: she had

jabbed the nail of her index finger into the cut she'd made with the keys.

He could no longer have the least question that she knew he was here. Indeed, he'd probably known it from the moment she'd noticed him. This was part of the fun, almost certainly.

Or maybe—just maybe—he was afraid. Or unsure. What if this was the first time he had acted out? All sorts of crimes like this misfired. "I just couldn't do her—I saw her bite her lip and all of a sudden—I just left." That was what had gotten Cobb behind bars.

Dr. Helen Myrer was not likely to strike any soft spots, she didn't think. She was about as vulnerable as Queen Victoria, she knew that. Too many years in the clinical setting had infected her with a mannerism of invulnerability that she could not easily drop.

Or was that really true? A good clinician was warm without being familiar, supportive without committing to the patient's self-justifications. She had been a good clinician, she'd had many successful outcomes. So maybe she would be able to diagnose this man and get a treatment regime going. Maybe she would be able to rescue him from his illness and so also save herself.

"All right," she said in a voice that was so calm it astonished her, "it's time for you to come out." She paused, raised her chin, spoke with all her authority. "It's time."

But it wasn't.

CHAPTER FOUR

The Trap

She sat in the Morris chair beside the dead telephone with the old *Reader's Digest* in her lap, her damned tears blurring its unread words. There was something quite unusual about all this, clever and unusual. His refusal to come out wasn't just a behavioral thing, she felt sure. What she was enduring now was consciously inflicted torture.

The profiling she'd done of compulsive murderers had been to build identification studies, not to effect cures. Interviewing people and administering tests to them was hardly the same as meeting them in a clinical setting. She might be able to predict his behavior pretty accurately, but as to *why* this particular man did this . . . well, that was the question, wasn't it?

Did he know she was a doctor? Sometimes these men

unconsciously sought help. Sometimes their very crimes
were cries for help. In 1946 the Lipstick Murderer,
William Heirens, had pleaded openly with the police to
stop him.

If only she had a catalog of actual patients to draw
from! But you could hardly specialize in compulsive
murderers; that was no way to build a clinical practice.

She'd had an occasional masochist as a private patient, some with rather unusual compulsions, but never
an active sadist and obviously never somebody capable
of violence on the Grand Guignol scale.

She took deep breaths, trying to regain some sort of
self-control. Surely there was something intelligent that
could be done. Damned smoothing, softening female
hormones. But hadn't it once been so nice to be smooth
and soft, to feel Al's pressing urgency, to delight in the
friction of love?

Thought of Al brought back the tears, but this time
they were not so much tragic as angry, and the clinician
in her said, *That's good, that's progress, anger is solving.*

In and out she breathed, looking down her chest at the
magazine. "Mother on a Mountainside: My True-Life
Adventure," illustrated with a painting of a young
woman rappelling a cliff in a lightning storm. A magazine from a lost world, from another age, from a time
when she was not being tortured.

Then she saw a bit of hope. The mere fact that he
hadn't attacked yet meant that she might actually have
some control over the situation. After all, maybe her assumption that he was actively tormenting her right now
was wrong. Maybe he wasn't moving because this *was*

his first time and he couldn't go through with it. Maybe he was back in that pantry sweating blood . . . or maybe he was even gone.

These were possibilities to be considered, and they implied experiments to be carried out. The first experiment would be to check the pantry.

Or no, perhaps not. She must do nothing that would trigger his emergence, because things would fall apart quickly from that point. When she saw him, she would probably be seeing her death.

If only she could establish ground rules so that wouldn't happen. She took a deep breath. There was no time like the present.

"Hello," she said into the silence. The past half hour of nauseated sweating had regressed her voice. She had not sounded so soft and vulnerable since young womanhood. Al had loved her voice, and her patients often commented on it, too. She forced it to go lower, get softer. "I'm a doctor, I can help you." This was her weapon. "I know what's wrong with you." She listened to the silence, waiting. Birds outside, the lazy bugs, the whisper of an afternoon breeze in the treetops, were the only responses. "I understand your problem, and I can cure it." As her last word faded, she sensed that another sound had also stopped. She waited, and soon it started again, very soft, very faint. But she knew what it was, and it was disturbing: she could hear him breathing. It was irregular, full of disturbances, even perhaps of sobs. More gently she said, "There are therapies that work. You don't need to suffer like this."

She heard the springs of a metal door opening and

closing. The refrigerator? No. She realized what it was and she didn't like it, she didn't want it to be that. Twice in her life she'd dreamed of being in a fire. As a child she had been trapped briefly in a burning tent, and the fear had come from there.

Okay, you bastard, so you opened and closed the oven. You can't know about my fears; the only person who's ever shared them is Susan Tuttle-Marks, and she's dead. She had done Helen's graduate analysis, had Susan Tuttle-Marks, with her careful mind and her ceaseless, compulsive smoking. Dead in an apartment fire in 1992, dead in her bed.

"Let's talk about it," she said, feeling a bit more confident that his silence was a sign of failure of nerve. She must personalize herself as much as possible to him now, must make herself human but not motherly—God, no, not that—must give herself a name and a background and a loving family, must make it necessary if he killed her, to kill a specific, named human being, not an anonymous mama surrogate.

She recalled a paper she'd seen on hostage personalization strategies and began trying to implement some of them in a more methodical manner. "My son and daughter are on their way up." But not arriving at any moment, no, nothing to panic him, nothing to make him act suddenly. "Be here tomorrow, probably." She put a smile in her voice. "Maybe next day, so we've got lots of time to get to know each other. My name's Helen, by the way. I have two kids, which I hope doesn't turn you off. My daughter is called Selena and my son is Michael. Grown children. I hope *that* doesn't turn you off." Be younger than his mother was, be girlish, be different from her. She forced out a giggle.

But then she heard something and she wasn't sure what it was. She thought for a moment that he was popping popcorn, but that seemed utterly ridiculous. Of course he wasn't. There came a smell, quite strong, that could be burning hair.

Dear heaven, what was happening in there? What was that thumping that had started and now also that high, frantic squalling?

She took a step toward the kitchen and then another. "Can I help you?" Another. "Are you in trouble?" Another. She was across the room now and standing on the bottom of the two steps that led up to the hallway and the kitchen beyond. The thumping was continuous, and that other sound was definitely something screaming.

As much as any part of it, the urgency in those sounds drew her. What was she not understanding here? Two quick steps took her past the pantry door.

Frankly, she'd expected to see him in the kitchen, but he wasn't here. It took only a glance to tell her that the sound was coming from the Royal Rose. She approached it and saw that the oven was on. The flailing noises from inside had reduced to an occasional bump.

She put her hand on the door handle. She didn't want to open it, didn't want to see what must be inside, didn't want this thing to escalate—oh, God, no.

But she did grasp the cracked, hot Bakelite, and she pulled, and the door groaned as it had for him. She saw in the blackness on the bottom, the smoking, still-jerking body of a large rat.

She cried out; she couldn't help it. Another scream came and then a third before she managed to regain a measure of control. Staring at the ruin, she backed away.

She saw it as a theater of extremes. He was dramatizing his potency, proving to her that he was horribly dangerous . . . perhaps, if he was very smart, trying to incapacitate her with fear.

It must be a response to what she'd said, to the controlled tone she'd used. But he must have had the rat already captured, so he had in some way anticipated that he would want to use it. How much insight did he possess, then?

The most awful thing about some of these monsters was their pitiful, wasted brilliance. She slammed the door and went back into the living room—and was appalled to see a change in her chair. The cushions had been slashed end to end. Stuffing bulged like summer clouds, and tufts of it lay on the floor like dandelion fluff, some still blowing about. But where was he? Nowhere to be seen, yet there was nowhere to hide. He had the clever deftness of the paranoid. Certain paranoids were almost mind readers, it sometimes seemed, and paranoid schizophrenics could be so quick and empathetic that they seemed to speak your words before you did.

The rat was a terrible sign. This was no game, and he was not going to be dissuaded by talk. When you find a child who tortures and kills animals, it is regarded as a clinical emergency. Animal torture is in the background of many seriously violent men, most notably the compulsive homicides. She was in the presence, she feared, of profound psychosis, of incurability.

Talk was the only weapon she possessed, and she was not going to abandon the only weapon she possessed—unless it wasn't a weapon at all, but a dangerous explosive about to blow up in her face. She'd said—what?—twenty words to him, and the chair had been ripped with vicious fury. Her skin crawled.

The sense of being in a trap now became very strong. As she had in the car, she froze. It was almost a physical thing and presented a dimension of helplessness that was new to her. She'd had one patient or another say that they had frozen with fear. It was something like what a mouse did when confronting a snake. Her analysis was that it was a survival mechanism triggered by extreme jeopardy. Animals that froze when threatened, such as opossums, did so because the reptiles that had threatened them in earlier ages could not see things that didn't move.

It was a dangerous response for a woman confronting a man who could see her perfectly clearly. Her eyes searched toward the front door. In the kitchen, the oven popped.

The fear that he would torture her with fire finally overcame her locked joints and stiffened muscles, and she emitted a great, wheezing gasp and broke for the door. Her feet thudded as she crossed the rug. She dragged open the sliding door with a grinding crash and dashed out like a deer in hopeless flight.

For a reckless instant she hesitated on the deck, trying to see if he was anywhere around. Then she climbed the rail and clambered through the ferns that grew against the side of the house.

Suddenly he was there, a shaded figure, completely

still, filling the bedroom window. He regarded her with folded arms. His stocking mask flattened his face and narrowed his eyes into the blurred image of monstrosity. She threw back her head and screamed as she lurched in the ferns. In her scream she heard the call of the ancient savage, forlorn at the physical weakness of her sex. She scrambled and struggled up onto the shale.

She went past the car, heading up the steep road. He was behind her, of course; he must be. She could picture him coming gracefully and quickly, fully in control of all the physical power of his sex, his male muscles rippling easily to the demented commands of his flaring, exploding mind. She could not allow herself to stop or even to slow down. This road might be an uphill mile, but it was the one long, impossible chance that she had, and after this there would be no more chances.

She ran as never before in her adult life, moving gracefully enough on her long legs but also very quickly toward the limit of her endurance. She climbed and climbed . . . and, when she was not overtaken, began to hope that the impossible was happening, that she was actually putting some distance between them.

She got to the first switchback and rounded it, moving along the three hundred level feet to the next upward-leaning turn with her breath coming white hot in her throat and her calves wobbling and her knees singing protest.

But he wasn't back there, he was not, and she was now officially and indisputably winning, she was easily a quarter of a mile ahead of him, he would have to run like the very wind to catch her. No question, he was suddenly at a disadvantage. She made another little sound, but this was not a sound of panic, it was a stifled, sup-pressed noise of glee and rage, the haughty snort of a deer who has unexpectedly escaped the wolves.

On either side of the road the pines were like walls. One side was a steep drop, and in that direction there were occasional mocking glimpses of the lake. The other side was practically straight up, a cliff choked with more narrow trees. The road between them was perhaps ten feet wide, and it was in these ten feet that she must seek her freedom.

But soon she could not make her legs go as fast as they had at first, could not force her feet to rise from the soft, impairing shale, could not prevent her breath from coming like the last breath of a dying soul. She went slower and slower, struggling with wet gasps that did not help, and she knew that she was going to have to stop. She dropped to slow motion, her legs going like the hands of an old watch, the road passing slowly beneath her. There was a sense now that it did not end, that she was not in New Hampshire, but in hell.

Very suddenly she went down. It wasn't a fall, not that, but a semicontrolled cessation of motion. She sank down and came to rest. "Shit," she said as if she'd had a flat or run out of gas.

Now she heard behind her the steady crunch of boots in shale. She took hard, frantic breaths and pushed herself upward with her arms. It didn't work, her legs would not obey, not really, but she did manage to get to a crawling position. Whimpering and cursing, she dragged herself along.

She found that she could crawl and by crawling keep

a fair pace. Soon, though, the sharp little shale bits were digging into her hands. Soon it hurt too much and she stopped again, this time pulling herself to the side of the road and even a little bit into the trees on the up slope. She dared not try to negotiate the other side. Not too far below the line of trees there was a lethal cliff, she remembered it from years ago, and below it black rocks. She was a little bit hidden now, up here in the secret shade of the trees. She toyed with the idea of getting to Kevin's, but how far it might be from here she could not tell. If she got lost in the woods, she'd be helpless.

He had to be back there, and in a few minutes he was going to come right past her. Then she thought: I've left tracks in the shale.

She crawled a little deeper into the woods, then clung to the trunk of a narrow pine as if she were being dragged by a wind, as if powerful arms were coming round her already, were tearing her away from her refuge right now.

She would be draped like a sack over his shoulder, she knew, and would feel that awful sense of absolute helplessness that she so deeply dreaded.

But he did not come. She waited a long time—how long she did not know—because one of her self-imposed conditions of relaxation had been to leave her watch at home. She waited, in the end, until the trees had grown long shadows. During this time she began seriously to entertain the notion that he had panicked and run off into the woods.

Eventually she became certain that she was not being

followed. He would have appeared by now even if he had himself been reduced to all fours.

Should she open the question of hallucination? Most people would not, but she had to look at some of the hallucinatory cases she'd treated. People saw things even more elaborately fallacious and just as vividly real. One man had described a railroad accident in which a train had come blasting into the waiting room of Penn Station so vividly that she had fleetingly thought to consult the papers, just to see if there hadn't been some tiny little accident.

Maybe the reason that she'd felt such an overwhelming need to isolate herself was that she had unconsciously known that she was going mad. Maybe she was calling out to herself for help, asking that she make herself a patient.

Should she go back down to the house, see if the chair was really torn, if the rat was really in the oven? She stood and wobbled back out into the road. But then she stopped. She did not have the ability to go back. In fact, she was finished with it and with all places like it for the rest of her born days. She might even start sleeping with the lights on again, something that she hadn't done since she was eleven and Dad had announced that night-lights were now kids' stuff.

The silence that had enveloped the place again had a very different feel to it from what she'd wanted. This was a cruel, dangerous silence, the terrified quiet of an awful place where owls swooped through the night and rats scampered in the crawl space.

Walking as quickly as she could, which was not fast

at all, she continued up toward the Tarleton High Road. Hallucinations or not, one thing was certain: Mr. Matthias was going to have to drive her out here and wait while she packed, and she would make him follow her all the way to the Deerfield Airport. If necessary, she would charter a plane to get down to Boston so she could take the shuttle home this afternoon.

She was going to spend the rest of her vacation time holed up in her apartment with the air conditioners roaring and watch every old movie in her considerable collection and call down to the bookstore and get them to send up nice, peaceful novels about social life in the English countryside.

It took her the better part of an hour to ascend all the way to the paved road, and when she began to hear the occasional hum of a passing car she found herself willing her legs to run and having nothing happen.

The last twenty yards of the shale road were the steepest, and these she negotiated with pain and difficulty, scrabbling in the sharp stones and ripping her already filthy skirt. She went clambering up the last five yards to the sudden growl of an oncoming truck, and at that moment the blue pickup came wheeling in from the main road, and turned toward her and turned on her, and came snarling down at her.

For the split of an instant she was too surprised to move, and maybe it slowed down a little then. Glancing toward the cliff, she noted that the trees here were so thickly grown that they formed a barrier as tight as any barbed-wire fence. She was forced to turn and run, loping and skidding back down the road she'd so painfully climbed, and the truck stayed right behind her, and this time she was sure that it was not a hallucination—no, it was not, it was entirely and totally real.

She had allowed an excess of professional knowledge to push aside an obvious reality. There had never been any hallucinatory process. There had been, however, a devilishly clever and cruel man, and that man was herding her right back where she'd come from.

The truck actually nudged her thighs as its engine guttered, and she thought she could also hear laughter, cruel, high, and—it seemed—young.

The truck hit her then, and she went sprawling and rolling and skidding in the shale. She skidded on her knees, then her breasts, then her left shoulder, and last her face, skinning herself where she was naked and ripping the clothes that covered her where she wasn't.

Then the truck was on her again, engine screaming. He would run her over, he would break her to bits under his wheels; that was obviously the alternative she would face if she did not get herself to her feet and get moving again, get moving instantly and go fast and not look back toward that chrome grill and that laughter-screaming shadow behind the windshield.

Down she went farther and farther, descending amid the song of the warbler and the lazy buzzing of the summer insects, while behind her came the snarling of the machine and the crunch of its tires and the laughter in the closed cab and, when the dear cabin came into view, the cheerful tooting of the horn.

CHAPTER FIVE

The Heat of the Day

I n the end, hopelessness steals everything. It emerges slowly, by degrees. First it steals the little efforts by which people care for themselves. They get dirty and begin to move listlessly. Next it robs them of their words, leaving silence in place of all that talk. Then passion dies; their very skin, untouched and unloved, loses the color of life. Beyond that there is the terrible plasticity of compliance.

When it comes fast, there is generally fight before surrender. The shock of the woman who realizes that she is going to be raped and cannot escape translates at first into some kind of effort.

If, however, she should be made to wait, a new psychological situation will result. Some will go mad. Others will become acquiescent with despair. Others will struggle until there is no struggle left, helpless to stop themselves even in the face of the absolute uselessness of their efforts.

Helen dashed into the cabin, slammed the door, and threw the dead bolt. Leaning against the heavy jamb, she actually felt a moment's relief. Then she heard the pickup's engine stop and she raced from window to window, throwing them down. She put down the bar that locked the deck door, she turned every lock on every window. She threw groceries onto the top of the trapdoor in the pantry, so at least there'd be some sound if he came in that way. She peered out into the soft afternoon.

Up the march of marigolds, behind a golden haze of mayflies, stood the pickup. There was nothing painted on its door, and she couldn't see the license plates from here. She could, however, see that there was nobody in the cab. That was a shame; she wanted very much to see her opponent.

She needed to at least engage in the first clinical act, which was to evaluate the appearance of the patient. What expression was on the face, was the skin dry or moist; did the hands shake, did the voice tremble; and the clothing—was it unkempt or neat, clean or dirty? Simple clues, but they would be the foundation of understanding.

She knew that he had an organized mind. But how organized? How much anticipating could he really do? A fair amount, she thought, judging from what had just happened out on that road. Then she thought, If he didn't want me alive right now, I would already be dead. Then she thought, I will not live through this.

But there was always that "unless," and her will, her love of life, her feeling that her own life was worth something to her and to others, kept arguing fiercely on its behalf.

There came a sound from the bedroom—a faint click. Rushing in, she saw nothing. She threw open the flimsy sliding door on the closet. Nothing there but her jacket, her two sweaters, some skirts, and some jeans—which gave her an idea. She took off the ruined skirt and pulled on a pair of jeans, then replaced her shredded blouse with a T-shirt.

It wasn't much, but she was at least doing something for herself, and that felt better. She also searched the back of the closet for that BB gun but found only a pile of old magazines that she would once have considered charming: copies of *Collier's* and *Life* from the fifties. She pushed them aside with her foot, seeking for something lethal or that could be made lethal.

She threw open every drawer in the dresser, but the ones that didn't contain her things or the spare bedding were quite empty.

From the living room there came another of the clicks. She rushed down the hall, but once again there was no sign of disturbance. So she continued her search here. Maybe she could pry a big stone loose from the fireplace. She pushed and shoved at them, but they were cemented in tight. Maybe the poker. Oh, yes! How obvious, how simple, how simply wonderful.

She lifted it out of the little stand of fire tools and

waved it around over her head. Oh, yes, this had heft, this had the weight of iron on its tip, this would knock a man senseless, this would kill.

Thank you, Doctor. Look what you've ended up with, you and your therapeutic promise—a weapon in your hand and a savage will to use it. With both hands clutching its neck, she marched to the kitchen.

The sun angled in the wide windows through hazy shafts of smoke from the still-running oven. Water dripped, the air reeked of burned fur.

The poker felt light in her hand. She could almost taste the joy her tormented state was bringing him, even feel the quick and mirthful beating of his heart.

She went back to the living room and threw herself into the ravaged Morris chair, the poker across her knees. It was tempting to consider that he'd left it here, at some level, on purpose. He'd certainly had plenty of time to remove it before she got back from the store.

What did this man want, and on what level did he want it? People do not express themselves simply; all human beings are complicated. If she'd learned nothing else in her career, she had learned this. The human mind was the surest and only proof of the existence of a hallowed beyond; there was a ghost in this machine.

Undoubtedly the conscious man did not want her to have this poker. But what of the ghost? The ghost had left it for her.

As she sat there, her physical needs began to assert themselves. She was thirstier than ever, she had to use the toilet, she was beginning to feel hunger. What's more, the skinned places burned and she felt filthy and she was itchy from being in the pines. She was tired in bone and muscle, and if she sat here in this quiet, she might fall into a doze despite the terrible tension, or perhaps because of it.

She hefted the poker. What would happen if she had a chance to deliver a death blow? What indeed? She didn't really know that side of herself. She'd never killed anything, certainly never thought about killing a person.

Placing her in this position was in itself an assault. All of her life she had been about healing and loving, making babies and having a career in caring work. And now here she was with this damned poker, not so different from the thigh bone an ape might wield. By just showing up here, he had taken her all the way back to the primitive beginnings of the species, and she must never forget that this was where his heart lived.

He would be capable of inflicting great suffering, because he would not identify with her humanity; his emotional structure would be too primitive for that. Unfortunately that did not mean he'd also be stupid. So far, what he'd done suggested a mixture of profound psychosis and normal or above normal intelligence.

There could be no more dangerous creature on this earth than a brilliant psychopath. Poker or no poker, she felt naked and exposed and very helpless.

All her life her body had been sacred, part of her own very private space. But not now; now she was suddenly due to be destroyed in the context of profound humiliation and maddening pain. She licked dry lips with little tongue darts; she felt her jaw crushing itself.

With a snarl that she hardly recognized as coming

from herself, she leaped up and dashed into the bathroom. She slammed the door and threw the paltry little lock and crouched with her poker jammed against the door.

Then she glanced over at the closed shower stall. Was there not a thickening of shadow in there?

He was in here, she had come right to him, he had known she would eventually, he had correctly deduced that and he was *right here.* Slowly she rose to her feet.

How should she handle this? Talk? Smash the glass with the poker? There were no references, no ideas, no notion of what would be best. Why? Because nothing would be best. She wasn't going to reach a man in this state with a few moments of dialogue. No, a man like this had to be captive to you, he had to be a prisoner before the slow process of therapy could even be tried.

Carefully, unsure of herself, she raised her poker and brought it slamming down into the shower door. The glass melted away like so much fog, and the top edge of stainless steel went clattering into the stall—which was entirely empty except for a large brown towel that had been left hanging in it.

It fell and lay amid the crumbles of glass, an intricate study in the stillness at the center of every violent act. Absurdly, she thought that this would cost Mr. Matthias more than the fifty-dollar deposit he had asked of her.

Now the bathroom felt like a trap. The instinct to escape suddenly overwhelmed the instinct to hide, and she threw open the door. Immediately she noticed that there was something new on the wall opposite. It was a photograph, a Polaroid print tacked up with a thumbtack.

She took it down, breaking her left thumbnail as she prised up the tack.

She carried it from the dim corridor into the sunlit living room and was sitting down to study it when she realized that the naked woman in it was trussed. The poor face was haggard, teeth bared. She was lying on what appeared to be a stone floor. The way the picture bled off into black suggested that it had been taken in a dark room.

Her hair was stringy, as if it had been made wet and then left to dry without any brushing or attention. There was a distinct red line on her lower abdomen. It smiled like a cesarean scar, but it was not a scar.

Her eyes were bulging, her brows raised, her mouth twisted in a snarl. Her cheeks were soaked. Helen realized that she was screaming.

She told herself frantically that this could have been posed. They sold far worse things on Eighth Avenue in New York. You could get a snuff picture for ten dollars, but it would be nothing more than clever makeup and bad acting.

She put the picture on the mantel. No sense in damaging it. Maybe she'd get out of this and be able to get it to the cops. Clearly it was important evidence.

She turned around and faced the back of the house, where he must be, no doubt just feet away. She could imagine him vibrating with delight.

She sighed. Sometimes it was entirely too easy to regard testosterone as the ruin of the world. Look at Naziism with its erect penis salute and stiff goose-stepping.

Helen Myrer, a white Anglo-Saxon Protestant, was

very aware of Hitler, being attached by marriage to the magical life of Jews. Ever since she'd met Al, the process of discovering the vast spiritual, intellectual, and cultural content of Judaism had been one of her great pleasures. She had so enjoyed the bar mitzvah of her son and bat mitzvah of her daughter, with all the dancing and the wine and food, and the pride she felt in her young people coming of age.

Now why was she thinking of that? Perhaps her effort to reach the miserable boy whom she suspected would be at the center of all this was turning her mind to memories of her own kids. To the disturbing thing she had just been shown, there could be no coherent response but silence. She knew that the woman was not made up in some Manhattan studio; she was lying on a very real stone floor, where Helen herself might soon lie. She did not want to find out the meaning of that mark on her.

Could there be any relationship more intimate than that between the torturer and his victim? What was that piece of Kafka's about the machine that etched the name of the crime upon the body of the criminal, etched and etched until his life dripped away and he perished in flayed agony? "In the Penal Colony." Yes, it had been about meaningless suffering, the curse of the world. In that sense, it had been about such a situation as this.

However, Kafka had not lived through the defining half of this century, had he? So he didn't know certain things, did he? He did not know that his machine would actually become part of the human soul, but that it would not etch the names of crimes on the quaking skin of the guilty. No, he did not know that it would etch instead upon the bodies of the innocent, and it would etch not even gibberish; no, it would simply etch.

She noticed the breath of the fireplace, cool and dank, flowing out against the back of the hand that clutched the poker. It caused her to realize that it was getting hot in here with all the windows closed and she thought at once, What use? What use, if he'd come right past the locks like this to torment her with his evil little picture?

She slammed her poker against the stone mantel, then strode from window to window, throwing them all open, getting a little air in the damn place. Then she slid open the deck door. Why not? The locks were totally pointless.

She glared out across the deck. "The stairs need some work," she muttered. Then she turned back to the room. "Let's watch a little TV, honey," she said in a stinging voice. "Okay, love? Since we obviously can't go down to the *dock!*"

She could feel a tension enter the silence. Back in the house somewhere, her tone had obviously communicated itself, and he had stiffened against the rage in it. The temptation was great, but she must not anger him. He was far from in control of himself; but then again, it might be merciful simply to be hacked to pieces at once rather than tormented over slow time.

"Let me see, what would you like?" she said as she moved toward the television that stood opposite the fireplace, just beside the doorway into the back of the house. "A baseball game, perhaps? No? Maybe there's a snuff film on—*Banzai Babes*—isn't that thing called?" It was a legend whispered about among clinicians, a tape of three women being tortured to death. There had been an enormous police investigation, many questions asked of New York's small coterie of psychologists who had knowledge of the criminally insane.

The filmmakers hadn't been identified, the studio hadn't been discovered, not even the bodies had been found. Dead anonymous women, who knew who they had been, addicts, probably, strung out enough to risk being hog-tied by strangers in the hope of making a few bucks.

She threw herself down in front of the television and hit the remote. A Red Sox game, an Oprah rerun (wives who tried to murder their husbands' mistresses debate them), a movie that seemed to consist exclusively of gunfire, a documentary about a hospital bombing, a show about bass fishing. There was also an old black-and-white movie, which she returned to. Montgomery Clift was in the process of upsetting Olivia De Havilland. Wasn't that called *Washington Square,* after the Henry James novel? No, they'd changed the name. It was called *The Heiress.*

It had been made in the forties, but it was truly like observing something from another planet. How could the world have possibly fallen down like this? What had taken us from *The Heiress* to the Manson murders?

There came a small sound from the hallway, a stealthy creak. She hefted her poker, came slowly to her feet. It would be now. Surely it would be now.

But no, all that happened was that Olivia De Havilland was charmed by Montgomery Clift, her father took it badly, they had words. It occurred to Helen that the film had been made while the Russian Myrers were ceasing to correspond with the American Myrers. All sixty-one members of her husband's Russian family had gone to the gas chambers in the time it took to make *The Heiress.*

Death didn't frighten Helen Myrer, it disappointed her. She feared pain, of course, but what she really hated about this situation was the meaninglessness. To die to satisfy the cravings of some miserable, failed creature who was barely definable as human was just so pointless.

"It's stupid," she said. She stopped herself. Shut up, you fool, that is exactly the wrong tactic. But her rage would not let her stop. "Stupid," she yelled, more loudly.

Oh, woman, shut yourself up!

But it really got to her, and she jumped up and roared, "You stupid, stupid bastard!"

She closed her mouth, crunching her jaw. She was not going to make another sound. She was not! "I'm a human being," she bellowed. "Can't you see that?" This was weakness, shut up, shut up!

And yes, he could see it; that was the whole sick point.

So she shut up, finally. She forced herself by absolute will to become calm, to cease to let the unconscious rule.

"I have a family, I have a career, I have patients, mister. There will be people who are concerned. Do you think they'll just let this go?"

How remarkably stupid. Where was the therapeutic

promise by which she lived? All she'd done was threaten him, thus reminding him that he had to hurry.

She heard something—a sigh. It was the sound a parent might make at a child's tiresome violation of some oft challenged household rule.

"I suppose you know what I am. Your friendly shrink. Ironic, right?" There issued from her throat a burst of what sounded almost like canned laughter. "That you'd pick a psychologist. To . . . do this with. Of all people, am I right?" She faced the doorway. "Listen, do you know my name? Maybe you do. Maybe I told you. But it's Helen, I'll tell you again. Myrer. Originally Helen Pennington." Again she laughed. "WASP, I fear. The human variety, that is." Without appearing an idiot, be open and warm. "So what's yours?"

The response was silence, of course. What else would it be? He'd have no more capacity for interpersonal interaction than a two-year-old. But when she was naked and trussed, you could be sure that he would turn out to have a powerful imagination, no doubt animated by a little boy's cheerful barbarity.

There just had to be some clever way of gaining control of this situation. She sat down—threw herself into one of the fluffy little chairs in front of the television. "My friend, you and I certainly are in a pickle. Or, let's be frank. I wouldn't describe you as being in one. Or is that really true? It cannot be pleasant. Hardly, to do this to yourself. I know that. I know a bit about you. You'd be surprised."

Now wait, what if he was paranoid? Why couldn't she at least do this well?

She paused, closed her eyes, gave herself a little space. Now, start again, focus on problems and solutions. "I know that you're suffering. Oh, I am suffering, too! Suffering terribly! Make no mistake, this is probably as terrible a torture in its way as—" Again, she stopped. She didn't need to address his fantasy. It was already sufficiently developed, thank you.

This was surprisingly difficult. There was none of the assurance she felt in her familiar setting. "I wonder, when you think of the way you are inside—how you feel about yourself—I wonder how you can actually— actually—" She had to stop because her throat was literally closing.

She took a series of deep breaths, then forced herself to go on. "I think that I could relieve your suffering. All kinds of ways. If you'd just come in here and talk. Just talk with me. Oh, you can still do everything you need to do. Don't get me wrong, I've accepted that. That's going to happen. But if you . . . just want . . ."

There was not a sound from him. Not a damned peep. Could she be getting through? She continued, trying not to sound as frantic as she was. "So, maybe we could start. We have to start somewhere. Like, what was the first moment you realized you had it in you to do this . . . sort of thing? It's an unusual sort of thing to do, you have to admit. Not everybody does it. Of course, that doesn't surprise you. You know how special you are."

"I am special."

His words—the three of them delivered very softly— hung on the air. And she thought, Sweet Jesus, I actually have a snowball's chance in a blast furnace. "Oh, that is very clear. You are bright, and you have a sense of humor. Honking your horn when you did, well, I was terrified, let me tell you, but I saw the cleverness. The moment you came driving up, I was impressed. It was clever. To say the least. Remarkably so. You know, my son is clever—not like you—but rather clever. I could get you some advantages." No, no, don't bargain *now*, wait until there's something on the table! Hostage Negotiation 101, you jackass! "Some advantages," she ended vaguely.

"I think I have all the advantages, Dr. Myrer."

He spoke with breathless excitement.

"What I'd like is to see you. I mean, you're like the Shadow around here. Are you young? You sound young." Eighteen to twenty-five would be her guess, allowing for the fact that the voice of a man in his state would always have an unfinished quality to it. At the point that the pain of his life had been at its greatest, he would have stopped maturing. "You know, I'm thinking. At first, I was scared of you. Then I hated you. I was pissed. Oh, enraged! But now that I've heard your voice, I think I'm beginning to see you're just as human as the rest of us, God only knows. And hurting. My friend—is it young friend?—you are in pain. And I've done what we psychologists call anger transference. I still feel hate, but it is now directed toward whoever hurt you so terribly that you must do this."

Now that was a reasonably good attempt. That had a possibility of reaching him. She leaned forward in the chair, thinking that she might try to go back out to the kitchen and finally get some water. What would that mean to him?

"I want to warn you," she said, "I'm going to get up and get some water. I won't come in your direction. I won't even look at you." Slowly she stood. Instinct was telling her that great care was now needed. It felt like walking in front of a coiled snake. But she had to; she needed the water, and she needed to establish a presence in the relationship for herself.

Everything in the kitchen was as it had been. She took a glass out of the cabinet over the sink and turned on the tap.

She was feeling the relief of the water when the glass suddenly plunged from her hand and shattered in the sink.

She stared down at it, briefly amazed. Movement, then, right beside her, made her jump away.

The stocking mask pressed his face into a nightmare. She thought, That's what they call a blackjack, that thing he has in his hand. Then his hand moved, and with it came darkness.

CHAPTER SIX

Vespers

She was aware first of the birds singing, then of the sensation of cool air against her naked skin. She reached up, feeling for the pain that drummed in her left temple. The skin was tight from swelling, and the spot was extremely tender.

How had she been injured, and how had she come to be lying . . . here? In fact, where was she? She opened her eyes, suddenly feeling an obscure sort of fear. Oh, thank God, she was in the bedroom, all was well.

How could she have done this? She searched her mind, but there was nothing clear at all. Her recollections of the day just passing had the half-destroyed quality of dream memories.

Traumatic amnesia: the short-term memory had been disrupted by the blow. She was lucky she'd managed to get to the bed before . . . but a blow like this dropped you like a stone.

It had obviously been a day of intense physicality because she ached all over, not just in her head. And her head—it could be concussed.

"How'd I get my clothes off?" she muttered as she rose slowly and experimentally from the bed.

The room seemed to go round, the floor actually to tilt. The pain in her head was like something from another dimension, another reality, a nightmare thing disguised in the trappings of the ordinary.

Without quite understanding why, she assumed a defensive crouch. The sun was low, and much of the house was in shadow. It was very quiet. Although, if she listened, she thought she could hear larks in the height of the sky.

"You've been struck a blow," she said to herself. Then, in rising wonder, "You've been struck a severe blow."

It was no accident, that was obvious. What did her mind keep touching in the hazy light of memory, what monstrous thing had happened to her?

Had there been an intruder . . . a robbery?

Had she been raped?

As quickly as she could, she went into the bathroom, which was so dark that she had to turn on the lights. She sat on the toilet and examined herself.

No rape evidence, but what was this faint red mark along her belly? Had it been made with a ballpoint? Or perhaps it was from the way she'd been lying—a cesarean scar pressed by a crease in the sheet.

There was a sort of unfocused flash, a senseless blur, like film that had escaped its gate. But still nothing definite. She soaked a washcloth in cold water and applied it to the side of her head. And saw, oh, that her temple was seriously bruised. The blow had been brutal.

A little water to get the encrusted blood off, and she could see a nasty contusion. A blow like this would have sent a shock wave right through the brain. No wonder her short-term memory was gone.

She found some Tylenol and took three, swallowing them carefully, trying to avoid moving her head. God, but it hurt.

She stood staring into the mirror at her haggard reflection and saying to herself, "This has been *done*."

She'd run. Yes, that was right, she'd run. But there had been no escape. She'd come back.

A horn had honked. Honked and honked and she'd struggled, she'd been desperate. Something awful had happened.

Then she saw the shattered shower stall. She stood looking at it in amazement . . . and then remembered her poker. She wanted it, she wanted it right now!

She threw the bolt on the bathroom door and leaned against it with her eyes closed. To rebuild memories disrupted by traumatic amnesia, you have to start with the small things.

All right, she'd come here on that plane. New England Airlines. She'd met Mr. . . . Matthias. Yes, filled out idiotic forms, paid and gotten her key, come out here, and—oh, God.

Oh, God.

She remembered that strange, gnomic figure with a sock full of iron filings or whatever in his hand, and his quick movements.

Suddenly there was a heave deep in her gut. She felt horrible; she could remember that he'd grabbed her as she fell.

She'd been in twilight shock then, a state that could come from the right sort of blow. A good hypnotist could probably recover some memories of what had happened after the blow, but she knew little about hypnosis.

Something tickled along the line on her stomach. She rubbed it, then looked down, and when she looked down she recalled a brief image of another woman. Her fingers went to the red pencil mark that traced the line of a cesarean. God, how creepy.

She clutched her belly, her eyes wide with horror. There was a picture, she'd seen a picture of another woman with just such a scar . . . a woman bound and lying on stone, her face distended by a scream.

Furiously she wiped at the mark. But it wasn't pencil or wax, it was ink. Indelible ink.

She'd been drinking water—so thirsty—and he had suddenly appeared beside her. He'd been standing there in a white shirt, looking up at her from the position of a largish child, but concealed in a stocking mask.

She must be dealing with a spectacular monster. Appalled by the evil intricacy of the mind that had conceived this violent, strange assault, she sat down on the floor and pressed her back against the front of the sink and put her feet against the door. With this leverage against him, he'd not be able to open it except by breaking it to pieces.

There was the window, of course, but it was small and high on the house. He'd go for the door first. She sat under the fluorescent light, waiting grimly.

But he might be gone. Of course, that was possible. She must have been on the bed for hours. Most of the day, actually. Where was that damned Slim? If he'd only come do what he'd been asked to do, her problems would be at an end.

She recalled the blackjack in the pudgy hand, the strange, slick face in the mask. He had hit her hard, and in a very specific place. Fingers trembling, she touched the wound. That evil little troll! He had not raped her, he had not penetrated, not physically, but this was as devastating a psychological rape as she had ever heard of. Over the course of this day she had been reduced, carefully and methodically. He was breaking her expertly.

She fought for control, fought against the various tides that were rising against her: panic, anger, irrationality, instinct. None was useful, none were capable of saving her.

Think, Doctor, go over in your mind the *Annals of Abnormal Psychology* until you come to the papers about . . . what? Psychological warfare? Because, dear girl, you've got to understand what has happened to this man to make him as he is, or you are going to die.

Detailed memory was returning. She recalled the sequence of events that had led to her escape attempt.

And oh, yes, that blue truck right at the last moment, and that awful run back down the road in front of it . . .

that was the source of the horn she'd recalled initially. Well, why not toot his horn? He'd been having fun.

The Gestapo had sometimes broken people with false hope. A cell would be left open by apparent oversight, and the prisoner would be allowed to escape and not hauled back until he had seen the sky.

She pushed against the door until it creaked. The breaking of the will . . . well, look at this, you evil bastard. Look at this broken will in here . . . on the floor naked with a face full of tears and a gut fluttering with sick dread. Yes, you know. You know how to break a will.

She could imagine herself in compliance, her limbs plastic like the limbs of a catatonic, submitting to his binding and then the enormous knife that was the first of him that she had ever seen. Yes, she remembered, she remembered it all now: going into the pantry with the groceries in her hands—oh, so happy, so glad to be here—and seeing out of the corner of her eye that terrible knife.

But why hadn't she simply gotten in the car and driven away? Oh, yes, but she had—tried. Tried to do that, too, didn't you, dear?

She slammed her foot against the door. "Scum," she cried. *"Animal!"* And then said to herself, "He is laughing now because you just did that. You are transferring power every time you show your rage. Every time, remember that."

What the hell did she mean, transferring? There was nothing left to transfer, it was all transferred. She sighed a long, angry sigh. She had to get up and go out there and see if he was even still here.

But of course he was. It might be possible for a non-professional to imagine that he had left, but she imagined no such thing. To locate and trap a victim like this would not be a commonplace achievement for him. So she was valuable property, and you don't abandon valuable property . . . especially not when you're having so damn much fun with it.

She heard a sound so completely from ordinary life that it seemed impossible. But it was not impossible, it was from the living room, and it was the phone ringing.

Hadn't she tried that? Yes, surely. Or . . . no. No, she had assumed that the line was dead. So she'd made a mistake. She had to go out there and grab it and get out just one word, "Help," that was all, but she needed to do it right now.

Too bad it involved leaving this nice, locked room, because if he hadn't left, he was certain to be *right there*.

It was still ringing, and she was not more than thirty feet away.

If he was here, where would he be—watching from the bedroom perhaps—or out in the hall with his enormous knife, waiting to butcher her if she emerged?

So she got to her feet, listening still to the ringing, listening to it sounding through the house like a summons from angels. She opened the door.

The hall was dark, the phone louder, and she was so afraid that it was hard even to put one foot in front of the other. But she couldn't go wobbling along. This had to be sudden, this had to be a mad dash and she was al-

ready wasting time. Like a gazelle, this lovely woman
ran through the house with her hair flying behind her,
her lithe arms swinging, her long legs pumping, her face
in its fully mature beauty flushed, the little light of the
evening gleaming upon the curves of her breasts.

She made it to the living room, sailed down the steps,
and went swiftly and with surprising silence across the
carpet, arriving at the telephone table all in a matter of a
few seconds. She leaped on the instrument with a fal-
con's quick skill and lifted the receiver and heard, "Carpets! Carpets! Carpets! Press one on your Touch-Tone
phone to get your carpets cleaned by King Carpet during our phone special sale days!" She thought, There'll
be an operator, and tried to press one, and discovered
that it was a rotary phone. New, they called this new!

"Hello," she whispered. She tried clicking the tongue.
"Hello?" She dialed the number one. Silence. She
pressed the tongue and kept it pressed, waiting to be certain that the connection would be broken and she'd get
the dial tone she needed. The town had 911, all she had
to do was follow the instructions. House number K-142
on the fire map, it was right here on Mr. Matthias's carefully typed emergency instructions.

She released the tongue . . . but there was no answering dial tone. "Damn you," she said, hitting it.

And then, finally, the carpet company's dialer gave up
on her and she was rewarded with a wonderful, clear
tone. She dialed the nine, hopping from foot to foot as
the rotor swung around, clicking ever so slowly back
into place. How had people ever lived with phones like

this? Finally it came to rest and she dialed one, then one again. There it was, 911.

There was a ring, then another. Hurry up, you idiot, this is the real thing! A third.

A click. "Hello! I need help! I've been assaulted, I'm out here alone—" Midway through the sentence she knew that the silence she was talking into was wrong. "Hello?" There was the flat, empty quality of disconnection.

She choked out a ragged moan. The bastard was manipulating the telephone. He was a little boy playing a prank—toying with her—being cruel, a little boy angry for attention. Oh yes, and she'd like to give him a bit of attention—throw him across the room into that stone fireplace and hit him until his blood was running down into the ash catcher.

Shit, shit, shit. Thoughts like that were worse than useless. If she ever expected to gain control of the situation, she had to gain and maintain a level of professional affect.

But this had really been devastating, it had really been clever. And it wasn't over yet: the phone, still in her hand, was once again emitting a dial tone. She said, "No doubt you can hear me." How her voice trembled. Had to control that. "No doubt you can hear me," this time from the chest, stronger. But where was the clinician's voice, gentle with concern, quietly authoritative? "You have a chance, you know. You have a chance. I know you want that chance or you would not have come to me. You are asking for help, whether you know it or not. Let it be clear, my message is therapeutic, it is heal-

ing. You can be healed. I can heal you. I have it in my
power to do this. I know the magic, I know how to reach
in and operate on your pain and relieve your agony, and
do it only with—"

A soft click and silence indicated that he had termi-
nated the connection. "Only with words," she said. She
put down the instrument.

She had to dress. No matter how much her head hurt,
how bad she felt, she had at all costs to meet him on
some approximation of an equal footing. The analyst
could not be unclothed, no, that would make the whole
thing absurd, another joke. She'd get nowhere with it,
analyzing him back to health from the position of a
naked victim.

She wished she knew where he was. Under the house,
perhaps. Possibly the telephone box was there. With the
hard winters up here, such things were not generally attached to outside walls.

Well, maybe he'd outdone himself. As long as he remained down there, she had a little lead time for anything she might care to do. Perhaps it would be best to
try another run, this one through the woods. Trust luck
to get her to Kevin's place. It would be night soon, and
at night even her random blundering might be effective.
But she couldn't do it naked and—especially—barefoot,
that was absolutely certain.

She opened her closet to get some clothes but found
things changed. Gone were her plain skirts and her
jeans, gone were her running shoes and T-shirts and
sweatshirts.

She ran her hand along the empty closet pole. This

had been a series of clever entrapments. She was being kept here without even a rope to tie her. And then she saw, lying on the floor, the shredded remains of her clothes.

She knelt. He had slashed these things to pieces with his knife—look at the way the breast of her jacket was ripped, as if he'd slashed and slashed at it. A sexualized, pumping motion, in all likelihood.

She peered deeper into the closet of his mind, to see if she might be able to find something more revealing, yet . . .

In the dark at the back of the closet, she saw an object that made her lunge down and scrabble. She pulled it out—an old flip-flop sandal, not hers, but . . . didn't it have a mate? No. She ran her hands back deeper—if he'd set a bear trap, God help her—but no—here, yes! Oh, yes, you beautiful, dear little flip-flop, you have found your sister!

She regarded them with the wonder, the elation, that she might have a suit of armor. She literally hugged them to her, hugged them and pressed their blue soles against her cheeks, reveling in them, in the escape they would bring.

She examined them. No, there was nothing wrong. These sandals hadn't been sabotaged in any way. They were a little small, perhaps, but she could manage. They were going to be perfectly functional, and she could negotiate the road again.

But that wasn't wise, was it? No, Mr. Brilliant Psychopath had the road covered, honk honk.

"And in the middle of his life, he came to a dark

wood. . . ." Yes, that would be the way to go. Although, not naked. She had to have something to wear to make it through that tangle without being skinned.

She sifted through the ruined clothes. "Damnit!"

So why leave the sandals—or rather, put them here? For she had not noticed them before, and she thought she would have. Were they meant as a token of hope lost?

Subtle ploy. He might be very bright. What if he was a mad genius? She'd dealt with more than one mind that had been too brilliant to remain sane.

"I am a bright woman," she said as she rose from the closet and saw herself in the mirror that was bolted to the back of the bedroom door. She did not often think of her looks, but now she saw that they might help her, they might be the reason he hadn't acted out yet. She doubted that she would be a good physical surrogate for the mother of a man built like that. His mother would have been short and stout, and if there were farmers around here back in the fifties, then also aged by the harsh conditions of her life.

She turned away from the mirror, tossing her head, a characteristic gesture that Al had adored. Usually it was pride that made her do it, pride in her beauty. But not now. Now it was anger.

Time to save this bright and beautiful lady—time for the next hopeless attempt . . . or, no, not quite time. If she was going to try the forest, she needed deeper darkness, and she had to have something to wear.

The evening still bore a certain light. A bad time to run, but a good one to examine the ground. She went to the bedroom window. It was steep out there across the road, but not impossible. She couldn't make out a trace of a path.

Ten minutes, Kevin had said. But look at those trees; they were literally shoulder to shoulder. By twisting and turning, she could probably get between them, but it would take a hell of a lot longer than ten minutes even to reach the top of the slope.

He'd have thought of the dark, too, of course. He'd know that she would have more of a chance then. What was that film—*The Most Dangerous Game*—wasn't it? Yes—Count Zaroff ran a place where he hunted human quarry.

So perhaps that was his next game, for her to run out into the woods and be hunted. He'd obviously made certain that she was handicapped, considering that she must do it stark naked, with only an ill-fitting pair of flip-flops to protect her sensitive city feet.

CHAPTER SEVEN

A Little White Light

The thing to do was to prepare and plan and make him wait for it. He could sweat, and she could make him do it.

She went into the living room. Damn jerk, just look at the way he'd destroyed that wonderful old chair. Destructive, bitter child.

Ideally she would make her move in the middle of the night. That was the ideal. In actuality there was the danger that he might at any moment run out of patience or simply change his mind. He must not be allowed to get to the point of binding her. Since he hadn't done it when it would have been so easy, while she was unconscious, it must be a significant moment of escalation for him.

Okay. First thing: Something to wear was absolutely essential. She glanced around her. Okay, wear the rug—

or no, how about the venetian blinds on the front window? Or maybe make a dress out of the stack of newspapers beside the fireplace. Wonderful. Or—yes—the ripped cushions on the Morris chair, a two-piece outfit.

She went into the bathroom. The only bit of toweling left was the washcloth she'd used to bathe her temple.

Thoughtful fellow; he'd been aware of how much more mobile a little covering would make her and taken the big towel.

Wait. The bedroom—hadn't she been lying on top of a coverlet? Yes! She went in and there it was, a cotton coverlet. Very well, she'd make it into a sort of cloak. Sister Helen. St. Helen of the Hills.

Now for food and water, yes, do this in a quietly methodical manner, do it as well as you can. She went into the kitchen, noticing that the glass that had broken into the sink was still there, suppressing the idiotic urge to clean up the mess.

She got another glass and turned on the water. It was a couple of moments before it became clear that he had cut it off. This was a cruel act, cruel and petty. Probably just giving back what he'd gotten all his life.

She went into the bathroom, her cloak swirling about her—and got water. "So, you're not perfect," she muttered. She drank, then had a second glass.

Acting from habit, she picked up the washcloth she'd been using and laid it neatly over the towel rack.

It was getting darker by the minute, and she should prepare as efficiently as possible. Food would help, so she went to the pantry and got out the Raisin Bran, poured some into a bowl. Now, to the fridge. Yes, the milk was there—but that was all. He'd even taken her four oranges, the miserable little pig-faced fatso. She wondered what he really looked like, wondered how mean he was. Then she thought about the girl in the Polaroid with her frozen scream and red smiling line across her soft belly.

She poured some milk into the cereal and took a spoonful to her lips. Eat, yes, no matter how hard it was, how unsettled her stomach, eat, because there is going to be a mathematics to this. He will be fully fed, she will be subsisting on carbohydrates and sugar. So who will go the farthest, who will be the fastest? The man in the stocking mask could be any age, from the robust twenties on. One thing was certain—he had quick hands.

She stuffed a spoonful of cereal into her mouth. She was chewing it when she realized that the milk was foul. Gagging, she rose and hurled the bowl against the wall. What had the jerk done—pissed in it or something?

She ran back into the bathroom—only to find that he'd now cut this water off, too. So she picked the cereal out of her mouth as best she could and just lived with the foul taste because there was no other choice. It was foul even to breathe. Piss or vinegar? Either one would have been appropriately childish, the practical joke of a very disturbed little boy . . . who was, right this moment, somewhere under the house.

So he wanted theatrics . . . phantom of the cabin. She could feel him down there listening, probably looking up, maybe crawling along under her as she moved through the house, shadowing her like a three-year-old did his mother.

Her short hairs shivered; she thought perhaps she was seeing into his mind somewhat more clearly at last. He was a little boy with the rages of a man. So he was out of control, and his fantasy involved denying that by controlling the victim. It involved the possession of a real, honest to goodness human being. But possession obviously meant more than simply capture. This was almost certainly a killing matter.

He'd have to break her first, then kill the shell. What thrilled him would be compliance. He'd want somebody who would lay her head on the block and simply wait. That would lead to his most thrilling moment, his sexual peak, watching her there, passive and yet imprisoned by the control fantasy of an out-of-control man.

Probably what all this waiting was about was that he could only move toward climax, never reach it. What would happen would be a protracted and savage sort of courtship, ending in an explosion of murderous rage.

As best she could, she went through the catalog of currently open cases. She couldn't think of anybody at large in the Northeast with a string of victims. But he was a killer for sure. She'd stake her rep on that. So maybe he was successful at hiding bodies.

The miserable taste suffused her nostrils every time she breathed. It could be vinegar, and she tried to convince herself of this. Unfortunately, however, at his arrested level of sexual maturity he'd have lots of unresolved issues involving waste matter. "Watch out," she muttered, "or Momma's gonna flush you down the john, pencil-prick." She wished.

The doctoring of the milk was probably an act of urolagnistic dominance. Had he been made to drink urine as punishment for wetting the bed, perhaps?

She ~~gritted her jaw. She was~~ willing to talk with ~~peo~~ple about things like this, but she certainly didn't care to be involved in this fantasy.

She wished that she could resolve this issue, but the mixture with cereal and milk had masked all but the sourness of the doctoring substance. Too bad, because understanding him depended upon the degree to which she understood his fantasies . . . and thus was the high road to freedom.

In the past, religion or some other moral restraint might have caused him to sublimate his urges or transfer them into a military career or something. But he lived in a very new kind of human society.

Everywhere you turned, there was the promise of moral freedom—a wonderful thing—a great and freeing change . . . except for the unpleasant little side effect that it encouraged a few people to be very, very bad.

It was almost fully dark now, but she thought that she ought to wait until late. Or, perhaps not. Like most country people, Kevin probably went to bed around ten or ten-thirty. If he was in the habit of turning out all his lights, she might never see the house.

She went into the bedroom and lifted the window. She was fairly quiet about it—as quiet as she could be given the wretched condition of the frame, which made a sound like sandpaper being dragged against tin. The latch on the screen was so overpainted that it could not be pried loose, not even by breaking another nail, this one right to the quick, and painfully. "How'll it feel if he yanks 'em off?" she said to herself.

With this encouraging thought, she knocked the latch aside easily. Then she got up on the bed and, as quietly as she could, went out the window into the summer night. Something had bloomed, and the air was dripping with fragrance. She wished it weren't, she wished that the world were as ugly as what happened in it; to have to escape a maniac by stealing past pale flowers beneath the light of a sickle moon was a peculiar ironic hell. "The damned darling buds of May," she breathed as she slogged up the hill.

Al's father's cousin had written a remarkable letter from Buchenwald about flowers coming up between the railroad ties. Twenty-five words or less on a Red Cross form: "The darling buds of May break the ties to the past. Spring here is the same, but so different. Spring in Central Park. I am not—" The rest had been censored. Over the word count limit.

She kept going, wishing that she didn't create this rustling din.

Would the wall that had restrained men like this one in the past have been breached if the cruelties of the camps had never happened? They were as septic as boils, the camps. The knowledge that we were capable of such deeds was now lodged in the subconscious of the world. "If the Germans could do their thing, then I can do mine. . . ."

Or was she being too facile, placing these various blames? Something was triggering these men, though, and it had to be something new. Jack the Ripper was an early anomaly; in general such crimes belonged not only just to this century, but almost exclusively to its second half.

She crossed the road, aware of how medieval and strange she must appear in this flowing cloak, of how ancient must be the feeling she had now, to be crossing the night in such dress as this, in sandals like those they'd worn a thousand years ago, in robes that admitted the caressing air. The woman as victim, the woman as witch, racing along the dreadful night, womb throbbing, legs pumping, head full of mysteries and healing.

Woman, heal the world.

She became aware of a sound—tinkling. Yes, and getting more distinct.

Oh hell, there he was! He was a hundred feet behind her, crabbing up through the flowers. There hadn't even been a two minute grace period. Didn't she have any luck at all, ever?

What would he do to her now, what would he *do?* She wondered if she could fight. She had no idea how even to begin.

She hit a tree hard, so hard that the skin peeled back from her forehead, she could feel the tearing of it, could feel also the blood coming down, could feel it entering her right eye. Her temple roared, almost knocking her out with the fierceness of the pain. She was no doubt concussed, maybe badly concussed.

She pressed on up an appallingly steep slope. Every step up brought a sliding halfstep back down. Soon she was literally wallowing in a haze of pine needles and forest dust, the idiotic cloak ripping and tearing on every branch it touched, and he was right on her, climbing steadily.

She realized that she would not get away. An instant later she also realized that he would not try to catch her.

This was very much worse than a nightmare. He wasn't trying to prevent an escape. He was simply running her to ground, exhausting her. When she could not move another inch, when she finally sank down, he would take her.

But what was that clanking?

He must have chains. She fought for more speed, for better purchase, but she could not go faster, she could not take longer strides or slip less. Then the cloak became caught tight and she had to stop and literally rip it out of a limb that appeared almost alive, a malign, grasping thing.

Uncinching the strap, she let the cloak go. Now it was just her and the scraping bark and thrashing branches. She gained a little distance, and there was soon louder crashing behind her. He'd become somehow involved with the cloak, but she didn't turn around, she didn't try to find out. Maybe he'd choke on it.

But no, here he came, clanking closer than ever. "Why," she breathed, "why?"

There was a response—she didn't catch the words, only their bubbly, brimming tone.

He grasped her left buttock, then was gone. He'd actually grasped her butt, he had put his hand on her, he was that close! She growled, she struggled ahead.

The hand came again, this time lingering a second longer. And listen, he's breathing hard now. He's just about as winded as you are, girl. He's grabbing at you because it's the best he can do, he can't do any better or he would.

Girl, he thinks you're winning. He actually thinks that you are winning, that you are going to get to whatever place lies beyond these woods, and he is not going to be able to follow.

Soon she discovered the reason. The slope got less, then ended abruptly, and she was suddenly staggering out into a wide meadow. Breeze tossed pale grass; the pines hissed.

This could not be more amazing; she was in a meadow on top of the hill. There had been this place all along, and he had known of it and had not wanted her to get this far, had obviously never expected her to manage it.

It was a Pyrrhic victory, though; she was lurching like a shot deer, wheezing and stumbling and taking the huge, wobbling steps of somebody about to collapse. But she must be going faster than she thought, because the tinkling of the chains or handcuffs was getting fainter, and along with it she could now hear little grunts of effort that sounded to her as if it might be extreme.

Kevin's place—God, please, let him have the light on! "Help," she called, and didn't it sound miserable—the croak of an exhausted bird, the cry of a dying dog. "Help!" A little better, not much, best to save her breath.

On she went down the long curving meadow lined by black shoulders of forest, went dashing and hopping amid the pale flowers and the lightning bugs, like a shadow of some goddess.

A long time ago this had been the sower's moon, the moon of the food planter, the belly filler, the mother who had borne this whole fragile race in her guts.

"Why do you hate me?" she cried. "Why, why, why do women take this shit! Why!" Then, more softly out of lungs too air hungry to do more than rumble, "Fuck, oh, fuck."

And then, then! Oh—impossible. No, no, entirely real. A white light gleaming, a porch light right over there, right in that clump of trees, yes, a porch light oh damn it yes, *yes!* What time? Couldn't be much past nine, so he'd be up, of course he would.

Not at home? Then she'd break in she'd get a knife get a gun use the phone, she would find some way. "Help! Help me!" Adrenaline came, and she began to really speed. She was dimly aware that never in her life before had she run naked in the night air and part of this was poetry.

And then she was coming up on the prettiest, most welcoming, most damned well wonderful little New England saltbox that she had ever seen, and there were golden lights in the windows and that white light over the kitchen door and even flower boxes in the window.

Dear Kevin, as prim and neat as you please.

Behind her, the tinkling stopped. He was hanging back, unsure of how to deal with this.

Well, she wasn't at all confused about it. There had to be a massive manhunt.

Once he was caught, she would study him. She would keep with him through the prison system and study him and write him up, this amazing creature. Killer, had killed before——ninety percent probability.

She knocked. Nothing. Tap on the glass, tap again. Tap tap tap. Then knock, knock, knock to the hollow of the house. Oh, the damn fool, he was at the Tarleton Ritz Theater, no doubt, or off playing some kind of country card game or at dinner. She hammered, but there was no answer, he did not come, he was not going to come.

She tried the door—and found that it was wide open, typical country. Well, when the story of Dr. Helen Myrer got in the papers, that would sure as hell change.

She slammed the door behind her but found that there was no bolt to throw—it was a double-keyed cylinder. She looked wildly for a knife, a gun, the phone, whatever might come to hand, because she had no illusions at all about him, he would come right in, he would bring the crazy viciousness of the madman thwarted, certainly.

She felt as if she'd just come out of a cave, just come out of the black primordial past, a tall, naked wild creature in this fluffy, busy little saltbox with its cozy overstuffed chairs and its old floor radio and . . . old magazines like at the cabin. Well, of course. Kevin had probably supplied them. No doubt he was a collector.

"Kevin," she called. *"Kevin!"*

There was no sound, not from inside, not from outside the house. She rummaged in the kitchen and was about to select the largest cleaver she could find when a voice made her turn around.

He was standing there with a sort of half smile on his face. There was a gun in his hand.

"Kevin?"

He nodded with brisk enthusiasm.

For a moment her mind simply stopped. He made a small sound, a sort of stifled laugh, as if he were a little boy wondering if he was about to get punished for some prank or other.

So he was—this. That innocuous, completely forgettable little man was a . . . what? How bad he was, she didn't yet know—but bad, certainly very bad.

She saw the cuffs hanging on his belt. She had a horror of restraint. She did not want that.

Then he raised his eyebrows and cocked his head to one side. "I'm sorry, Doctor," he said in his breathless voice. The way he dwelled on that last word, as if it were some sort of loathed food, made her flesh crawl.

"I'm not a doctor, I'm a psychologist."

He came closer to her. "Come on, let's give you the grand tour." He bustled past her into the living room. "What this whole place is, is a 1958 collection," he said. He seemed completely unconcerned that she might bolt, but the pistol barrel never left its target, which was the center of her belly.

She became aware of her nakedness and covered herself as best she could.

"Venus on the half-shell," he said. He waved the pistol, drawing her closer. "Come on down," he said. With his free hand he pointed to the floor beside him.

She squatted as women must have when they gathered tubers, squatted and grunted as if torn by her many pains.

"This is the beginning of the greatest journey of your life, naked lady."

He began bringing magazines out of the basket beside the floral-upholstered easy chair. May 1958. March 1958. December, 1957: *Saturday Evening Post*. There came sobs, quick as a motor, one after the other, and with them shaking that seemed somehow deeply broken. "Oh, I'm such a sentimental goof!" He sniffed. "And hardly a good host, am I? I think not!" He stood, drew her to her feet also. He took a step back, regarded her up and down. Then he waved his free hand around a room that spoke of the distant fifties, the period when this man had obviously started spinning out of control. "So, you're very welcome," he said. "It's not much, but it's home."

CHAPTER EIGHT

All through the Night

"Y ou were herding me," she said. He blinked and backed away from her, as if she were something dangerous—just a little, though. Arm's-length dangerous. She noticed that the handcuffs on his belt were worn and old.

As if surprised by something about her comment and considering it more carefully, he cocked his head to one side, a gesture that was quickly becoming characteristic.

Seen like this—much more carefully—he presented a very strange picture indeed. His hair was jet black, which made his skin seem almost powdered. His broad forehead was smooth, his cheeks gleaming with sweat. His eyes were big and wet, the eyes of an ill-treated dog. The glint of the animal conveyed another message, of something that saw itself as cornered, and that was a very dangerous message. Rosebud lips pouted beneath the unfinished nose of a boy; his heavy eyelashes seemed to wave like palm fronds when he blinked.

He laughed a little, and the tone seemed to say that he knew secrets about her.

How long had she been unconscious with him when he'd hit her with the blackjack? Hours, two or three hours.

"Put your hands down, I want to look at you."

Forcing herself to comply, she dropped her hands and stood before him, feeling the wary helplessness of the captive. She knew that she had to think quickly and well, but she could not think, there was nothing to think about. She'd been herded here like a cow. How could she possibly outwit somebody who could control her like this?

She could have run anywhere, so how had he known? Then she thought how painfully obvious it all was. The cliff that overlooked the lake was impossible. She'd already tried the road. And there'd been that little conversation at Matthias's place, just enough to draw her here.

"You're smart," she said.

He nodded, politely acknowledging her admission.

She also understood that will was the issue here. The longer hers remained intact, the longer she would live. He was here not just to kill, but to prove his superiority. So fighting would keep her alive—until he lost patience, of course.

He was like a creature from another world, this eerie little man in his black shorts and suspenders, his open-collar shirt and high-top basketball shoes. There was more than a little of the boy in his dress, and like his magazines, it spoke of a childhood that had been murdered.

With a graceful gesture he reached down and pulled a ring in the floor. A creaking trapdoor came up, and suddenly she was looking down into a black elsewhere.

He gestured with a pudgy hand, as if welcoming her down. His gesture was accompanied by a stretched smile that entirely revealed the fiery emotions it was meant to conceal. Horrified, she took a step back.

"Don't even think about it," he said in a tired voice.

She had literally felt the kitchen door back behind her somewhere, had tasted the night air.

He came up to her—two dance steps. Delicate fingers touched her temple. "If I have to do that again," he said in a sort of sardonic singsong, "you're gonna get brain damage." He might have been describing a cold or a bout of the flu.

She could not go down in that dreadful hole. She had to distract him—talk about him—get him on the subject of himself. "How old are you?"

"Old enough. Now if you don't go down there, I'm gonna show you why you should."

She tried the clinical practice of drawing him out with a question. "Why?"

"You better do what I want, lady."

"My name is Helen."

"I know what your name is, Dr. Myrer, I read the stupid forms." He gave her a level stare. She stared right back.

Seeming almost surprised with himself, he dropped the hatch.

The explosive crack made her scream. His eyes widened and he looked unexpectedly pleased, as if he were nine and had hit some sort of a ball exceptionally well. Then laughter burst out of him, as it did from a child who had accidentally invaded another's privacy.

Now she saw the front door. It was solid wood, with a reclining half-moon of a window that looked out onto the dark. Was there a road out there—cars, people, rescue?

The next thing she knew, she had raced over to it and was dragging at the handle—uselessly. The lock was double keyed just like the back.

She stopped. Maybe the back door, which was mostly mullioned glass, could be broken down. She noted that there were key locks even on the windows.

Now she turned around, faced into the prison of a little house. To her left was the living room. He was sitting down, actually sitting in a chair even as she tried to escape. You've done this many, many times, she thought.

She returned to the back, going through a kitchen that smelled of bacon grease and oranges. She plunged her fist into the door. The glass was held together with surprising strength by the lead mullioning and gave way rather than shattered.

Even so, there was blood. She backed away, amazed at the spray of it coming out of her left forearm. She hadn't done anything to the glass but break a small hole in it—but she couldn't continue, not with all this blood. If an artery was cut, it had to be dealt with at once.

She went to the sink, grabbing what turned out to be an oven mitt from the counter. She stanched the bleeding.

He already had the water running, and he was taking the forearm and holding it under the stream, which made it sting, then looking up at her with crinkling around his eyes. "You missed the vein."

He wrapped some paper towels around the arm and led her—ushered her by the shoulder, actually—along the hall to the back of the house and into a blue-and-white tiled bathroom. "We need the Mercurochrome," he said. "We've gotta doctor you. You need a tetanus shot, too." He patted her left buttock. His hand lingered there a moment and she could feel it was very soft, like a deerskin glove. He took down an ancient vial of antiseptic and with the glass dauber daubed it on the wedge-shaped hole in her skin. "Lucky you," he said.

She heard the bathroom door slam and realized that he'd closed it with his foot. He locked it, too, muttering as he did so, seeming almost embarrassed.

As he bandaged the forearm—a expert job that seemed calculated to induce pain by a bit of excessive pressure here and the dig of a fingernail there—she saw with dismay that there was even a lock on the tiny bathroom window.

He folded his arms and seemed to be trying to stare her into submission.

"What?"

"You need a tetanus shot."

"Well, you haven't got a tetanus kit, and I wouldn't

let you give me a shot if my life depended on it. Which it would."

"You don't know what I have! What if I have the anticancer drug of the world, don't you want that, you dope?"

She decided that he was arrested at about age ten. She'd never encountered a case like it—a man who acted like this but demonstrably was not retarded.

His arm came striking at her, his hand like the head of a snake. She fell backward against the edge of the tub, and as she did he gave her a vicious kick, the edge of a boot against her right shin.

She gasped, sucked air, gasped again as the pure fire of it swarmed down her legs. Damn, but that had hurt. Oh, *damn!*

Then she realized her right thigh was stinging.

It was probably the single most terrifying moment of her life, and she rose up roaring and clutching it in both hands. "What is it?"

"That's for me to know and you—"

"What in hell have you done to me, you vicious little turd?" She went for him, she went for his fat-ringed neck. She got there, too, she actually pushed him up against the door. But all of a sudden her throat had taken a blow and she was coughing and could not raise her chin, and as she went forward a knee came up and snapped her jaw closed so hard that she felt her appliance break. She ended up spitting it out on the floor in blood-blushed pieces.

He reacted with a child's curiosity. "What's that thing?"

"TMJ appliance. Was."

"TM what?"

"It's because of tension."

"No tension here."

Her heart was beginning to change its beat, her legs felt heavy and the terror was surging in her blood. He'd hit her with heavy drugs. "Oh, God, I'm dying, I'm dying." Her voice seemed distant, as if a memory.

He raised her head, his hands on her cheeks. "Is this the Green Mountain State?"

She knew that he was testing her, gauging the effect of his dose. "That's Vermont," she said defiantly, struggling to control her tongue. "This is the 'Don't Tread on Me' State."

"Tha-a-at's right, and don't tread on me, *honey bunchie.* Can you still walk?" She felt him dragging her, felt herself move as if she were attached to him.

The bastard had fast hands. She'd known lots of fast hands, beginning at Harriman High, the fast hands of Richard "Oh, Helen, They're Just So Beautiful" Turner.

Then she knew that she was lying down, that her face was pressed against a sheet and the sheet wasn't real clean. She tried to cry out but there were weights dangling from her vocal cords, preventing her cries of protest, preventing even moans. Heavy sedation.

It was all right, it was warm. . . .

Hell, it wasn't all right!

"Bastard . . . bastard . . . What the hell . . ." In her mind she said, What is it, what is it? but nothing would come out of her mouth, and these gray blankets were soft, nice and soft.

Don't go to sleep!

She heard someone talking, reciting a poem, but not one she knew, and anyway she couldn't follow the sonorous words.

The hypnotic voice took her into a half-lit corner of her mind, and she saw the face of the full moon come down to earth, and the face of the moon was grinning as if it had engorged the world, grinning as it carried her across the dark river.

Don't go to sleep!

" 'From the full moon fell Nokomis . . . ,' " the voice said. Dimly she remembered that Nokomis was the moon-mother from the *Song of Hiawatha,* but that was as much work as her mind could do at the moment, and instead she saw Nokomis falling through the blue night, her hair aglow with moonlight.

This was interrupted by a great and inappropriate tightening in her chest, and she wanted to tell him that his drugs were paralyzing her diaphragm, but she could not tell him, she could not now make words travel up her throat. The tightening continued, and then she knew that some part of her had failed, and she could see his moon face rising and falling and hear the slap of skin on skin and was aware not so much that he was jumping up and down and clapping, but that jumping up and down on the bed had been part of the aesthetic of her childhood, also.

He came then like a cloud down upon her, and she thought for a moment that something huge was crashing on her, the *Hindenburg* on its burning flight. He was so close that she had to inhale of him.

"Bye-bye, baby," she heard her mother singing, "day will be dawning . . ." Oh, the "Moonshine Lullaby." She hadn't thought of that song since childhood's end.

Last, last, she thought, this is the last of Helen Myrer, oh Al, I could not cry because I am not the type to cry and I know your mother was shocked by my dry eyes looking at your mahogany coffin. But Al, I sure did love you, and I love you, kids, this is Mother, Mother is dying.

I held you, Al, I held you when your head went back and you could not raise it. I gave you all the dignity that I could.

"Breathe!"

I don't really understand you, I could never slide a needle into somebody without knowing anything—any-thing—

She could not tell what he was doing, but suddenly there was breath again, hot breath going down her throat. Off at the numbed edges of her consciousness, she was aware that fingers had begun to hold her mouth open. What was this, was he forcing his own breath down her throat? What about killing her?

Oh, no, it was CPR. Sure, she knew CPR. Slowly two black-clad nuns came up the hill. One of them said, "It's the Ark of the Covenant," and she thought, The Covenant, but could not complete the thought and so closed her eyes to the merciful nuns and to the covenant that was forming between her and the man who was so intricately at once preserving and taking her life.

She did not know that she'd been purposely dosed almost heavily enough to kill. He played the CPR game for eleven fascinating minutes.

For her there was only blackness. She did not know that he came to her when her breath finally settled and lay with his head on her shoulder and his hand lightly on her breast, feeling her breath coming and going, and prayed to his dark god to make her last.

All she knew of the night was a dear and familiar scent: the smell of Al's sweater, rich wool and leaf smoke and pumpkins, and the deeper scent of Al himself, that beautiful, kind, and so very powerful man whom she had admitted to her soul by the widest door in the universe.

He lay cuddled up to her like a puppy. "Oh, Al," she sighed as she had on indolent Sunday mornings for twenty years, when he had turned to her and so gently come slipping across the sheets.

When she heard a chipper, "Hi there, Helen," she realized that the scent was only a filthy old blanket and remembered that Al had been dead for years. She threw off the blanket, clanking when she moved her arms.

It hit her with overwhelming power, the whole dreary mess at once: she was here, he was here, and now she was in the handcuffs, and that meant that the end had begun. She could hear them in the statehouse: "Helen Myrer, ironic way for her to go."

She clanked her cuffs and moved her feet and was relieved beyond all sense to feel that they, at least, were still free.

"My, it's such a pretty day," he said, elongating the word for emphasis into "da-a-a-ay." For whatever reason, it made her want to cry. "We need some breakfast," he added. He fluttered his eyes at her. "Sweetheart."

"Sweetheart . . . sweetheart . . ."

"*You* needum coffee *mucho. Mucho grande*." He dragged at her and she came up instantly. Another nod—cold, quick—and she was on her feet.

Her alacrity was absurd, but she couldn't control it. She was submitting to him . . . and then she thought, The hell you are, lady. You are doing what you have to do to stay alive, but you are not, and I repeat that, *not* going to give in to this creep.

There was still a clinician in here, and she was not defeated, no. A toss of her head brought an immediate narrowing of his eyes. She saw that he knew quite clearly what he wanted from her and that her gesture had told him she wasn't totally compliant yet.

This was so much more complicated than the blank banalities that she had learned from witness testimony, from the few women who had escaped compulsive killers.

Or from the killers themselves: "Well, all of a sudden the knife was kinda in my hand, y'know. And she goes down like a sack a bricks."

"And what did you feel then?"

"Like I killed her."

But had it not been more like this—violence transformed into an art?

She let him push her down the hall and across the dining room, shoving her as he might a wheelbarrow. What was art but a reflection of being? So this was art and very new art, because it reflected a level of violence that we had only recently discovered in ourselves.

Maybe that was why this crime was so fresh minted; maybe what we were looking at here was a new art, one tailored to the aesthetics of the era. Now his eyes sparkled, and she thought that only an artist could have eyes that spoke so clearly. "You get off on this, babes? Want to make it with me?" he said.

She clanked, managed to conceal her revulsion. "I want—I could make breakfast. For you."

"Yeah, you mean you want outta them cuffs. Uh-uh. You're still thinking. You can get out when you stop thinking." He laughed, a booming hurt-lungs sound that hurried away on a flood of giggles. "Would you like some Raisin Bran? I know you like Raisin Bran." His voice dropped, as if he were trying consciously to lower it: "You beautiful babe."

"I feel awful."

His shrug told her that it just didn't matter and reminded her powerfully of what was happening here.

What about the clinician? Remember her? She is who you are and what you have, don't let this poor little psychotic strip away the clinician. So address her, what does she say about this?

"Do you know what I am?"

"Sure. A psychologist. Why I went in there."

"In there?"

"To the cabin. I never took one outta there before. 'Cause of, I'm the caretaker, obviously."

He went about his business, putting bowls on the table, getting down some glasses. "It's nice to have somebody to talk to, Helen," he said. Then, "Usually they don't feel like talking."

"Usually?"

"Do you have a nickname, Helen?"

"Just Helen." She did not care to tell him that her intimates called her Cooie.

"No," he said with the bored assurance of a self-righteous child. He poured cereal into the bowls. "You do have a nickname. A Helen would have to."

Slowly she sat down before one of the bowls and watched the milk sluicing over it.

He shook his head as if to say, "You are just too much."

"Is this seasoned?" she asked.

"I just wanted you to get to know me a little better, is all."

"I sure did!"

"You spit it out." He ate. "This isn't as good because I'm not in it. If I was in it, you'd like it better."

She used a struggle with her spoon to cover her disgust. What an incredible thing a distorted ego was. "You think about it a lot?"

He held up his spoon. "Raisin Bran?"

"Urine."

"It was a joke!"

"Am I laughing?"

He folded his arms, regarded her with those eyes of his. "I think you're gonna be a lot of work, you are."

"Before I'm broken? Why not just kill me?"

He ate more quickly. "I was raised by a wolf." He

threw back his head and howled and ended it in gargling and giggling and cereal spewing.

"Now that would have brought me trouble when I was a kid."

"Doesn't surprise me. Why you became a shrink. Figure out your mother."

"We could figure out your mother."

"Figure out what?"

"What she did."

There was a steadiness in his eyes when he looked at her. Then he went back to his cereal.

"May I know why I feel so horrible, Kevin? What kind of drug did you use last night?"

"Who am I supposed to be, Dr. *Seuss* or somebody? Sheeshola!"

"I'm scared, is all. I think it's natural."

"You're fine. It was just some lousy phenobarb."

He could do just about anything to her that he pleased. That was the reality of the situation. She dropped her eyes.

"Depressing, isn't it? I know." He smiled softly. "The waiting's awful."

"What am I waiting for?"

"That's for me to know and you to find out, ain't it?" He picked up his spoon in his right hand and inserted it into the end of a tightly closed left fist. The fist resisted, but he pushed harder, and as he pushed he groaned and then pushed harder yet. Then he pushed harder and groaned more loudly. Her fingers went to the mark on her own hand, the wound she'd made clutching her keys. He pushed harder and started screaming, and she screamed, too, she could not help herself.

"Shut up!"

Instantly she obeyed.

"Shut up and eat. You're a slow eater. Did you know that in the Inquisition they used to burn people at the stake—"

"Yes, of course."

"For, like, a little while, just till they were, like, with their hair gone." He took another mouthful and chewed like a rat for a moment. "Then take 'em down before they was dead, and dress 'em up and make 'em go to dinner and things. Then after a supper where they had jugglers and all manner of follies like that, they'd take 'em back to the stake."

She noted how he reverted to a child's voice when he spoke of torture. "Did she burn you?"

"My mother was a really wonderful person, and I would very much appreciate it if you would shut up with this your-mom-made-you-crazy fuckface *shit!* Maybe, my dumb-bunny, some people had good parents who they loved and did not have crazy sicko parents like you!"

"Did she scar you?"

"No!"

The mother had been a major problem, obviously. He was too defensive about her for anything else to be true. But what of the father? The silence on that point was becoming impossible not to notice. "Your dad a good man?"

"Farmed this place for thirty years. Died in the friggin' sweet corn."

"Was it a good living in the fifties?"

"How could a hundred-acre New Hampshire farm be a good living? We were filthy poor. Poor as rats."

"But you kept it? You've been here always?"

" 'S paid for."

He had begun looking at her with appraisal. It made her stomach go to acid, made all her injuries sing. "What is it?" she asked the concealing eyes.

"Thinkin'."

"About?"

He inclined his head toward the back hall. "You know. Down."

Oh, God, that *basement*. She'd forgotten all about the damned thing.

He would not simply carry her down or she'd be there now. What this was all about, she felt, was getting her to the point where she would go down there on her own.

"Your mom punished you in the basement?"

"Who?"

"Your mother."

Blinking, he regarded her. "No."

"I doubt that."

"Look, I know exactly what you're trying to do. You're trying to get into my mind, and your very pitiful professional guess is that my mom was a number one bitch or my dad was a homo and used to do hits on me or something. But you're wrong."

"Wrong?"

"I was raised by Ozzie and Harriet, Doctor dear."

"Then why are you like this?"

He shook, as if to shake her off. "Maybe I'd *like* to know why I am such a unique and gifted man. So smart, but so completely a flub at school. So far ahead I was fucking behind!"

"You're furious at the world, then, not your parents?"

"Doctor, can't you face the fact that you've got a little old big fat mystery here? You think you know so much about me, so why am I like this?" He gestured with his spoon. "C'mon, Miss Shrink, let's see how good you are."

"Somebody left you with a rage that you can't control."

"Oh, yeah, I'm outta control. Okay. I sure got on top of you, for a guy who's out of control."

Had he raped her? No, thank God. Probably couldn't. "You're very . . . considered. Just as *she* was when she hurt you. There was a ritual."

"Well, I guess I have to tell you, I have a mystery for you. I must be a medical mystery because my mom was a very nice lady and my dad was a good old New England farmer, and they never laid a hand on me, and I swear to you, there was not a voice raised in this house in all the years we were a family."

"Tell me how much phenobarb you gave me."

"A half bucket!"

"Am I still tranquilized? Is that why I feel like just giving up?"

He leaned toward her and delivered a fish-face by sticking his fingers into his cheeks and pushing out his lips. "Var de var var," he said through the fish-face.

My Diary "Got Her!"

So now I put the pen to the page at last, in the green notebook you chose for me. I look at you and you sure are pretty.

You know the biggest secret in Tarleton Corners, which is that I am me.

I have got so many surprises!

Mother, you wore heels, you were surrounded by magic air. The magic air, and you in white and your face smiling, and I am left in the land of Never Love Me where dwell the children of the empty.

Helen Doctor, do you get why you are here? You put it all down on the state forms, you are going to fix me somehow if I can be.

Why am I alone? Why am I like this? Why am I fallen down this hole?

I look over at you, you who are so pitifully trying to figure me out when I am so many thousands of miles ahead it is not funny Mrs. Head Shrinker Dear.

When you put your arms around the air and close your eyes, maybe somebody was there for you, Helen Head Chopper. Fucking bitch, fucking bitch, fucking bitch.

Hey lady, you see, I used to put my arms around the air and say, this is the Castle of Never Love Me.

Last night I looked at the pictures, the one of me standing on the stone pillar with my balsa wood Piper Cub in my hand. I already had the cave when they took that, and that day I smelled like burned hair.

CHAPTER NINE

Beyond the Diagnostic and Statistical Manual

Helen was completely at a loss as to what might be the matter with this man. He was more than childish in his affect, he was profoundly unformed. But he was so well organized mentally. The control he had over the situation was quite horrifying. Yet he seemed like a patient, and *she* was used to being in control with patients.

Involuntarily she groaned.

His eyes went soft with pleasure.

Damned drugs, they made her so weak when she needed to be so strong! With a choked gasp she mastered herself. Every time she had previously lost even a little bit of control, matters had deteriorated that much further.

As the heat of her rage slowly subsided, cold, dank, choking fear replaced it, deeper than before, because she knew they had just come closer to the end. "I need a doctor," she said. It was a miserable sound, and the defeat in it surprised her.

He kept eating. "You might need a doctor, Doctor, but it ain't on my account. You just got a few cobwebs in your belfry, is all. That was a vet shot, kiddo."

"A *vet* shot?"

"As in nice and sanitary."

"As in drop a horse."

A quizzical raising of one brow, then, and she thought that the expressions that flowed across this simple, child-haunted face were vastly more varied and subtle than those of all except the rarest of human beings. This was not just a clever man or even a smart one. He was brilliant, and that was so very dangerous.

But what was wrong? Didn't brilliant people generally find brilliant solutions to their problems? It came down to an issue of pleasure, she suspected. He had become addicted to what he did and so lost all feeling for his victims.

A mechanism was revealed: the ego had become a fortress. Feeling was now self-directed. This was why people who tortured and murdered were often themselves so incredibly sensitive to pain: every human feeling that they possessed was turned inward. It was why they could inflict so much and why they suffered so terribly when it was inflicted on them.

What she suffered just didn't matter to him. He felt only his own pleasure. But there was an even more important question—the "why" of it. That question . . . that was a question from the deep mystery of mankind. The *DSM* did not even begin to approach issues like this. This was more than mental disease. This was a whole, twisted being.

He hunched over his bowl, snapping up his food, rushing it to his mouth in neat spoonfuls. His chewing was rodent-like. Had he been starved as a child? Starved and beaten—was that why he held the spoon like a club?

To what degree did his present behavior reflect childhood? Well, to a great degree. Otherwise he wouldn't be stranded in late boyhood. His affect was that of a prepubescent. "Kevin," she asked past her ashy mouth and cotton tongue, "how old were you in 1958?"

"You sound like Donald Duck."

"Let me guess. I'd say twelve."

He flipped a spoonful of cereal at her. She was too slow-witted still to react, and she ended up with wet Raisin Bran on her forehead. She tried to laugh. "Hey," she said, "we get punished for that."

"What're *we* gonna do, rattle our cuffs?"

"What we could do is find out what's wrong with you. We could work together, and you could be helped."

He stopped eating and turned his smooth face away from her. She was surprised to realize that he had downy cheeks. He mustn't even need to shave, poor creature. She wished to hell that she could see a workup on his hormone chemistry. " 'And there was there an herd of many swine feeding on the mountain: and they besought him that he would suffer them to enter into them. And he suffered them.' " He leaned far back in his chair and stared at the ceiling. " 'And the devils went out of the man, and entered into the swine, and the herd ran violently down a steep place into the lake.' " He seemed to be laughing, or were those tears? She could not be sure just from the shaking of his body, and he kept his face turned away. "'Oh, what a beautiful morning,'" he sang in a breathy, soulful whisper, "'when the stars are going to fall.'"

"Why did you pick me?"

"You're the fucking doctor."

Her heart started going faster. "So you think you need a doctor?"

He rolled his eyes.

"You're very practiced at what you do, Kevin, and I think you're too smart to take this risk for no reason. Taking somebody out of the Old Secret."

"They'll drag the lake, search the woods."

"Then why?"

"Guess."

"My guess is that you know you need help."

He made a tent with his fingers. "Everything's a game for me. You're a game. Just another little minor nobody nothing game. How d'you like that?"

"I'm not a game. I'm a human being, Kevin. I have feelings, and when you cut me I bleed. I have a family who loves and needs me, and patients who depend on me."

He got up, scraping his chair noisily along the worn white linoleum of the kitchen floor. After rummaging in a drawer, he came up with a gun-shaped implement that was not familiar to her. He plugged it into a socket behind the drainboard and left it on the counter. Then he got a chair and put it down beside the counter with a decisive thud. He motioned with his head for her to come.

She crossed her legs, sat tight. "What is that?"

He picked up the instrument, made an adjustment.

She could smell the heat.

"Come here to me, Helen."

She shook her head. She had recognized some sort of soldering iron thing. There were black smoking bits on the tip.

"You really are a baby, Helen."

"Pain . . ."

"What?" He cocked his head.

"I'm too scared!" She'd not known that the potential for this quivering, gurgling fright even existed in her. She'd always had such presence of mind, such poise, such a sense of capability.

"Okay," he said in a bored voice. He came over and wound his hand in her hair—and then yanked with a furious, shaking motion that made her cry out and lurch from the chair and go to her knees and scrabble frantically along after him.

She came up against the green painted cabinets, still kneeling. When he directed her into the chair, she obeyed instantly.

With those strange, soft hands of his, he drew her legs apart. The tool smelled like hot plastic. She could see smoke coming up from it, drifting in long curls into the morning light. She had to distract him, had to move his mind away from this terrible hot instrument. She thought, her mind racing. "What about if they have dogs?"

"Oh, dogs." He waved the hand that now held the instrument. "That won't matter."

She wound her ankles around each other. He came closer. "Want it to be the face, hon?" His own face was empty.

It was impossible to bear this, she could not, not for another instant, and she found herself on her feet before she knew what she was doing, and when she did know, she still shouldered him as hard as she possibly could.

He lurched back against the counter, his expression never varying. She was on him instantly, bringing down the cuffs against the top of his evil head, bringing them down with a crunching clank—and then feeling a hideous, stabbing pain against her side that made her go staggering and lurching backward, and in an instant she was lying down, curled around the agony.

The instrument in his hand was now pouring smoke from its tip. His face remained as empty as a doll's, but a little smile appeared, fixed like paint. Snarling agony swept up and down her left side. She crouched and looked and saw a long scorch mark, raw red inside, tan at the edges.

"Stinger," he said, holding the little device up in front of him. "One of my working tools." He blinked, regarding her as he might someone interviewing for employment. "Do you play cards?"

"Shit, it hurts!"

"Do you play cards?"

She fought back the rage that the pain was bringing, fought for composure, fought to suppress the instinct to twist away from the agony, to jump up and try again to run. How far would she get this time—now barefoot, naked, and handcuffed? The rational part of her mind said it urgently and said it clearly: Each escape attempt will hasten the killing process, because each time you're caught, you are a little further broken.

"Cards," she said, "cards, oh, cards . . ." The false smile was a mistake, and she dropped it.

He helped her to her feet. "Living room," he said. "We usually play some cards about now. Spite and Malice, naturally."

By attempting to engage her socially like this, the man within who wanted to be healed might well be declaring himself. Despite the fact that she had no idea how to heal monstrosity on this scale, her only hope was to reach that man. Heal or die. "Spite and Malice," she said. The pain, though, the *pain*. How could she concentrate on clinical strategies when she was suffering like this?

She threw herself into the chair he'd pulled up for her at the card table. What was Spite and Malice? She'd better not say she didn't know the rules; he might abandon cards, and she was desperate for anything that delayed that trapdoor opening.

He sat down across from her, got a deck from a drawer in the table. "Stop that moaning."

"I can't help it!"

"Then I can't help it, either!" He slapped at her, and

she yanked her head back. But she also forced herself to go silent.

"Finally."

What a stupid, pointless, idiotic mess. Chance had entered on so many different levels: the chance decision to take the vacation, the pleasant memories of the Old Secret, the sheerest chance that Mr. Matthias's phone number had remained in her possession all these years.

Why couldn't she have gone out to Jamaica or over to Paris or London? Why come to this miserable, third-rate corner of nowhere to stick her toes in a hideously cold lake and cook her own supper at night?

As he dealt out the cards she tried to get used to manipulating them in handcuffs. Then he got up and went to the tall teak sideboard with its elaborately carved drawers. He returned with a package of Benson & Hedges cigarettes. She looked at them, silently wishing. It had been a long, long time since she'd smoked, but she could sure use a cigarette right now.

He lit one, and she watched the smoke pour from his nose, then stared at it lying between two fingers of his left hand. Picking up his cards, he raised his eyebrows in her direction, then nodded toward the table. "Ever wear men's pants?"

"No."

"Would you like to?"

"Never thought about it." She fumbled with her cards, trying to read them through the amazing waves of agony.

Because of her side she sat rigidly straight, her gut

sucked in, breathing in short breaths. She had an ace of something, a couple of fours, a club, and a spade.

"I dealt, so you go first, babes."

What did it mean to go first? She took out the ace and put it down in the middle of the table. He put a two and a three on top of it and the play began to develop. Just as well that she couldn't beat him playing a game she didn't know. A man with his developmental problems would have difficulty dealing with loss.

"You played right into my hand, dumbhead." Triumphantly he placed the top card in his pile on top of the four of diamonds she had just added to the center stack. "And you forgot to draw new cards."

"About what happened in the kitchen," Helen tried. "I lost it and I'm sorry."

He laughed a little. "My dear, you are really in good shape. Mostly, I have to tie 'em up like mummies or they will not stop that squirming and going on. And do they cuss! I have heard *language!* I gotta gag 'em, mostly." He took a furious series of drags on his cigarette. She was reminded of a kid smoking for the first time.

"Do you think about them between times?"

"Sure. I think back."

"To some more than others?"

His face grew more rigid, revealing that the answer was yes, communicating the small but substantive fact that he was able to tell the difference between remembered people. Again, it wasn't a good sign. She needed symptoms of psychosis, but this was normal behavior.

She tried to see how much detail he possessed. "Which ones, mostly?"

"Look, lady, I'm not hardly sentimental about it! I don't think, like, oh, that one was so pretty or this one sure cried a lot or I could have really loved that scumbag bitch or that one bled like a fucking *pig!* Okay?"

"Okay!" What a terrible anger was there; and right at the surface. The cards were just another of his shields, nothing more. In actual fact he was probably barely able to tell one woman from another. This meant that it was easy for him to claim, each time, that his victim was his mother. "I didn't want to offend. I just have . . . you know—professional interest."

"You know what? I'm gonna do you harder and longer than I ever did anybody because of that. You fucking shrink."

That was a new direction, and one she really did not like. She inventoried the possibilities, tried one. "Did a shrink hurt you?"

"Did a shrink hurt you did a shrink fucking *hurt you?* Oh, yeah, a shrink put down that I was *not sick* just to get me off the budget and I went back home. Then one day I find this hat, see. I find this hat in the middle of the living room and I look down and wonder, Whose hat is this? So then I smell the blood. It has a strong smell, you know."

"I didn't."

"So now you do. And I go down in the basement and find this beautiful mess with a lady in the middle who is real cut up, and she is just—she died screaming. Oh, boy."

Women are the sacrifice of the world. "So the lady
. . . was your psychiatrist?"

"Stupider than me."

"Say again?"

With swampy eyes he regarded her across his cards.
"You. Are. Stupid."

"I can't understand what you're driving at! You cut up
your psychiatrist or you didn't cut the poor woman up?
What?"

"*What* is that you put down a six when I've got a
seven turned up in my pile, you stupid, fucking moronic
fuckface FOOL!"

His cards came fluttering past her face. She lowered
her eyes, tried to stop shaking because of the signal it
sent and the way it made her injuries sing.

"The rules state, 'The winner is the player who is able
to eliminate his face-up stack first.' That's what the rules
state. You work for the state, don't you?"

"State of New York."

"No wonder you're so stupid. Most of your patients
get crazier, I bet. Like what happened to me because that
Sylvia Doctor Nothing-Head Flournoy was such a *fucking idiot!*"

He'd roared so loud that she could smell his smoke-
sour, rotten-toothed breath. When she flinched away, he
got up, marched around the table, and placed his mouth
full on hers. Self-absorption on his scale would mean
that he wouldn't miss the slightest flicker of an eye or
twitch of a finger that concerned him, so she bore the
kiss, forcing back her loathing. Finally he drew away.
Folding his arms, he cocked his head. "One thing I've

always been is a good kisser. Mother taught me. She said, 'Every man ought to know how to kiss.'" He crooked his finger. "So come here and kiss your mother." He closed his eyes as if in bliss, then put his hands on his heart and swayed as if swishing an imaginary dress. "Kiss her, do." In his face she saw more clearly than ever the face of the child, and was reminded that the beauty of mankind was disclosed in its children. In this face, though, the beauty was corrupted, the savagery disclosed. "Kiss the empty hole!"

Pathology at last—an unresolved Oedipal conflict that had led to oppositional defiant disorder and probably antisocial personality disorder.

But no, such people were impossible to deal with, and Kevin had apparently been perfectly normal in the office setting.

So it was compartmentalized. Also, it was only a bit of muddiness in the general murk of his being.

As her stomach curled in on itself and she fought to keep her lips from twisting with disgust over the taste of the vile creature, her mind raced. Her job right now was to stave off the beginning of the fatal sequence. At some point he would, she felt sure, begin a series of ritualized actions that served to impose his fantasy of retribution over the reality of the person he was tormenting.

At some point she was going to become his mother, and when that happened it would be over for her. She had to gain time, even a minute, even ten seconds, because any time more was more than she had now.

Somewhere out in the world, machinery would inevitably start to grind. There would be an emergency at the office, and when the phone didn't answer they'd ask Mr. Matthias to go out and get her to call them. Or one of the kids would need something or have a success to report. Boss would be missed, Mom would be missed. They would come.

She found herself listening to the silence . . . and, in that moment, also saw that there might be a way to reach him revealed in his kiss. He had delivered it with real heat, he had loved it.

"Oh, Kevin," she said. She constructed a smile. She opened her lips slightly, gave him the best big-eyed invitation that she could.

He responded with a twinkle. "It's a funny feeling, being helpless, ain't it?"

She nodded, trying to conceal her rising distress, unable to do so. "What're you going to do?"

"You're with a guy who bides his time."

"Because it makes me suffer so much to wait?"

He touched her cheek. "The waiting's the worst part, baby."

"I'm not your baby," she hissed. She thought: Shut up, Helen, you damn fool, *just shut yourself up!* She clamped her jaws until they cracked.

"No-o-o . . . but I still know how you feel. So scared . . . but it's not all bad, is it?" He was stroking her cheek with fingers that felt like fat worms. Her eyes were closed, she was getting tears. "Want another kiss?"

She said the only thing she could think of. "Sex and violence are brothers."

His breath washed her with its sourness. "You're gonna go all the way, you know, Doctor. You're gonna suffer for me, and then when I am damn good and ready, you are going to feel every tiny bit of me taking your life away from you." He was inches away, as if absorbing her anguish on some unnatural level, and she was reminded of how little we know of the human mind. "This is no game, Doctor."

"I know it, Kevin. I never felt like this."

"Like what?"

She let herself sob. "Like you're suffering, too, and I don't know how to help either one of us!"

He pointed a finger at her. "You're smart. Good actor, too." He took her arms. "Come on."

"Where?"

"You don't ask questions!" He raised his open hand, glared at her. "Learn this!"

She tried to shield herself. "Okay!"

"Now come on."

All she could think about was that trapdoor waiting for her.

He pushed at her shoulders. "I'm just gonna clean up your icky burn, now come on."

She went with him into the bathroom and let him wash her with a white washcloth with teddy bears running around the edge and made no move to stop the water sluicing down her chest, between her breasts. "We're getting smell-eee! When you're scared for a long time, you smell like sour cheese. Did you know that? I have to bathe 'em if I'm not gonna puke. Ever been bathed, baby?"

She knew that goose bumps of revulsion were rising on her arms; she could feel them. He could see them also, and he stroked her left biceps. "I thinkie we likie this crazy guy, huh?"

It was beyond her ability even to pretend agreement.

He lifted her chin, looked down at her. "You are filling me with weirdness, strange lady."

She swallowed, managed to raise her eyebrows in a parody of casual question. "Can the strange lady get up?"

"So get up. Anyway, I don't like you, Helen."

"No. I understand that."

"Do you know how much I don't?"

"Not much at all."

"Not totally much at all! You are a fucking fathead shrink what's got no brains. Say that."

"Say what?"

"You say to me, tell me you got no brains."

"I have no brains."

"Naked, smelly bitch. Say that."

"Naked, smelly bitch."

"Louder."

"Naked, smelly bitch!"

"Like me, doncha?"

She didn't know how to answer. She nodded.

"Oh, you do, do you? Well, Madam Head *Shrunk,* that is a fuckface bitch lie!"

"No!"

"You don't like me! You think I'm stupid!"

"I certainly don't think that!"

"Then you also don't think that I'd buy your crappy, childish, shitty lies!"

"I like you."

"Woman, I am murdering you! Taking the life from your body, and I am doing it for fun. That's the fucking truth, and if you like a man who is doing that, you are one hell of a lot crazier than that man ever was or will be! Sheeshola!"

He thrust with his hips. Exhibitionism, another symptom of maturational failure. "Like to look at it?" He yanked down his zipper.

"Oh, I—I—" She hadn't seen rape as something he could accomplish.

"Blown away?"

She shook her head.

"What? Mine's not good enough for you? What'd you expect, a spike like the devil's got?"

He had not exposed himself, but she didn't point this out. Probably he was very undeveloped sexually, and this was central to his anger, poor man.

He was winding tighter and tighter, and she could not prevent it, she could not see what she could do to soothe him.

"You loathe, you hate, you despise me!" His words resounded on the bathroom walls. "Just a minute." He got the washcloth and daubed her face carefully. She realized that he was drying tears. Then he hurled the cloth into the sink. "Fuck you, fuck you, crying on me! Crying all over my fucking floor!" He shoved her, knocking her back almost into the tub. "You sick bitch! I would get a sick one!"

This was a damn disaster. But what in the world had she done wrong? Where was this behavior coming from?

"You know how hard it is to get one of you? I only done two since April!"

Dear heaven, he was hideously active, that was more than one a month! But where were the bodies? No serial killer was recorded at large in New England.

"I have to get a stupid, sick fuck bitch like you. I thought you were a doctor, but you need a fucking doctor!"

"Why sick?"

"Why? My God, woman, you're trying to get into me with sex! Whaddaya think, I'll throw my arms up in the air and say, Oh, God, I gotta marry this sex queen or I'll die? Hell no! You're the one who's gonna die, sexy."

"Sex?"

"Kissing me! Staring—" He pointed at his groin. "I can *feel* that!"

"I'm sorry."

Another blow came down. Shielding herself, she tried to crawl all the way into the tub, struggled to avoid knees, fists, open palms that seemed to strike from everywhere at once.

Even under the onslaught there was a small part of her that was analyzing, trying to understand the errors that had led to this deterioration. By trying to extend him the therapeutic promise, she had, it seemed, only condemned herself to a more horrendous death.

She began to cry and could not stop even when he snarled at her, and when at last he took her head upon his shoulder, she wept as did a mother whose child was lost.

My Diary "The Furnace"

When they're scared they make me mad, and when I get mad I put on hard crunch. I get wet doing them. They are so huddly and they yell inside their throats like they're trying not to. She gobbled against my tongue in her mouth. That was cool.

The thing is, if there was once this little kid who had never done none of this, then why do I got to suffer them and kill them now?

I am writing this, she is looking like, what is he putting down in that binder I bought with her right there? See, bitch, I already knew what I was gonna do, I had you on my list from when Henry says, we have a shrink rented the Old Secret.

I seen them shake like Jell-O under the knife and that is different.

Pain makes us naked, that is no lie. They are all been so naked. I have this idea I am on a sailboat with a crew of these girls with smooth hands and smooth breasties, see, and I make signals with their panties to all the other boats, that I am the dad of the world, and every time I do one, I hoist her panties high.

Why is the doctor so scared? She is crumping up and got wet eyes and that makes me want to hit her. I got a furnace in me, and it is lit up now, burning like a oil burner with a hi-pressure blower. The furnace is iron. It is around my heart.

Hey, it's getting on toward time, we are going to have a fun day today, even though this dumb whiner bitch doesn't know fuck-one about how to play cards.

CHAPTER TEN

Slim

He'd taken her out of the bathroom, sat her on the dirty maroon couch in the living room.

He had been scribbling in a green binder very much like the one he'd bought in the store, and she had been thinking about Selena and how very much Selena really relied on Mother. He had been writing, she had been thinking. She had tried to see his hand, to just see if it was tight or loose, when he threw down the cheap plastic pen he'd been using and came roaring straight at her.

He was slamming her, cuffing her with open palms, and she started yelling, she could not help yelling, but he kept on slapping her head from side to side.

The blows took on an impersonal, inevitable quality, like hail from the sky or a shelling from distant enemy lines. Although she tried to shield herself, the cuffs impaired her, and more than one landed solidly. She thought maybe she was going to be beaten to death. "Tell me what I did," she heard herself wail.

Gradually, as the careful blows continued, she understood that this was not meant to kill. It was a new kind of terror, not only distant but also intimate, and the pain of it seemed to gather a meaning unto itself. He hit her skull, her arms, her jaw, her shoulders, working at it as methodically as if he had been doing an exercise routine.

Finally and abruptly, he stopped. "Had enough," he said in a high, breathless voice, "had *enough?*" Then he muttered, "You turned on the furnace, bitch."

"I'm sorry if I angered you!" He'd hit her temple where it was still so terribly sore; he'd made her other injuries throb.

"Now you gotta take the heat."

She could do no more than make miserable little sounds, the whimpers of the victim that were inexorably becoming central to the definition of Helen Myrer.

He cocked his head. "I didn't understand you, and I think I asked you a question a second ago. Answer me, fuckface bitch!"

She gasped, she gagged, she hardly noticed when he glanced at his watch.

"Cat got your tongue? Okay, then it's time." He dashed into the kitchen, and she literally leaned toward the front windows, so intense was her desire to get out of this terrible hell. Then he was back. She groaned, tasting blood from cut lips.

He had equipment with him—rope and a big roll of duct tape.

"Oh, please," she said when she saw it, "please give me a chance."

"You turned on the furnace."

"Listen, I believe I can help you. I know you're suffering—"

He slapped duct tape across her mouth. "I know you're suffering," he mimicked in a sing-song. "Bitch asshole primo. Sheeshola!"

She sobbed past and around the tape, a gagging, astonished noise. Hardly seeming to be aware, he bound her wrists with rope, then put a belt around her middle and attached the rope to it so that she could not raise her hands. "Okay, we're goin' back in the john," he said.

She complied as he pushed her along. By this time she was afraid to resist. She was in shock, she was falling before him, she did not know how to stop him. He got her down into the tub and lifted her legs and bound her ankles together. Then he went round and round her mouth and nose with tape, until she could do no more than groan and to suck in a breath took a conscious effort.

He removed the cuffs and pressed her into the bottom of the tub. "Every time you move, it means another hour. You get my drift?"

She nodded, her head thumping on the old gray porcelain.

"You don't make a sound, you understand?" He dug his fingers into her side.

She nodded even harder, as hard as she could.

He got a grip, pinching her until she thought she'd go mad. "You make a sound, if I can hear it, you will get your living heart cut out of your body, you understand that?"

She managed to nod again, even from the depths of her pain. Abruptly he released her. He stood up and removed a last section of silver-backed duct tape. She saw it coming toward her face and closed her eyes against it and was left in darkness.

Fear literally shot through her, burning her to the deepest unconscious. Terrors marched out of her depths, and she imagined red hot tools and started to moan in her misery—but stifled it instantly. She lay blinded, trussed, as still as a corpse, barely breathing.

Because her ears were now all she had left, she began to listen with a kind of fanatic desperation. His breath swept in and out, in and out. There was a creak, a soft click—

She thought, Either he's just left or he wants me to think that. For some time she listened. Nothing but the faint gurgling of the toilet running and the very distant singing of birds. There was an occasional sound out in the house, a thump or the creak of a floorboard.

She inventoried her situation, but only very briefly. I've come all the way, she thought. This is how they end up, as trapped as a human being can be. She was aware of the pain of the injuries that had been inflicted on her, but in a strange, distant way, accurately reflecting the fact that her body had ceased to be her entire possession.

She had never been tied before in her life, had never been rendered unable to speak, never fallen into the physical control of another person this completely, and it induced a deep change in her, causing her to withdraw from herself almost as if his assault had infected her very blood with something of him, or as if her spirit recoiled from her own body, because of its submission to someone so loathsome.

She understood these dissociative tendencies and sought to reclaim herself as her own possession. However, the thought that emerged was that she should quit worrying about survival and start preparing for death.

How do you do that, though? Should she reembrace the religion of her childhood, make a decision in favor of the existence of the soul? Should she pray or simply retreat into herself and await extinction? Even now, at this very end, she could not find a satisfactory resolution. Deep instinct, she had thought, surely told you at the end what to do, but it did not come to her aid now. The questions upon which her unsure spirit was founded only grew more intense. She did not have a faith to sweep them away or the kind of courage that, at a moment like this, could embrace oblivion.

Then she heard a sound, very far away but as distinct as a voice raised in alarm. There had been two beeps of a horn. Yes, she knew it, two beeps. But that meant a road, that meant people! And so near!

She listened, her breath held, her ears like instruments of science. It came again, the sound, and she knew it was the crunching of tires on gravel.

The bathroom was along the side of the house, opening onto a hall that led to two bedrooms, and the driveway must be just beyond the wall. On that driveway there was a vehicle, the same one that had honked a few moments ago.

It sounded very much like somebody had arrived. Oh, yes, that was exactly what had happened, because now she heard the tinny bang of a door slamming—a truck, she thought, yes, or an older car. Then she heard the humming of a voice, then footsteps on gravel.

Spontaneously, without thinking, the trapped little girl in her cried out. The trapped little girl made a sound, a sort of soft, moaning sound.

Instantly the bathroom door opened and she knew he was right there.

The front doorbell rang.

He said not a word, but she heard movement closer, the scrabbling of fingers in a box. Then she heard a scratching sound, horribly loud, right under her nose. And then the hissing flare of what she knew by its acrid, searing odor was a big, fat kitchen match. She made suppressed little sounds of terror; she could not help it. Her whole body was electric with tension. She could hear the faint crackling of the flame.

The doorbell rang again, two buzzes that seemed devastatingly loud.

She felt him lift her left breast, felt whispers of heat along its tender underside, knew that he was sweeping the match back and forth. For just an instant she felt a ripping pain. Involuntarily she made a sound. She arched her back, trying to get away, and the agony stopped.

"A person can be burned at the stake," he said. "That's ten awful minutes. But they can be torched slow, inch by inch." He rattled the box of matches. "It takes ten hours to be burned to death with matches."

He left her, drawing the bathroom door closed—but not, she suspected, all the way. Somebody was here, oh, yes, somebody from the outside world—that strange, unreal paradise.

He had not closed the door all the way; she knew that he had not. So maybe there was a chance for her. She heard his voice in the distance of the house, heard him say, "Hiya, Slim, come on in." His voice was quite loud. Did he want to cover up any sound she might make?

"Well, you're lookin' better," came the other voice, much softer.

"Gettin' over it, gettin' over it."

He'd called in sick, of course. Had to explain his absence. She was so excited that she could barely control herself. It was the proverbial Slim himself and he was here and all she had to do—the only thing that was necessary—was to make one hell of a lot of noise at just exactly the right moment. She was going to be free, she was going to be safe, she was going to go home, thank you, God. No questions now, she felt that presence, felt it singing in her blood, calling out to her from beneath her unconscious, the sharp voice of deity, and knew once and forevermore why there was worship and why faith did not admit of reason.

She was saved, resurrection, hallelujah. She'd help the poor madman, of course she would. She'd testify to his insanity, save him from rotting, get him into a facility where he could find integration and live out his days behind decent bars, not cruel ones. Oh, resurrection!

The poor mad creature did not understand that she would not let this moment pass, that no terror tactic could prevent her.

She might be tied like a goose on the way to market, but she could make one hell of a banging against the sides of the tub, she could roar through her nose, she could definitely make enough noise to be heard anywhere in the house.

"So, where is it?" Slim said. She hadn't seen or heard him in twelve years, and the voice was older, a little heavier, but it was still very definitely the same man. The two of them went banging off into the house, off toward the back, and their voices became much more faint. "I got a job, I need a helper," Slim said. There was clanking in the pipes.

"What kind of job?"

"Them steps're gone, down t'Matthias's rental. You can't get to th' dock except the pathway, and the renters ain't gonna take the pathway no way!" He laughed.

"There's that lady staying there now."

"Say what? Turn around, where I can see you!"

"There's that doctor staying there."

Helen could hear the nervousness in his voice, even the fear.

It was lost on Slim, though. "Oh! Yeah, that'un. She left a note, she's gone camping upcountry. Matthias says she came here last with a husband and kids. Now she's by herself. Divorce! Well, we need to do it next couple days, anyway."

"I was over there for the garbage, I didn't see any note."

At that moment there was a shuffling sound and suddenly she felt a cold nose on one of her knees, which jutted up beyond the edge of the tub. A dog, he had a dog with him! She was in anguish, come find your dog, your dog's in here, Slim, in here with me!

She tried to move her fingers to somehow come into contact with its collar. But she could not, she could not reach it, and now the dog had stopped sniffing her. Your dog's gone, Slim, please come looking, oh, Slim, Slim, come looking I need you, I am so desperate, Slim, *please please*.

And then she made a sound, a long moan, which got louder on its own, and which she then made louder, even trying to turn it into a scream. She banged the tub, too, banged and struggled, heaving her whole body up and down.

The dog must have been frightened, because it was suddenly gone. No. No, puppy, come back, please, puppy, Slim has to look for you, Slim has to find you here.

"That's just a joint," Slim's voice said faintly.

"I'm gettin' lots of leaks."

"House's settlin'. Built the way it is, got to happen."

He must not have realized what her sounds meant, if he'd even heard them. However, if Kevin had heard it, even the faintest suggestion of it, then later . . .

That later must not be allowed to happen, *must not!* No, not for Dr. Helen Myrer. She had walked the halls of power, she was responsible for the welfare of thousands of helpless patients, she couldn't be extinguished like some sort of lab rat.

She had to get the dog back in here. The thing to do was to muster every iota of command that she had, every bit of appeal, every faintest suggestion of demand, and make the sound that would cause the dog to come to her.

She took a breath, she concentrated all of her force, she strove for the kind of demanding yet cajoling tone that dogs responded to best.

"Hm." Not much. "Mum mum, mmmm."

What meaning could that have for a dog? None whatsoever.

Kevin's voice, startlingly loud: "What's it gonna cost me?"

"Oh, what say ten?"

"Five and parts, Slim."

"Six, then, and it's done. And you take fifty for working on those steps, and not a penny more."

They must have agreed, because the clanking in the pipes got louder.

The dog did not come back. But she had another idea. Once Slim was finished, he was going to come back through the house, and when he was just outside this door, she was going to erupt into the most stupendous cacophony of roaring and thudding that she could manage. He would be bound to stop, bound to take notice. Her only danger was that he would go out the back door. But he'd come in the front and his truck was on this side of the house, so he wouldn't, surely not. No, Slim, you mustn't, you *must not*, because there is a human being here who is depending on you, a human being who needs you more desperately right now than any human being ever has or ever will.

Then she heard the click of the dog's nails outside the door, and another plan formed. She might be able to help herself a lot. "Hm?" The clicking stopped. "Hmmm? Mmm." She pushed herself backward until her head was against the drain knob on the front of the tub. For this to work she had to be in a sitting position, and she had to get that damn dog back in here. "Yfff! Fff! Mmm!" Oh, God, that was loud, that was too loud. If *he* heard, he'd come close the door all the way and destroy her one chance.

Painfully she forced herself to a full sitting position, dragging her back along the drain knob with its protuberances and edges. "Yfff! Yfff! Mmm!"

Click, click, click. The dog came in. Again she raised her hands away from her waist, raised them as far as the belt through the ropes would allow. She extended the fingers, she wiggled them.

She was rewarded with the sensation of a wet nose against her fingertips! Oh, doggie, doggie, come closer, sniff closer, let me get these sweet damn fingers in your collar! And the dog did sniff closer, it sniffed her ropes, it sniffed downward, becoming interested in the unaccustomed odors of a human body. Yes, oh—just inches—yes—

The dog did not wear a collar, but she got a bit of fur between the middle and index fingers of her right hand. Pressing them together, she could—just barely—hang on to the animal. It realized that it was caught, though, and started to pull away.

"Mmm? Uuuhhh . . . mmmm . . ."

She thought she had it. Yes, yes, she did. She had the dog, now the fur was between her hands, was caught more tightly.

Call it, Slim, call it and it will not come, and you will look for it and find us. Slim, you will find me. Oh, yes, God help me, yes.

He seemed to tinker with the kitchen plumbing for an hour, for a hundred, a thousand hours, for whole long cycles of time, the passing of the seasons, the precessing of the equinox.

Perhaps ten years passed of struggling with the increasingly nervous dog, until finally there seemed to be a putting away of tools.

Then there were murmurs, then the water went on for some time. They were testing it, yes they were, this was just about to end, this horrendous chapter in her life to be over. She gripped the dog more tightly, and the dog stiffened, started to want to pull away. "Mmm . . . mmm . . ."

"Chaps! Hey, Chappie, girl!"

The dog lurched. With every bit of pressure she could bring to bear, she held the fur.

"Where's that damn dog?"

"Under my bed, maybe?"

"Chaps! Chaps!"

The clank of tools, the creak of footsteps.

Now. It had to be right now. *"Mmm!"* She banged her feet as hard as she could, so hard the shocks shot up from her heels to her head. *"Mmm! Ffff! Mmm!"* Banged them and banged them and Chaps lunged and growled and got away from her, but it didn't matter, Slim was right outside, he was passing the damn bathroom!

"Chappie, there y'are. Drinkin' yer pot, probably. She's a bad'un about that."

He chuckled. Helen set up the most spectacular crashing and groaning that she could manage, but he continued on relentlessly, his voice dying as he went to the end of the hall.

"When'll you want me on the steps?" *he* said.

"Oh, lessee. Miss Nibs'll be back from her camporee Tuesday next. Say, Monday?"

"Sure thing. Monday."

The front door slammed. A moment later there was a crash of tools being dropped into the bed of a pickup, and the tinny door closed again. Then the pickup ground to a start, and she heard it moving off.

She cried, desperate with terror, completely mystified by her failure.

And then he was there and God only knew what was going to happen to her. He ripped the cover off her eyes and she could see again into the brightness of the bathroom.

"I guess you should've been told," he said. "Slim's stone deaf. He reads lips." He folded his arms and looked down at her. "You are a bad girl, Helen. A very ba-a-ad girl."

My Diary "Tragic Beauty"

This is the best one ever, this one is so much fun it is just hard to believe. I mean, she is so easy to scare, she is like a little kid. I can't remember when I got one that wasn't always just fighting and trying to get away. It's dull.

You are trying to figure me out, that is what is so wild. I want you to. Momma figured me out. It felt good, when she told me I was what I was, she was never wrong about men.

You are so funny. You are both smart and dumb. I am going to dance with you. I am going to put on my records like I did with that Gloria. Gloria, she danced. She really tried hard. She had a lot of character.

It's lucky most people don't know how much fun this is. You go out and hunt, and you get you a person. Yours to seal to you in blood forever. That's why, if you are not put out of your misery, you are going to keep on. I mean, because this is art and I am an artist like God, mixed up in creation and death and things.

She is real beautiful. It would be a comfort if only I could lay my head in her lap, and look

up at the sky above her head, and see the
snakes that climb in the clouds.

But she won't, the bitch, she won't and she
won't stop me no matter how hard I do her!
Fuck you fuck you!

She is very dignified even naked and covered with blood and tears and even though she
got a swollen side of the head. She never wants
to yell. But you hurt her and she sure does yell.

She can get a lot scareder. (Is that a word, I
think so maybe.) She can realize that she is
under the hand of the master. She is trying to
talk her way out of it. But there is no way out
of it. It just happens. Nothing to do with me.

It's just like bringing in a fish. It's real fun if
you have a good fighter. Dr. Shrinkola Shit-
head is a good fighter. That is why it is so sad
in a way. She is trying so damn hard, and she
is going to lose. That is the tragedy of beauty,
I suppose, to always in the end rot in the grave.

So let's have a party. Dance. She's so pretty
in the old death-shroud robe. Boy, if she knew
how many had been in that robe. But it's still
new, it's only been worn about fifty times. Like,
that's a month and a half old.

She thought I was going to burn her to death
with matches. You can't burn nobody to death just
with matches, it takes wood—loads of it. If all you
want is bone left, try about a quarter cord.

CHAPTER ELEVEN

Dancing

She expected to burn, but that was not what happened. Instead the whole process seemed to take a breath, to pause in a curious way. He seemed almost kind as he unwrapped the duct tape from her mouth. "That's awful, isn't it," he said. "Here." He wiped her sodden lips with a bit of tissue, tossed it away. "Slim's been deaf for about five years. Ears just went on him, but he's still the best plumber in the Corners." He untied her feet. "Now, I think you've learned your lesson, you won't be doing any more kicking and banging. Not that it matters." He unbuckled the belt that held her arms to her waist, then replaced the cuffs and took off the rope.

He laughed. "You'd never have held on to Chappie. Chappie's a lot stronger than a pair of tied-up paws."

Then he sighed. "You *will* try." He cocked his head. " 'Course, it's what makes the world go round." He drew her up. "Cat got your tongue?"

"I'm sorry."

"Oh, no. No excuses. What's done is done."

He moved them into the living room and drew her to the floor beside a dark green easy chair. She was silent, waiting now for the worst of it. She closed her eyes, took her mind to the place where Al lived, tried to somehow push away the terrible despair that was coming over her in waves.

The thing to do was deal with it on two levels. Accept, that was one. When he hurt her, she'd let herself scream; if she could, she'd hurt him back. But, on the other level, she should not give up what had always been her only real weapon, her mind, her knowledge, her ability to analyze this man.

He sank into the chair. With his toes pointed toward the floor, he smoked and stared into some inner distance. From time to time he scribbled in his binder.

She inventoried routes of possible escape, found nothing new. When she glanced at the phone he said, "It's turned off."

"You're observant," she responded.

He said nothing more, but when she stirred, testing to see if she would be allowed to stand, he pushed down on her shoulder. "You're gonna get boring, you are. It's not a good idea to bore me. It's a good idea to keep me interested."

"Like a fish fighting on a line?"

He gave her a merry look. "Yeah! That's exactly right. I guess I kind of like to fight."

So she'd fight. She'd think and consider and evaluate. And she would watch, watch, watch. But look at all the locks—very discreet, very natural . . . but also very there. This little house would have been an efficient prison even if she hadn't been in handcuffs.

As the minutes passed, she experienced waves of relief and waves of horrific anticipation, and there was nothing that could reconcile them. She wanted to plead with him, but she would not because she guessed that they all did that. Obviously her most important weapon was to stay interesting, and that meant making herself as different as possible.

As the pain from his blows faded, the agony in her side grew until it overpowered her other injuries. As the wound tightened, it became excruciating. If she lived— and she was not yet willing to abandon that possibility—she would bear a scar an inch wide from her underarm to her hip.

He could sit and stare and scribble for a long time, as it turned out. "What're you writing?"

"My stuff."

"You keep a journal?"

"Nah. Just lately. I got a head for poetry, but I can write nothing myself."

What might the diary reveal? Was he running on rails, a sort of mad robot, or was this all considered action? He had a dysfunctional upbringing and possibly some physical problems, but she continued to have the sense that he was not essentially symptomatic.

Certainly nothing that would explain this. "Could I read them?"

" 'Course not. And shut up. Speak when spoken to. I might just decide to use you as a toilet, Miss High-Mighty Shrinkola."

What she had to do was to remember every paper and book she had ever read about sadism, every talk she had ever heard, and all the interviews she'd done with compulsive murderers, detail by detail.

This whole situation had acquired a strange, dreamy quality, as if it could not be happening to somebody who was a familiar in the governor's mansion and counted among her friends some of the powerful and great. She couldn't be brought this low, to be crouching naked and half-destroyed beside a raging psychotic with murder on his mind.

She reviewed relevant papers: Ellman's "Sadism and the Dark God," with its excellent discussion of the overdeveloped ego; Klein's "Failed Development of the Conscience in the Child," which told of the process by which moral discrimination was killed in the young; Dupree's "Libido and Reality in Masochism," which discussed the very sort of provocative sexual aggression that Kevin McCallum displayed.

And then there were those men. Helen: "Would you do it again, Guy?" Guy Cobb: "You don't do it. It does you." And another one, the boy T. T. Fair: "I didn't believe they was killed. I am thinking, This is a trick on me." He was thinking that with the shotgun still in his hand and smoking pieces of his parents scattered through the living room.

She watched her captor. Where did choice lie, what part of the self made choices? She could theorize elegantly about that, but here and now things were different. It was suddenly urgent to solve the mystery of the will. Do or die.

Could the discriminating part of a person be killed or fail to be born? What had really captured her, a human being or something from the dark past, the implacable reptile out of which our species was born?

Noon drifted into memory, and the quality of the sunlight began to change.

Through all these hours she remained as quiet as possible. If he fell asleep, she told herself that she'd have the nerve to rise up and bring these cuffs down on his head with all the force she possessed.

The house was very quiet, not even a clock ticking. He laid his hand on her head. His eyes were open. He was like a lizard sunning itself on an afternoon stone, and she came to think that he must be locked in a kind of hypnosis. What must be giving him his pleasure was knowledge of her anticipation—and now she knew why he had spent so much time at the cabin in hiding. The waiting thrilled him.

What else went on in that bobbing, round head of his, behind the maze of expressions that passed through those eyes?

Like all perversion, his actions were parodistic: this was a parody of courtship. He was courting by torment instead of charm, and she was drawn to him by fear and handcuffs rather than love and flowers. This courtship would also end in a wedding night, but it would not be a night of pleasure, and the consummation of their marriage would be ghastly indeed.

Then she thought, What is the mystery of death? And at once: No, don't go down there. Focus on him, he is the door, not death, death is what you do not under any circumstances want to think about.

Pain, then? She knew that there could be far greater pain, unimaginable pain. What happened when a devastating injury was inflicted with slow deliberation? Did shock finally overtake your suffering?

She squirmed, she sighed, and every time she did, she felt his hand pat her or twine deeper into her hair, and the feet knocked the front of the chair and the face stayed like stone.

Slowly, back and forth, his feet kicked, his heels making a dry sound. Through the haze of his cigarette smoke she watched him, but not in a way that might challenge. She gave him short glances, for the most part keeping her eyes down like a geisha.

All the windows were closed, and the air grew thick with smoke. She lost her desire for a cigarette and began to wonder how she had ever lived with them in her life.

Ideally she would find, somewhere in her clinical persona, an effective combination of neutrality and openness that would finally establish lines of communication.

He began to look at her, and she did not like the looks. She thought that the killing process could be about to start, from the merry sparkle in his eyes and the color that was flooding into that gray, empty skin.

"Come here," he said at last. The words were spoken

softly, but after these long hours she reacted to them as she would to an explosion.

She struggled to her feet, stood in front of the chair. He pointed at the floor, and she went to a squatting position.

He patted his lap. "Come."

"You want me to . . . sit?"

He chuckled but did not explain himself. He wanted something intimate, it seemed to her, but lacked the ability to express himself. He was like a randy boy, all stuttering and muttering.

Finally she returned to her former position, and he began stroking her hair. His touch was so light that it felt like small, smooth movements of air. He had extraordinarily gentle hands.

"Do you want to know?" he asked.

"About . . . what?" She started feeling a little sick. She did not like where this was going.

"I just wanted to tell you. I mean, you've gotta be wondering."

She wanted to say that she didn't understand what he meant, but she did understand, she understood very well. She contented herself with a strong denying shake of the head. He must not articulate his fantasies. That was terribly dangerous.

His hand caressed her cheek, his fingers touched along the edges of her lips. Firmly, she buried the impulse to bite the goddamn things right off.

"We'll do a little after supper."

She thought that she must get out of the heat and stink of this room soon or she would be sick.

"A little what?"

As if he knew her feelings, he leaned over and was suddenly peering into her eyes. Nobody had ever looked at her like this, not Al on their wedding night or in the hour of his dying, not her babies lifted for the first time upon her breast. She thought that he was a very remarkable human being, a perverted saint. She saw the hero in the madman and knew that his actions were a sort of defiance. By killing others, he was fighting death in himself. Embracing what he feared.

In this sense he was a more raw, more real human being and far less of a freak.

He drew her to him with one strong, short arm and resumed stroking her long hair. She lay rigidly against him, her hands in their cuffs twisting together. Her mind leaped along paths of escape that never seemed to lead anywhere. She could break a window, but he'd be on her long before she was out. The doors were hopeless. He was too close to her and too alert for her to get a weapon, let alone use it.

He drew her closer yet, forcing her to lean across the arm of his chair until her cheek was against his chest. She could hear his heart, hollow lubbing and smart, quick dubbing, and in his lungs the long, sad wheeze of old rales. He'd had pneumonia, probably, that had not been properly treated.

The picture was growing more complete of a brutalized, forcibly sexualized, and also ignored child. To add to it, he had tasted the agony of becoming pubescent and . . . not. She imagined a short, feral being scurrying through the shadows of town and school and farm, now abused and now ignored, spending longer and longer periods alone with furious, helpless thoughts and fears that all came true.

Since he'd talked, she might as well try again to engage him. He'd wanted to tell her of his plans for her, so she gave him an opening. "Kevin, I do want to know."

"Lovey," he said, "I've changed my mind. I think we better not talk about it. For your sake. What I want you to do is just keep thinking, Kevie knows what he's doing, all I have to do is wait. Just keep thinking that."

From the way he shifted in the chair, she suspected that he might be experiencing sexual excitement at the thought of such submission. So her helplessness was a triggering mechanism, also. Part of his pleasure must come from the cannibalization of the other's ego. "Kevie?"

A pause. Then, expectantly annoyed, "Yes?"

"I think I want to know . . . just a little bit."

He sighed. "I want to tell you, Doctor, that I just cannot stop. I mean, I have no idea how to do that. It's just—all of a sudden—there she is, and it's over. It is so over." He fell silent.

"Amnesia?"

"No, I remember." A rising intonation: "I remember them all."

The dark god was the one who actually enacted the fantasies, the dark god was the one who did what the man did not dare.

She went up to a full kneeling position. "You're innocent."

He held out his hand, as if he were a little prince expecting it to be kissed. She did not respond. She wasn't about to kiss this man's reeking paw.

"You're just fascinated by all this, aren't you, Helen?"

His conversational tone suggested that he felt a sense of complicity. Could they be colluding in a way that only he could see? There was something about the power of the killer that was leading her into unexpected places in herself, that was true.

"It's making me . . . new," she replied, trying to find words that would acknowledge the hate, the contempt, the gagging terror . . . but also these other, much more elusive emotions that seemed to be in the direction of not only saving herself, but also—and very genuinely—rescuing him from his fall.

"Kevin, what I think is that I'm not finished with my life. I'm not finished with my family or my memories, or even love."

He ran his fingers through her hair. There was a strong impulse to draw away, but she did not.

They were descending together into the cavern of his mind. She was becoming aware of new feelings, quite beyond description, that were not from her known self. There was a curious quality to them—a sort of angry nostalgia for the life that had not yet been taken from her. Was this the anger of the murdered soul, cheated of its time in the sweet of life?

He had robbed her of one of the most fundamental of the innocences, stealing from her the deepest, most basic assumption of trust that exists between the sexes. From now on every man would for her cast the shadow of Kevin McCallum. If she by some miracle survived this, that would remain true forever.

The anger, though, was not directed at him. It was deeper than that—perhaps directed at the essential mystery of the situation—perhaps at the whole darkness that had spread out from the great suffering heart of the age into all the small, broken hearts it had produced.

So her hate was larger than the man who had inspired it. She could lie in his lap, she could give him the compliance that so excited him—in other words, serve his perversion. In simple terms she was bonding with her captor. She thought of the witches who had, in the end, lit their own fires for their inquisitors, and of the Jews who had been deceived by the relentlessness of the accusations against them into assuming the passivity of guilty prisoners.

The mind sought to explain its suffering to itself, and innocence was always stolen, not lost.

Now that this was actually happening to her, now that she was living it instead of reading about it, she was awed and amazed by its power. She was bonding to an evil maniac, right here, right now. In the mystery of the moment she could feel it: despite all her intelligence and competence, her knowledge and judgment, she was beginning to comply.

His hand petted her, slowly, slowly. The only sound in the room was the hiss of his palm against her hair.

Thus did her death draw near, on the uneasy drift of his touch.

She found that she was beginning to talk to Al in her

mind, as if she expected to see him again. She was start-ing on the journey out.

"Come on, now, honey," Kevin whispered with the gravity of a man at a funeral.

She felt his arm come around her waist, felt the sense of being guided, of being controlled—and thought, No.

As if tied to the flitting of her thought, he deflected her to the love seat that stood by the door into the hall. Putting his hands on her shoulders, he said, "Please, Helen, sit."

She complied, head down, as if in some way under accusation. He came beside her, raised her face. "You're the loveliest one," he said. She realized that his eyes were not black, but deep mahogany brown. They were human eyes, after all.

He gave her a nervous kiss. Immediately she tinkled her cuffs, then raised her eyebrows expectantly.

"I'd let you go, but I can't make that decision."

"You don't have to do anything you don't want to do, Kev." Please, please let him agree—just one subtle, in-direct indication that would reveal some level of choice.

"You don't understand one little tiny thing, baby."

"I understand that I'm good for you, Kevin! I under-stand that!" She shook her cuffs. She had brought him right to the *edge*, only to see him pull back. Dogged now, she went on. "We can defeat the dark god together. I have the tools, believe me, I do. You just have to let me use my tools."

"I am becoming the servant of the dark god. And when he opens his wings and rises up from the caves of the depths, I am no more than the leaf snapped off a branch of autumn."

She threw herself against him, kissed his lips as she fell, and ended face upward in his lap, smile constructed on the way down. "You are unique!"

He raised his head, pushed back a black bang. "'Look upon my works, ye Mighty, and despair!'"

"Says Ozymandias, king of kings."

"'. . . as on a darkling plain . . . / Where ignorant armies clash by night.'"

"What's that?" She didn't know much poetry.

"'Dover Beach,' Matthew Arnold. 'Ah, love, let us be true / To one another! for the world, which seems / To lie before us like a land of dreams . . .'"

He leaned his big head back, closed his big eyes.

"Where did you learn that?" She had visualized him as being far too much of a cast-off to have gotten a decent education.

"'Hath really neither joy, nor love, nor light . . .' I would have been a poet, Helen. I sent some poems to magazines, but they came back." He gazed wistfully away. "That was about fifty lifetimes ago." He waved his binder. "I write like a kid."

She suspected that "fifty lifetimes" probably meant fifty victims.

When you dealt with the statistics, a man like Kevin had no social worth. He was a danger free, a liability incarcerated, that was all. But if you looked into the individual life, that same man was revealed to bear a deeper value, broken but—as in the case of Ted Bundy, for example—obviously substantial.

"Helen. It's a name without a nickname. But you must have one."

It now seemed useful that he should know. "I'm called Cooie."

"Cooie?" He laughed in his nose, then gazed down at her with the gaze of a normal man in a happy moment, and she felt an acute sense of the long gone, as if the coming of men like him had brought with it a whole ashen world.

"Cooie patootie," she said, "is the full nickname."

"From what? What got you called that?"

"Being able to coo like a dove. I had a pet dove when I was a girl. He was a boy dove, he was named the King of Russia."

"I got my tail spanked off for pulling the feathers out of Mother's canary. His name was Cuttle-Bud."

It had been very early on, then, when that first serious symptom had appeared. She tried to take him deeper into the violence of his past. "What was it like getting your tail spanked off?"

"Want to find out?" He rubbed her knee.

Although she loathed his touch, she closed her eyes as if with pleasure. She was thinking hard, analyzing. "What was done to you? Exactly?"

"She had a punishment chair. She sat in the chair. I stood there and she unbuttoned my shirt and took it off."

Again, Helen tinkled the cuffs. Again, he did not comply.

"She undid my pants and pulled them down. Then she . . ." His eyes closed, and Helen saw the pain in the man. She clung to her professional impulse in the direction of rescue.

"Then?"

"If I had—if it was hard—she—" He breathed between clenched teeth.

"She, Kevin? What did she do?"

"Oh, we had us a clothespin, I guess. . . ." Out of the side of his mouth had come a long stream of drool, which he flung away with a finger. "It was very painful for me, Cooie."

It was a typical pattern to invent things like this as a means of self-justification. Patients had to be led to the real truth, which was usually that the parental acts had been much less physically awful and more psychologically devastating.

"That makes my blood boil." She delivered her actor's line with an actor's conviction and like an actor discovering the truth of a role for the first time.

Whether this particular abuse was real or not, Kevin certainly had been to some degree created and had suffered horribly in the process. Maybe if she could deepen her compassion for him, she would be able to reach him. "Would it make you mad if I said something that I really feel?"

A little twitch at the edge of his mouth may have revealed disappointment. "So, what do you really feel?"

"That we've said the word 'love' a lot in the past few minutes."

In the crinkle of his eyes she thought she might detect an answer to the question of choices. He might be trapped in his acts and past, but if he was shown some light . . . maybe.

"There's no accounting for taste, Coosifer." He laughed a little. "I mean, I ain't exactly Bruce Willis."

"I ain't exactly Julia Roberts."

"No, but you're in that direction. You want to sum me up, I'm a cross between Michael J. Pollard and Yoda, for chrissakes."

"I don't mean lovemaking-type love. I mean the love of two people who have respect for each other. Respectful friends."

"While I am doing you, will you think that?"

There he went down the wrong path again.

"What I want is for us to find out how to be friends. Part of you wants to feel good about himself, wants to . . . well, to grow up."

His hands came together. It was the spontaneous, eager clap of a delighted little boy—but silent. "You know what, Cooie, you know I really— Oh, gosh." He looked down into her face, very seriously. "Cooie, I get to know people by watching how they are when they suffer. So that's how I get to love 'em."

Her blood ran slowly, but very certainly, dead cold. She was talking to the dark god right now, and the dark god was sensing by his dark instinct *exactly* what she was trying to do and was not buying it for a single instant.

"Kevin?"

"Yes, Cooie?"

"What if I said it's not about suffering any more than it's about lovemaking? It's about . . . well, things like talking through the night just because you like each other, about finding in each other the special part that is completely true."

He cocked an eyebrow. "If we fall in love?"

She closed her eyes and drew herself deep within, because the next thing she was going to say would either end the game for her or put her on top. "If it happens, then we deal with it."

There was a silence, and in that silence she heard his fear: She is a liar; there can't be a single crumb of sharing or affection, let alone love.

"Cooie, you're crazy."

She lifted herself, kissed his chin. Her burn nearly brought tears to her eyes, but she kept smiling.

"You don't know how crazy."

She sat fully up, leaned against him. He arched his back like a pleased tomcat.

"I'm torn, Kevie. I want to find some kind of reconciliation. I guess I want to learn a new level of compassion, when you come down to it." She touched her side. "Why don't you stop the physical stuff? Can you?"

He lifted her arms, looked down at it. "I did a job, didn't I?" He touched it lightly; all she felt was dull pressure, but she flinched away automatically. "Do wacka," he said softly. He pressed his finger into the center of the wound. "Wacka." The pain went deep inside her in a series of curdling throbs. "Wacka." He was watching her face. But what was he seeing? What, for a man like him, was the actual, final meaning of pain? "Wacka do wacka do—hurtin'?"

She nodded vigorously—and realized for the first

time since this had happened that she was still wearing those pretty emerald earrings from Rosenoff's in Albany. "Like my earrings?" she hissed. She could barely speak, could barely breathe. Inch by inch he was working his fingernail along the wound, opening the scab. It was an act of remarkable cruelty. But look at him, he was smiling so sweetly! The love was plain to see, but what a love. It was turned inside out. The finger was like a brand, like a steel spike.

Finally he hit a nerve and a white hot explosion seemed to tear her chest open and she jerked back and screamed, and even she could hear the despair.

"Wacka do wacka do!" His nostrils dilated, and for a moment he appeared arrogant to a degree that was almost inhuman. "Would you like to dance?" he asked quietly.

She could not form words. She was lying against the back of the couch, biting her lips, lost in her pain.

"Would you like to dance, I said."

"To . . . dance?"

"I rumba, fox-trot, waltz, and do swing."

He got up and went into the bedroom. She was on her feet in an instant, instinct causing her to look wildly toward the nearest window. But then he was back, and in his arms was a black silk robe with a golden dragon embroidered on the shoulders. In his precise, almost prissy manner he laid the robe on the love seat. Then he withdrew a small, knobby key from his pocket and unlocked her cuffs.

She rubbed her wrists. Despite her intense desire not to reveal herself, her eyes flickered from window to door to window. She could almost taste the air out there, the sweet Jesus evening air. He laughed, a sound as if of plastic cracking. "You're like a pet squirrel, you're fine till you get a shot at the outdoors." He put the robe on her, and it felt awfully good to be clothed. "So don't even think about it."

"Thank you."

Then he withdrew a small chain from his pocket. "Hold out your hand." It proved to be a thumb lock, a device that she had never seen before but that undoubtedly had a long history in the prisons of the world. The chain to which it was attached went to a leather bracelet around his wrist. He looked her up and down. "Well, whaddaya know, you're a beaut in clothes."

He led her to an ancient floor-standing Victrola, a combination radio/record player that looked as though it came straight out of about 1952. He put on an LP called *Cocktails for Two*. Soon music came out, a bland foxtrot. He turned to her.

She found that she was grateful almost to weeping just for the damned robe. There was also a curious feeling connected with the thumb lock, a kind of relief. A moment's thought told her it was because she didn't have to worry about escape.

She was dropping into deep compliance, and it was terrifying because there seemed to be so little she could do about it. Even though she was obviously weakening in deep ways, she must not allow herself to overlook chances.

Then they danced. He did not dance well, but there was something about his fumbling boyishness that was sweet and pained her, because of all it revealed about his suffering.

He danced with his victims, as he had not danced with the girls of the town. Here he was, living the dreams of his failed self.

Like it or not, the slow movement in the gathering dark took her back, made her drift with the drifting of the feathery silk robe, to other days.

Listening to the music, watching the room drift around her, she considered all the references to the fifties.

"What were you doing in 1958?" she asked.

"I was a boy in 1958."

"How old?"

"You keep asking that! So I was thirteen. Thirteen on June 13. My lucky number."

"Yours and Satan's. So, why is everything in here from then?"

"Oh, no particular reason. Mom died on the fourteenth."

"Mom died?"

Step one two, step one two. "They have a tendency to do that, moms."

As he ran his hand along her back, she made herself tremble. Let the poor creature feel liked. Step one two, turn, and step. She could imagine what most of his dancing partners were like, stiff with terror.

It was stuffy in here, and look at the long light of the sun outside, the sky glowing, the horizon gold and deep orange. Step one two.

Maybe she could do something with this damn thumb

lock, maybe get the chain around his neck somehow.
One step, two step—he crashed her into the dining room
door.

"Sorry," he said. His eyes, when he looked up at her,
were bright, and she saw as clearly as if she had beheld
there the core of the man that they were bright with an
absolute light that was death.

CHAPTER TWELVE

Into the Dark

They seemed to be dancing more smoothly together now. She allowed herself to think that progress might be possible at last.

His abnormality expressed itself into every dimension of his being. The smooth, ambiguous body and strangely ageless face signaled deep physical dysfunction; the profundity of the psychological illness confirmed his status as a true freak. But a freak, not a madman.

So there would be no diagnosis and no cure. But could there not be something else, something more?

The tempo of the music increased. " 'Our hopes are high 'cause we live on love,' " a girl sang as a big band thrummed. They began dancing the swing, which she remembered only dimly, but which he obviously knew fairly well. He kept glancing up at her and looking more wicked every time he did.

The next song was the much slower "Memories of You." Its forlorn verses drew her toward contemplation of the pointless end that awaited her. Even the order of the music might have been a careful choice. Certainly it told a story—her story—she feared.

The record finally stopped, and once again he gazed at her with his careful eyes. "We have some champagne."

She smiled—not too horribly, she hoped. "What're we going to celebrate?"

He twitched the chain, and she found out that a pressured thumb is an astonishing bondage. The merest flick made her bite her lips to keep from crying out, the pain of the swelling that had quietly developed was so great.

He let her calm down, waiting with the patient indifference of a man at a bus stop. "It's time."

Her blood told her, Make a break. But where was the opportunity? There just wasn't any!

"Time?" Her whisper was raw.

"To break it out."

"Oh, the champagne!" Her heart went to clattering, and she shook uncontrollably.

He reached up and touched the tip of her nose. "You get red. Blushie blushie."

She had to follow where he went; the chain was only three feet long. They entered the kitchen, and he got the bottle out of the refrigerator. The pop of the cork made her touch memories of good times. She'd last toasted the New Year with the kids. It was freezing, and you could look down from her Manhattan apartment and see windswept figures and hear, faintly, the revels of Times Square.

They drank out of wide champagne glasses from another era, sitting together at the kitchen table. If only she could somehow get the chain around his neck; but he was so watchful.

The champagne roiled in her stomach. She hadn't eaten since breakfast, and that had been just a few choking mouthfuls of cereal. She was thirsty again, too, and all of her wounds hurt like miserable hell, especially the poor dark red thumb. "Will you look at it!"

"What?"

She held it up.

He sipped from his glass. "It's not even ripe."

"Ripe?"

"When they're ripe, they're black and shiny. That's just dark red."

Being destroyed like this must be like watching the timer on a bomb: the progress was slow and fast at the same time. When you took stock, you were shocked by how far things had gone.

"Here's to ripe thumbs," he said.

She looked sightlessly into her glass. Again, she tried to analyze. They knew that child abuse led to an abusive adulthood in some cases—but why not in all? Many people suffered ghastly upbringings; they were punished brutally, sexually assaulted, emotionally devastated. But most of us, no matter how bad our childhoods, did not do things like this.

Was it that men like Kevin indulged themselves somehow, starting with small acts of savagery in childhood—dropping a can of beetles into a fire, plucking a living bird—that slowly escalated to the sorts of cruelties he was inflicting now? If so, there had been original choice . . . and that brought up the issue of original evil.

She had never really entertained the notion of an evil power. But perhaps she was in the presence of something very like that. And she thought: Evil is never captured, evil is never tried. It escapes in its own destruction.

She tried to draw some more information out of him about the all-important early days. "Did you ever have torture sessions with animals?" she said to lead him. "Besides the bird?"

The mockery in his eyes was plain. Could he be sensitive, perhaps, to subtle body language or even to some sort of odor? He could smell fear; he'd said as much. What else could he smell? The study of odor cues was still in its infancy, but there was a growing realization that they were important. In the background the record came to an end, clicked twice, and fell entirely silent.

"On a farm, you respect animals," Kevin said into the sudden quiet.

"How did you feel after you were punished?"

He raised his glass, toasted silently, drank from it. "Were you ever punished?"

She shrugged.

"If nobody ever spanked you, you haven't lived."

"How so?"

"It hurts so much you can't stand it but it keeps on and you can't do nothing, and all of a sudden, you just totally give up. You totally belong to that person." Reverent with memory, he closed his eyes. "Then it's cool."

This was the most familiar symptomology he had yet reported. The man was seeking to be controlled. For him peace would not come until he was under the very sort of domination that he sought to impose on others. In this sense his assault was fundamentally a plea to be stopped.

But what strength it would take! The center of Kevin's hell was the fact that nobody—no woman, primarily—could control him as his mother had. This was the source of his anger; it must be.

At that moment she heard a sound in the distance, the unmistakable bark of a dog. She fought back an excitement so intense that it almost made her gag. "Why cool?" she asked in a level tone, calculated to impart mild interest.

A dog—and listen, more than one dog!

When he spoke, it sounded a thousand miles away. "Try it."

When she did not react, he lifted his right shoulder— a tiny, acceding shrug that said that it didn't really matter—he'd do what he pleased in the end.

Dogs, they were looking for her with dogs!

Giving no indication that he heard, he refilled their glasses, then lit himself a cigarette. He raised his glass. "To tragic beauty." His hand came across the table, patted hers. Their eyes met, and there it was again: she

could see the brilliance of the man. He must not be un-
derestimated, not for an instant. In his own way he had
discovered real truth, which for evil or good was always
powerful.

"Then die," he said.

Her face must have flushed again, because he smiled
a little. He'd heard all right, and he was going to kill her
right now!

"It's from a poem. 'Then die that she the common
fate of all things rare, may read in thee, how small a part
of time they share . . .' "

"Where did you learn poetry?"

"*Great Poems of the World.* I have a sponge memory."

"But you never went to college or anything like that?"

Again, she heard it, the unmistakable baying of a
hound on scent! She prayed, calmly and intently. Please.
Please come. Come to this house, come to me, O hound,
Hound of Heaven.

He shrugged. "My favorite is Emily Dickinson. I
know fifty of her poems. 'We paused before a house that
seemed a swelling of the ground.' Remember that?"

"I'm at a loss."

"Really? 'Because I could not stop for Death, / He
kindly stopped for me—' You never heard that?"

"Has death stopped for me?"

"Yeah, babes, I guess . . . kind of. 'The Carriage held
but just Ourselves / and Immortality.' Do you believe in
immortality?"

She felt tears descending, cooling as they fell.
"You're such a smart bastard!"

She had pleased him, and he smiled like a kid. "Oh? How so?"

She fought her wild hope, fought her trembling voice, her racing mind. "Just when I think I'm understanding you a little, you make it harder."

"Am I smart, compared to most?"

She labored to pay attention to him. But the dog—the dog was moving off! Frantic not to reveal her inner turmoil, she glanced at the green binder—that treasury of Kevin McCallum. "Do you write poetry, incidentally? Is that what you put in that binder?"

"I put what I want to put! And no, I don't exactly write poetry! I am a lousy writer."

"I could read it, if you wanted me to."

"Shut up or you'll eat the damn thing for fucking supper!" He drew closer to her, his mouth slightly open. He was like a man eager to eat.

And the dog bayed once more, but farther away, farther yet! She ached to scream, to bellow, to somehow go to them, to the state police who would be with the dogs. But she could give not the slightest sigh or her life was over. She spoke calmly. "Will you tell me something I'm curious about?"

"What are shrinks curious about? I thought you knew it all."

"Why is this place set in 1958, really? Is it because of your mother? A memorial?"

"In a way."

"Was she your first victim, Kevin?" She had to get outside, had to move fast, or they were going to be gone forever. It had been easily a minute and she hadn't heard—or no, there it was! Coming back—yes, the hound was coming back!

"Look, I think it's time to be frank. You can try to shrink my head all you want. But you are not going to get through this, Cooie. So all the answers to the mystery of Kevin McCallum are going to just—" He snapped his fingers. "My advice is, try to make your peace. It's about now that most of them realize they have to. Nothing's worked, and it's time to pray or go into a panic . . . or start cussing, which a lot of 'em do." He sipped from his glass. "We're running out of time, Cooie."

The words hung. She raced from strategy to strategy. Got to get out, got to haul and do it *now!*

He shook her chain. "Achy?"

It hurt like hell. "No, it's fine," she snapped.

"Oh? Mind if I take a look?" He took her hand, suddenly kissed it, his lips lingering on her knuckles. She could feel his breath tickling the skin. "You have beautiful hands, Cooie."

She held them both out, inviting more submissive acting out. He ignored her.

"Come here," he said, getting up suddenly, causing her to cry out with pain when he yanked the swollen thumb. "Oops, I thought you said it didn't hurt."

"It hurts, oh, Jesus!"

"Then." He yanked. She shrieked, amazed at the tide of agony that swept up her arm. "Do." He yanked harder, and she bellowed. But he was louder: *"Not!"* She howled and kept howling because she could do nothing else. *"LIE!"* He bellowed it over her cries.

She lurched at him, fell at his feet writhing . . . with her arm drifting in the air to keep the chain loose. He waited, gazing down at her as she fought herself. She was appalled to find that she could not stop groaning, could not stop twisting with the ceaseless agony.

"Okay," he said, "get yourself together." He came down to her, she saw his face push itself into hers. "Come on! Put it together!"

She scrambled to her feet in a billow of black silk, stood there gasping and choking, still hopping, still clutching her thumb to her chest.

He led her by the chain into the living room and unhooked her from him. He examined the thumb while she sucked air between her teeth. "Maybe this could be a little tighter, even."

She closed her eyes, but the expected torment did not come. When she opened them again, he was watching her with a patiently bland expression on his face. "Put your hands behind your back now, Cooie."

She hadn't heard the dogs for a long time. Why did they hover out there, why not come to the damn house and at least check it out!

If he was really, really smart, the bastard had put pieces of her clothing in the woods and the dogs were getting confused.

There were dogs, there were! It was *not* a hallucination; she was a woman of importance and she had been missed and there was a massive manhunt out there right now!

A blubbering sob came out of her, sank into gobbling

sounds. She had been disgusted by his drooling, but now she did it.

"Watch the rug," he said. The softness in that voice!

"Putcha hands behindja back, boobala. We better do the cuffs again, I guess."

When she heard the clinking she could not prevent herself dashing down the hall to the back door. She just could not.

She grabbed a picture off the wall this time and used it to smash the glass, which came down in a curtain of spiked shards. She stepped through, ripping her robe, feeling bits of glass pressing dangerously into the bottoms of her feet.

Behind her there had been a roar of purest rage. He grabbed at her robe as she stumbled out into the night. She had no head start at all; he was getting his arms around her waist before she even reached the edge of the porch.

"Don't do this," she said in a choked voice. "You don't have to, you can be free!"

As if by accident, his arms opened. She sprang away from him, thinking in awe: He just made a choice. Then he was a pale shadow back in the dark because she was running as hard as she could, running and screaming her name into the night, "This is Helen Myrer, the lost woman! For the love of God!"

She was unable to really run, was forced instead to jerk along from the pain in her side. The evening had descended to its last pale light, and she was hardly able to see.

Where the hell were they? *Where were they!*

Her breath was coming harder and harder, and every jostling step caused agony. Even though it hampered her, she clung to the miserable shred of clothing he'd given her as she negotiated the weeds. She would not lose this, not as she had the cloak in the forest. Being naked had become a horror for her; if she survived this, she doubted that she would ever enjoy it again.

Without warning, a boiling, bone-twisting agony rolled up her from her thumb and she went flying in a heap. The chain had caught on something and gone tight, stretching her arm to its full extension. The torment was beyond belief, and she screamed savagely, screamed a desperate, incoherent bellow toward the night and the silence, and the god-be-damned lost dogs!

Rustling came, and he was there. "These mantraps are simply awful," he said in a bland voice. He shone a flashlight on her face. Then he bent down, and she felt a slight lessening of pressure on the thumb. "Lord, this is like hooking a trout through the gill. These things are supposed to trip you, not tangle you up."

When he drew her up by the hand, she came fast to avoid any extra tension.

"It's amazing the way a dumb old thumb can control a person."

She was more scared than she'd ever imagined she could be. At least the hand was now somewhat numb. She tried to talk, could not make the words come out.

"Hey, calm down. I'm not mad. A person in your situation's gonna try. I had one girl, she did seven tries. That's the record."

She managed a few sullen words. "I'm getting special treatment, aren't I?"

"You think so?"

"Because I'm a doctor."

"You think I'm being . . . nicer?"

"Slower!"

He turned and started for the house, his arm over his shoulder, the chain grasped between thumb and forefinger. She scurried, frantic that it not be pulled tight. " 'Hi ho, hi ho, it's off to work we go,' " he sang in an eerie, trembling voice.

As they walked he yanked the chain from time to time, and she yelled. Suddenly he stopped. "Shut up!" he whispered. Then he was right in front of her, and there was a straight razor in his hand, its steel blade gleaming brightly. His voice was low and harsh, and she knew that he was well aware of the dogs. "You keep your trap shut, or I am going to cut your eyes out of your fucking head!"

She cried as she walked.

There were so many lightning bugs in the field that it seemed as if heaven had descended. Then they reached the house, went up onto the front porch with its moth-choked light. Such an innocent little place! He unlocked the door. "Ta-da," he said. "Back to camp."

Then they were inside, and she gagged from the thickness of the air.

"They used to dress 'em up as clowns when they came back to Auschwitz," he said. "Then tie 'em to a board and break 'em with clubs." He kissed her forehead. "So I guess I'm really a pretty nice guy." He put a cigarette in his mouth. "I smoke too much," he said absently. He pulled up a few windows. He didn't seem to care anymore if they were locked. He seemed suffused by a kind of glow.

Crickets sang in the night, the high screams of bats came in on a restless breeze.

"Now, my love, when I go to cuff you, what's gonna happen this time?"

She backed away, she could not help herself, she was amazed at herself, she was so scared of this man. He took control, went behind her and swept her hands back, stood her as stiff as a soldier. "That's a good girl."

Her suffering hand felt so huge, it seemed that it would be impossible for him to manage it. But that wasn't the case, and she was soon bound.

There was a hideous stab of agony back there. She howled.

"Just testing," he said. "That thumb's nice and ripe. We can unlock it now."

There followed the most horrible sensation by a degree of perhaps a thousand that she had ever known in her life. Fiery tides swept up and down her body, ending reason, personality, name, almost eradicating consciousness itself.

Dimly, as if it were happening in another universe, she was aware that he was supporting her body and that she was staggering, that the floor was coming up, and—above all—that blowtorches were blasting her arm, her whole side, her neck, her head.

She was entering, it seemed, an area where the edges of reality were less sure, a frontier where she was not

Helen or Cooie anymore, certainly not Dr. Myrer, not anybody, really. She was her fear. Her first, middle and last names were all the same—Pain.

Off in the dim world, somebody was talking. " 'We passed the School, where Children strove, at Recess—' " It was a child's sacred whisper, something from the freedom of younger days.

"Help me," she whispered to the child. She was aware that she was kneeling now, that the room was turning a little less, that the pain was a little less, and for that she was grateful to good heaven.

He was singing, the child was singing: " 'We passed the Fields of Gazing Grain—We passed the Setting Sun—' "

"Sun," she said as if it were a word that would restore her to the formed, sensible, and orderly world from which she'd fallen.

She felt a hand on her forehead, felt herself in Mommy's care now. Mommy had her in her arms, and she sure felt awful, she had the flu.

" 'Since then—'tis Centuries—and yet . . .' "

She gagged and up came white froth, the bile of an empty belly.

The voice of the angel said, " 'Feels shorter than the day I first surmised the Horses' Heads . . .' "

"Emily Dickinson," she managed to whisper.

"Ol' Emily. I've quoted this poem fifty times, it seems. Maybe more. 'The Horses' Heads Were toward Eternity—'" He uttered the line like a prayer.

Then he was drawing her up away from the john.

"Finished, love?" She understood for the first time that she was hanging over the toilet, that she'd been sick.

"The dogs," she heard herself moan.

"Yeah," he said ruefully. "We're in a hurry, babes."

" 'Save it for the sunshine,' " came a crooner's voice from the Victrola.

"You put another record on."

"Yeah. It's better, covers our noise."

It was as if her youngest days were unfolding on some nearby cloud, while hell proceeded around her. Hell had her. He was no dark god; he was worse, a demon come up from chaos.

Then she heard, " 'She's my pony pony pony-tail . . .' " and it took her back. She'd had a golden ponytail, she'd worn pedal pushers.

He was wearing a red-and-white checked apron that smelled of starch, that was as clean as something from the past.

" 'When she's dancing . . . ,' " he sang with the singing Victrola, then wiggled his fingers in her face. "Come on, babes, come with Daddy."

"I was a ballerina," she said, snatching at a vague memory.

"Sure, sure."

"I had a pink tutu."

"It's called a tippet, that kind of robe. Emily Dickinson says 'gossamer gown.' "

"Is this a shroud? Have you given me a shroud to wear?"

"You've torn it, too."

" 'She's got rings on her fingers, bells on her toes,' " the Victrola sang.

His hands tightened on her hips. He was guiding her toward the pantry. "Raise your foot," he said from the height in which he resided. She did it. "Now." He pushed, she stepped—

His arms felt like steel. It just seemed impossible to cease to *be*. But it had happened to Al, it had happened right before her eyes. It was happening to her. He was doing the damned killing and she wasn't ready, she hadn't expected it, she hadn't gotten a chance to try everything!

"Wait," she moaned, *"wait!"*

She tried to stop walking, but she could not stop.

He kissed her ear. "I love you, you beautiful thing. You really are a beautiful one, you know. Very beautiful."

"I'm so tired," she said, and she heard the little girl she had been so long ago, needing to be put to bed.

"Well, that's perfect, then, 'cause it's your bedtime." He folded his hands, bowed his head.

She let him guide her. They stopped before the trapdoor he had opened previously. "Uh-uh," she said. She backed away.

It came up with a heavy creak. The darkness was total.

"Down you go," he said. His hand was on her shoulder. She could feel the compliant self saying, *Don't make him mad, you mustn't do that.*

She tried to fight the compliant self, but it took the fact that you were being punished as proof of guilt. The compliant self could lead even an innocent man into a gas chamber.

The angel with the fiery sword was the adult oppressor of the wild Eden child, who drove him from holy country of innocence. This was why returning home was the great theme of the world.

"Is there a bed?"

"A very nice bed, Cooie. Your own bed in your own room."

"My room?" She knew she mustn't do this, not if she loved her life. But that was knowledge way up at the top of the tree, and she was looking down at the roots.

"Nice, clean sheets and no more Kevin until tomorrow." He handed her an old penlight that barely glowed. "Use it sparingly," he warned.

Shining the frail light on the long ladder, she went carefully down.

My Diary "That's My Baby!"

We are rockin' and we are rollin' and she is down, she is down just as sweet as you please and I am gonna get her back real deep where we will have nobody but each other and no matter how hard you scream or who looks for you, you are not going to be found.

It's the thumb does it. Now, that hurts. You hurt them enough, they always go down.

But this one got dogs looking for her, for shit. I mean, why did I take you, Cooie? I knew there'd be trouble. Old High Sheriff Decker and the State Police and all. You are a high person, you don't belong with the likes of me who usually catches whores on the streets of Boston. You belong in limos and tall buildings. You wear such expensive perfume I can still smell it today.

But I am way ahead of you! You are smart, too, and you have the benefit of education, but I am still the victor.

I brainwashed you, and I am just really amazed at myself. I did this to a major shrink! This is an achievement that should go down in *the history of the world. I wish it would. Who would think that I could be this smooth? But I was smooth, I was very smooth. I played all the right songs.*

It just makes me so fucking mad that you WILL NOT stand up for yourself! You are just like the rest of them and I am fucking all alone and this thing is going down forever, it looks like. All the way to hell I guess.

You fucking stupid cock-tease bitch, you haven't got a brain in your dumb-bunny head!

SHIT SHIT SHIT she went down there! Why? I mean, goddamn, how dumb can you get? She went down there! Fuck you, Cooie, FUCK YOU!

I won.

CHAPTER THIRTEEN

The Hour When
Most People Die

T he bed was a narrow bench of bare boards, which would have mattered more to Helen had she not been in shock. Although there had not yet been the sort of gross hemorrhage necessary to cause a severe drop in blood pressure, her fluid intake had been cruelly insufficient, and this, combined with the pain, was making her lethargic. Her mind—the only weapon she possessed—was well on its way to total failure.

This vital, wonderfully alive woman was now frankly dying. Even so, in the part of her soul that was still functioning—the little light that remained at the core—she was surprisingly calm. Where she ought to plan and strive to save herself, though, she was beginning to dream.

The dim penlight did not allow her to look around much, and she was not thinking clearly enough to try to find a light switch. She lurched out into the small room. What was under her feet? A rug. It was a room with a rug. Or—no. She had something on her feet, didn't she? Yeah, slippers. He'd given her some slippers.

She wept because he had given her slippers.

She stood in the moonlight, in the slippers Al had given her on her last birthday before he died. She stood beside the bed, looking down at this brilliant Alfred Myrer, whom she had taken to be her husband. Look at that wonderful face—the sharpened visage of the litigator and those taut, narrow lips. How effective he appeared, even in sleep. But there was also, in the repose of the face and, above all, the soft shape of the closed eyes, the sweetness of the little boy who still lived inside.

"Al," she said in mixed wonder and amazement, "Alfred Myrer." She could see the Jewishness in him, in the curve of his nose and the ridge of his brow and in something else—a sort of luxury of expression that reflected his rich personality. To know a Jew, as she had come to know this Jew, was to understand why the evil of the world wanted them so badly.

Jews had flooded the place with light: they had discovered the one God and civilized half the species with His Ten Commandments; they had dared to imagine that God could actually become man and redefined civilization again in the image of the resultant discovery, Christian ethics. They had made staggering contributions to the economy and arts and letters of every nation they had entered. Time after time Europe had risen up in terror at the freedom of spirit that Jewish ideas promised. When they actually attempted to extinguish the whole race, the Jewish spirit responded by escaping to America and devising the atomic bomb . . . which turned out to be the essential defense that saved freedom in the world.

All this was for her embodied in her precious Al—Al, whom she needed so badly right now. She reached for him, longing to just once more touch his warm, hair-dusted chest. "What happens when we die, Al?"

"We become memories."

"No afterlife?"

"In the hearts of the people who love us."

She had assumed, always, that you could find the whole mystery of man in the electric meat of the brain. But now, in this world of spirits, with Al seeming so close . . .

A clammy hand came up, ran along her cheek. It was pudgy, so unlike Al's hand.

"Al, are you feeling okay?"

"Not really."

"Why did you die so young?"

She could feel him considering. "Well," he said at last, "it doesn't feel like I died. It feels like you and I became one person. One of our bodies shut down, so now we're sharing."

"Like a dorm room?"

"Like a dorm room."

They had been rather scandalous back in college days, openly sharing a room at Columbia. In the sixties people still disapproved. But her mother had said to her, "I have to tell you, Cooie, I think this guy is wonderful." And Dad had said, "Living together is fine. It's a good preparation for marriage."

Very late she had heard her mother moaning, had heard her father's comforting rumble. The truth emerged, as it always did in their family, in deep privacy. She had then heard, in the quiet of the night house, a despairing, ragged cry: "Why is she doing this to us?"

The next morning Mom had gotten up early and made pancakes with fresh blueberries and squeezed a dozen oranges for juice. "You need a healthy breakfast, you look like you never sleep."

"Oh, Al, remember those days? We were like a couple of little hamsters, weren't we?"

"Gerbils, actually. Hamsters do sexual battle with each other. Gerbils cuddle." He raised his arms and she went down to him, down to their firm, friendly old bed.

"I love our old marriage," she said.

"Me too."

He had planted one of those sloppy, indolent kisses of his on her lips or, rather, on the bottom of her face. They had rolled about in the bed, they had giggled and cuddled under the sheets, they had blasted away at each other, staring into their lovely, dear faces as they delivered the pleasure of the body.

"Al," she said to the bench, "oh, Al, I'm coming home, honey. It's Cooie, it's me." He had hardly known her in the last days. The failure of the liver is a devastating illness; it causes vast and complicated trauma. At the last, he could not even speak. "But the light did not go out, Al. I just closed your eyes for you, is all." She had done it because she hadn't wanted the kids to witness their father as a staring corpse.

"Oh, Al, look at the stars. There's the Great Bear."

"Where?"

"That bunch of stars in the southwest. See the shoulders and eye?"

"Which eye?"

"The bear is a lady bear, Al. Those are women's own special stars."

"Are they now? My star is Orion."

"She's a lady bear because of the two little stars over beside her knee. Those are her children, and she protects them fiercely." She put her hands on her belly.

He had come gently to her on that starry night in their first month together, and he had kissed inside her ear and laid his long artist's hand upon her breast. The plan was, she would not wear her diaphragm, but she would not tell him so he wouldn't feel too pressured.

Women's stars in a summer sky, women's bellies, heavy with the future. "A baby can live in a drawer, Al. A baby doesn't need much."

"Harvard is twelve grand a year."

"Oh, Harvard." She stretched her long self out beside him. They had done this before, come to this hillside in the deeps of Sterling Forest and guerrilla camped. Al yelled the rebel yell, and they listened to it go racing off through the trees. She kissed his cheek, as proper as a nun . . . in high heat.

"I never thought anyone beautiful would want me, Helen."

"You're beautiful. You look like a Brooks Brothers ad."

"I was referring to what is inside the suit, dear."

She stroked it. "Why does it get so hot? Does it get fever?"

"Good God."

He had come rising up over her like a jolly male storm, and they had sweated and bounced beneath the tossing trees and the women's stars. She had felt it come into her, the living life of their first baby, the very moment that it came.

Oh, she knew. She knew for certain and she knew right away. "We did it," she'd said, her voice shaking. "Al, we can't let all these people be here, there's too many!"

The hospital was practically overwhelmed with Myrers and Penningtons, mother and dad and her sister and his uncle Ted and aunt Rose, and somebody had brought liquor—probably they all had. Finally the problem had been solved by making the serious cases waiting room the temporary and hardly serious Myrer/Pennington birthing bash room. It had been a long labor, and the longer it went the drunker they got and the louder they roared, and the more Dr. Magruder's veins stood out on his bald head.

When Al wasn't goggling at her and yelling "Breathe!" so loudly that it confused the other couples, he was helping relatives smuggle in bar supplies.

"Oh, you hurt me, Mikey, you made me so mad!"

"I made you mad when I was just born?"

"Mad but happy, my son." How wonderful it felt to hold a baby and feel him suck, to hold a boy and feel him nuzzle, to kiss the bristling cheek of a young man.

She remembered his question at the breathless age of eight: "Mommy, what is the Secret Society of the F.u.c.k.?"

Oh, the F.u.c.k., she had said into his wide and absolute seriousness, oh, the F.u.c.k. "Well, when Daddy gets home, tell him you want to join the Secret Society of the F.u.c.k. He'll get you enrolled."

Al had said of Selena, "You've given birth to a banana this time."

"A banana?" Her head had been distorted by the birth canal and she'd been colored by bilirubin. Selena Banana had been her nickname until she got old enough to put a stop to it.

"Selena Banana," Helen said. She was aware of the shadow of the man standing over there, but there was no point in using her light, she didn't care about him. Who was he, anyway? He must be just some ghost, he wasn't real, he couldn't be real. Al would never let a robber get in the house; the last thing he did at night was to lock up and check the windows and set the alarm system. Al Myrer kept all the Myrers safe, he kept Mikey safe in his bunk-bed room and Selena in her canopied-bed room, and Helen in their four-poster with the well-oiled springs.

Michael had asked, "Why does the house shake at night?"

Al had said, "It means Mommy and Daddy are having a happy."

"What kind of a happy?" He was most dubious.

Al had taken him in his lap and whispered in his pearl white ear, "It's something you do in the Secret Society of the F.u.c.k.," and that had explained it.

Michael had said to his sister, "When the house shakes, it's a sign that Mommy and Daddy are having a happy."

"Oh, Al, the years are passing, they're flying, Al."

"On happy wings."

She had lain beside him in their house of children, the boy who was tall already and the girl who was asking, Am I pretty, why are the boys so weird, am I ever going to get married, Momma?

Oh, yes, of course. And why did you name me Selena, it's hideous! Rebecca and Marielle are wonderful names, Momma. Rebecca and Marielle and the rising and falling of the sun, and Al in a long succession of black suits, pleading in that precise, resonant voice before the benches and the bars.

A man wiped her tears and she said, "I'd be more comfortable with a female nurse."

She and Al had cried all through the first night of his descent. He was still so strong and so much hers, she could not understand why. There was no why or, at least, not one that had to do with the part of life that they understood.

They found that getting older did not mean that you lost your needs or your feelings. You might not be what he saw originally, but you were still there. You were still yourself and you felt like you always did, a bundle of love and desire.

The shadow man was attending to her belly, and it hurt. What was he doing? "Just ignore me, Cooie, don't even think about it."

Al came trotting down from the upstairs bedroom of their suite. He was in his white tennis shorts and he looked oh so very desirable, her sensual litigator. The deep running of the ship, Caribbean blue passing outside, this amazing suite on the SS *Chanson,* the ship of song. On the Ship of Song, they had recovered the sexual life that had gotten lost in the busy years. She had finally learned to quit contemplating him clinically, and he'd stopped threatening to sue.

"Al, we have to run the deck six times before dinner."

"We ran the deck six times before breakfast. I didn't buy a suite to run to Bermuda."

He was funny, she was funny, their kids were funny, too.

"Al, I have an official declaration to make. My official declaration is that we are having a happy life."

He had taken her to him in her bathing suit and both of them smelling like suntan lotion—and the nurse was hurting her.

"I know it hurts, honey. It'll be like this for a while."

She couldn't see a thing in the dark. Why didn't they have any lights in this place? No decent maternity ward was dark like this; what if there was an emergency? It smelled like mildew. It smelled faintly of animals, as if they hadn't been exterminating the rats.

"Al, I want you to tell Dr. Magruder to keep that male nurse out of here at night. He's creepy, I don't like it."

"I'm your gynecologist."

She had toxemia with Selena, she was in for the whole third trimester and dopey on phenobarbital. Al entertained her by playing cards with her. "Am I any good?"

"Pick up the queen, honey."

"I'm not any good. I hate this. I hate toxemia!"

"You're fine, you're under the best care in the world."

"Oh, Al, I have such dark feelings. I have this dark feeling about this baby. It's like a baby that's not meant to be."

"Well, the Myrer side is meant to be. We've gotta make up for all the lost Jews, you know."

"Half Jews."

"Michael is all Jew."

"Well, half of his genes are from England."

"Your genes are like water. That's why your empire sank without a trace. Put down that jack."

"I don't want to play if I can't!" She noticed the male nurse again. "Al, he's *hurting* me!"

Al slipped softly into the dark and she had to laugh at his silly little mincing wave like Oliver's in Laurel and Hardy.

"Doctor, I feel so strange! I feel like I'm floating away." And then, the wonder of realization. "I'm dying. Oh, I'm dying, aren't I?"

"Yes, Helen, you are."

She sat up, she looked down at herself, and she saw that there were marks on her belly. What were they?

Somebody had drawn lines on her, she needed that damned penlight to see what was going on, what the hell was the bastard up to now?

She got off the bench, closed the robe, and began searching for it. Her feet whispered along in the fluffy house shoes, her robe felt warm. What in hell had the doctor done to her?

She was so weak! If only she could get a little sugar, maybe it would clear her head. If only she could get some meat. Oh, a nice stick of beef jerky would be wonderful, all salty and greasy, oh, Lord, yes.

Salty? All of a sudden the thirst was on her; she realized that her mouth was drier than it had ever been in her life before, that her tongue was like a chapped heel. She swallowed, tried to bring up some moisture, couldn't.

She knew what happened when the electrolyte balance was disrupted this profoundly. She knew about the dementia that came with severe thirst.

The combination of the thirst and the disturbing knowledge brought her back to reality.

She spoke aloud. "I know you're in here, Kevin. Kevin, I know it won't matter what I say. But I want to tell you that I have two children, a boy and a girl. I think I've told you this. I have wonderful grandkids. Kevin, you can let this family live and be happy. We have already lost my husband to cancer. Don't make them lose me. Please, their names are Selena and Michael, and there is no reason why they should suffer a loss like this."

She went down to her knees. "Kevin, can you see me?

I am on my knees. I am pleading. Kevin, if you don't give me water, I am going to go into deep and irrecoverable shock. I am going to die of thirst, Kevin." She muttered the last, "Before you're done with me."

Was he really even here? She'd been hallucinating on that bench, hallucinating until the stillness and the lying position restored a little strength. Al had been there, and Al was dead. She'd been having her babies again. They'd gone on the Ship of Songs cruise.

Was this what they called your life passing before your eyes? "I'd like a steak dinner," she announced. One of those lovely, stolen evenings at Sparks Steakhouse in Manhattan. Oh, the wonderful crust on their sirloins, the juices, and the deep, steaming blush when you cut in. "And the salad!" Dark green lettuce crumbled with fabulous blue cheese and olive oil so fresh that it tasted as if it had been pressed that morning.

And wine. Oh, *wine*. A wonderful Château Giscours or a Talbot, dark purple and cool and so absolutely, sinfully rich.

Now wait. Now, what had she been doing? She was in terrible trouble here, and she had been dreaming while literally standing in the middle of the floor!

She had to regain control. Yes, control was the key. Come back down to earth and find the damned penlight. See what all this strange prickling was on her belly.

Well, finding the penlight was nothing—the penlight was in her damned pocket. She took it out and opened the robe—and what she saw in the failing yellow light made a shriek burst out of her.

He'd been *etching* her, making shallow cuts along the smiling cesarean line he'd drawn earlier.

Anybody could see what would be next, and it was too terrible to think about, to bear, to have to wait for! As if she'd encountered the hot edge of a stove, she went skittering backward. Unable to maintain balance in the dark, she toppled to the packed earth floor.

She hardly noticed the fall, did little more than grunt. Her nostrils dilated, and she found herself sucking air with the avidity of an animal. The animal within had smelled a scent of vital importance; it had smelled water. She fumbled the penlight on and cast its beam about.

It was just a small, square basement room furnished by a backless bench. *He* was nowhere to be seen, and certainly there was no water.

In fact, the room seemed exceptionally clean and dry, so what were all these smells? She was inhaling the scents of a wild underground place that wasn't here.

More hallucinations, probably. She went back to the bench and lay down. There would be no food. There would be no water. Soon he would come back and make the incision implied by the smile he had etched.

She came to her feet, yelled toward the ceiling, "You can't do this! Don't you know they're looking for me? Don't you know they care about me?" She touched her injured belly. You had to be careful with a woman's body, you couldn't play games.

Every few minutes the darkness seemed to grab at her, and she waved her arms and turned on the rapidly dimming light.

Life was arbitrary. It was meaningless in precisely the way that Sartre had claimed. There was no consciousness behind it, nobody watching over things, just a small, wandering planet full of humanity . . . and, growing deep among them like a hidden tumor, the occasional monster.

It was thoughts like these, of the arbitrary nature of her suffering and the empty accidents of life, that sparked her mind again and reconstructed her as a thinking creature. This, and the anger.

Some people had good luck, and some did not have such good luck. All of her life she'd had good luck, things had moved according to the clock of success . . . until the death of Al, then this dark woods and Kevin.

How could it possibly be this way, that a psychologist would get caught in one of these horrible, stupid, tragic situations?

She opened her mouth, cracking her jaw. That was a bad one; it had made her ears ring.

Well, what difference? The meniscus wouldn't wear out before the damned cesarean was done! Her hands clutched her belly. Her *womb!* That cockeyed piece of shit, he sure knew just where to take his hate!

She'd been heaped with it throughout her career by men who had trouble with a female boss or considered a female colleague an opponent.

Women's stars, the fierce, the protecting Ursa Major, bore them and held them and raised them up . . . for what recompense?

Then she heard a sound, a sound so distant that it might as well have been on Mars. She listened, but it was not repeated. However, she was fairly sure that she had heard that dog bark again. "Oh, puppy," she whispered, "puppy, come on!" She would have cried for help, but she did not dare, not and excite Kevin's immediate wrath.

Nevertheless, this faint and perhaps imagined sound from the outside world was what she needed to add a little hope to the restoration of the thinking being.

The bark did not repeat. Neither did Kevin come.

She got up from the bench and paced, holding her hands out before her to avoid slamming into the walls. This thirst was driving her nuts, it was making her want to claw into the floor, dig a crazy well. She understood the meaning of that phrase "crawl the walls."

She understood also Arthur Koestler's description of the prison in *Darkness at Noon,* remembered the haunting cry of the old prisoner who had forgotten parts of words. " 'Arie,' " she whispered, " 'arie ye wretched of the earth.' " She hadn't thought of Koestler in years and years, but his vision of oppression had been one of the things that had inspired her to embrace the humanism that had led to her career. " 'Arie,' " she yelled, " 'ye wretched of the earth!' "

He had given her the robe to keep her alive. He probably hadn't even heard her yammering about the dangers of shock. Knowledge of the thirst that was consuming her was no doubt a gut-deep thrill for him.

She touched her thumb, which replied with thuds of agony. In the half-light it appeared to be streaked with lighter areas of infection.

Wait a minute, was she nuts or what? She could damn

well see! She jumped up, ran to the center of the room. She could definitely see, there was no question about it.

It must be morning.

Hardly daring to entertain further ideas of escape, she nevertheless looked around for the window. But the light seemed to come from everywhere. No, it was a little brighter on the far side of the basement.

Superficially this room was very simple, just a concrete square with a trapdoor and a ladder and the bench. There wasn't any effort at soundproofing. Why bother, in an isolated place like this?

She found that the wall at the lit end of the room did not go all the way to the ceiling, and the glow was coming from the other side. There seemed to be no way to get to the top of the wall. It was more of a concrete shield. She tapped it. Thick.

Then she thought, Dear God, this is his graveyard, it must be. No wonder the basement was so clean; he put the remains behind the wall.

But if his kill rate was as high as he claimed, the whole place would stink of fresh corpses. That faint animal smell was alive, it wasn't coming from corpses.

A sound came, then, from far away. It was a high, mournful wail that never seemed to end, a wail that made her want to clap her hands over her ears.

A dog again, howling?

No, she thought not. She listened, trying to tell its direction. Eventually it trailed off like a wind dying.

It had come from behind the false wall. She touched it, realized that it was damp. Without the slightest thought she slapped her tongue against it and licked. It didn't help, though; the damp was nothing.

The thing she had to do was jump up and grab the top, then chin herself until she could see over. Oh, yeah, that was believable, that was something she could manage.

She jumped, but she didn't think that she came closer than six inches from the top. Anyway, her arms weren't strong, she couldn't even begin to pull herself up.

Morning. Outside the sun must be pouring down, outside the birds, the breeze, all of dear life going on without her.

Morning. He was waking up, he was stretching in his bed, taking a piss . . .

She jumped again, felt the tip of one finger touch the top of the wall. The light definitely came from behind it. What if the wall was there to keep you away from a window? What if she got to the window?

A squeak stopped her, made her look up. It was followed immediately by roaring so loud that she cried out in fear.

As the sound continued, she fisted her hands in her hair. Her debilitated condition caused her to come to understanding only slowly. But when she did, she stopped screaming at once.

The sound was only Kevin running his morning shower.

She began to breathe in panicky bursts. She dashed around the square room, slapping the walls like the caged animal she was. She rushed up the ladder and slammed on the trapdoor, thinking in the confusion of her terror that she could maybe break out with the shower covering the sound.

It would have taken a sledgehammer and a strong man to accomplish that.

Time, she was running out of time! Oh, God, God, please, if you're there, do something for me! I've never even asked you, God! So please, please listen to me now. Listen to me! "Listen to me, *listen to me!*"

The water stopped; she heard the final squeak of the taps being closed. Then she saw, running along the ceiling near the trapdoor, pipes. In four steps she was back at the ladder, then she was up and stretching as far as she could toward the beads of condensation that had formed on them.

Closer she stretched and closer yet, but not quite close enough. She groaned. It was fully eight feet to the floor. She mustn't risk a fall. A sprained ankle would mean the absolute and total end of all hope.

She snorted. Hope!

It was so quiet.

Then she noticed something that she hadn't seen before, visible across the wall from the top of the ladder.

There was considerable space back there, and the light didn't come from any window, it came from an inchwide opening between the foundation of the house and the stone face on which it rested. This face sloped quickly down behind the wall, but not close to it, not close at all. There was lots of room back there, a whole dark area at least the size of the basement itself.

Above her there were thuds and creaks. She rushed down the ladder, went to the middle of the room, and ran at the wall. She tried to run up it, to somehow get high enough to catch that edge.

She sank down, resting against the wall, hugging it as if it were a protective old friend. Another odor came, and with it a faint hissing sound. She let her head loll, watched her hair come down around her face, stringy and ugly, her beautiful hair. Washed, but not properly attended.

She stroked her hair, trying almost without realizing it to improve matters a little . . . perhaps also to keep her mind off the succulent, commonplace, precious odor of the bacon Kevin was up there frying.

CHAPTER FOURTEEN

Escape to Darkness

She opened her mouth, did not realize that she was lifting her fingers as if eating. She imagined the bacon curling in the skillet, popping and sending up smoke as the middle turned dark and the ends became golden curls.

She moved about, nervously touching her injured belly, becoming aware of her other pains.

Suddenly she stopped. Had that been another bark? Couldn't be sure. Then creak, creak—he went across the house, down ... to the back door. Yes, he was at the back door! Oh, it *was* a dog, there was a dog out there, there was the search party at last, *finally* getting it into their thick skulls that good ol' Kev had a big problem!

She was screaming, jumping, crying ... and then she heard another sound. Something scraping, but what?

Then a clatter, another scrape . . . and the very distinct sound of glass being poured into a trash can.

All that was happening was that he was cleaning up the mess she'd made of the back door. There was no rescue on the way or he sure as hell wouldn't be doing a thing like that.

"Everybody's got a dog," she muttered. All along it had probably been just some family hound out chasing deer.

She listened to him up there, his footsteps on the floorboards. He moved around a lot, and every time he came near the trapdoor, her heart started hammering so hard that she was afraid she was at risk for cardiac arrest.

Again and again he came over. Once he even threw the lock back with a sickening, decisive thump. She almost tore hair out in hunks, waiting for it to open. But it did not open.

Her fingers flitted along her new injury, adding it to the other hurts, especially the thumb, which was very sore.

She moved ceaselessly back and forth, back and forth. As if struck by a critical idea, she rushed over to the bench and tried to lift it over her head like some kind of ungainly club. It weighed far too much.

She dropped it and sat on it in a defeated slump.

Were they all this cruel? John Wayne Gacey had been, judging from the testimony of the survivor. Anybody who killed was cruel, but the ones who did it slowly . . .

She could understand people acting out of sudden bursts of helpless inner violence, but not the level of consideration and planning that she was seeing here. Choice was not only available to this man, he was making elaborate and careful choices, torturing her with extraordinary attention to detail.

She considered the mother—had she been sane enough to be held responsible? What had gone on in her childhood—had her father inspired the rage that she carried against men, perhaps by coming in the night to her bed?

How long were these chains that linked us to the past? Evil had been man's partner always.

At that moment the trapdoor creaked loudly and a searing sheet of white light came down, forcing her to shield her eyes as he quickly descended the ladder, his sneakers scuffing along the rungs. "Mornin,' Cooie." He had something in his hands, something wrapped in canvas. "You manage to sleep any, hon?"

She couldn't stop looking at that canvas. She watched as he laid it on the bench.

"I guess we'll get going at about eleven," he said affably.

She backed away from him. "Kevin, I want to beg you. I want to beg you to let me go."

He raised his eyebrows. "Hey, I thought we were past that."

"Well, we aren't! I want you to—"

"Look, this thing just rides the rails from here on."

"Listen to me!"

"Come on, Cooie, you're a shrink, you know I have to do this. *I have to!* There's no way to stop me. I never found none, and now it looks like you didn't, either."

She hardly heard him; she was edging toward that canvas. Under it there would be some evil tool, and that tool could be used as a weapon . . . if she was quick. She swallowed. "I'm sorry—my throat is so dry."

"Oh, I know it, I worried about you all night. It must be so awful for you."

"Give me a drink!"

He stared at her as if he had no idea how to do that.

"Go upstairs, get a glass, go to the sink, fill it with water. It's not hard."

She held her robe tightly closed, as if trying to conceal from him the strange new cut that he'd made, as if he might forget it.

She was closer now to the canvas, close enough to reach out and throw it back with one quick motion. All right, remember that you have no strength, no staying power. This is a one-shot, and then it is over. And when he binds you this time, in those bindings you will die.

He sat down between her and the canvas. She almost burst into tears. "I know you're upset," he said.

"Upset!"

" 'Cause if you're not, you're crazy. What you need to try to do is stay cool."

This was impossible. It couldn't be like this. "Will that help me?"

He grabbed her by the throat, glared into her eyes. "I made you some breakfast," he said.

Then he was across the floor and up the ladder. The trapdoor slammed, and for a moment she was blind. When her eyes adjusted to the dimness again, she ripped aside the canvas—and spilled bacon and eggs all over the floor. There was even a carton of orange juice. She crouched down, grabbed the food off the floor, ripped open the juice, and drank it—and it was as if it had been poured into her throat by the hand of an angel.

She scraped up the bits of egg that remained on the floor and put them in her mouth. The tastes were incredibly detailed, of yolk and the lighter egg white and hot bacon grease. Very wonderful.

She was grateful to him, she was ready to kiss his filthy feet, she was abject. But she also straightened up.

Eleven o'clock, he'd said, but had, of course, omitted to tell her what time it was now. She'd had a watch, a lovely watch, a platinum Cartier given to her by Al for their twentieth. So what had she done with it?

She was coming unraveled; she couldn't remember the simplest thing. Real life seemed like a distant, fading dream. She could not even tell whether or not the thinking she could manage was clear. "You're just sitting here, you've gone passive, you're letting this happen to you, and it doesn't have to happen. It does not have to happen."

She'd spent the night in hallucinatory shock, come out of it after an apparent period of sleep, and now that she had this food in her she was actually feeling a little better.

Why would he feed her? Why would he help her in any way? Again, she must be the victim of some kind of deception. But what could it be?

Probably he simply wanted her conscious and in command of her faculties so he could enjoy her suffering more completely. Last night he had expertly broken her to compliance and had no doubt taken great pleasure in it.

Had she remained broken? She didn't feel that way. What she felt was trapped. But he had seemed incredibly powerful when he came down here, a small god, perfunctory and commanding.

Her breath stopped, and she came slowly to her feet. "No!"

But the answer she felt in her heart was yes. The compliance was so insidious. You didn't know what you became. This had happened in the camps, even to vital, intellectually powerful people.

Overpower, degrade, render hopeless. Then you will have compliance even from somebody who is very strong.

She jumped up. "What time is it?" she called. "Hey, what time is it?"

It was so strange to find that you could not believe in your own death. Her new submission seemed as natural to her as skin.

Except that it wasn't. Except that it was an illusion.

So break the illusion, crush it, escape from its hypnosis.

The trapdoor opened again, and again she was pinioned by the light and by his movement down the light.

How could a human being appear more ordinary? He was odd looking, true, but in that gray shirt and those frayed jeans, a cigarette dangling from his lips, he presented not the least appearance of a dark god.

"You haven't told me everything about yourself," she babbled, coming quickly to her feet.

"I told you plenty."

"But this life you described—your mother—"

"It was a hard life, but I survived."

"If you'd just open up, you could find out something about yourself. But you won't. You just won't!" She was shrieking, she couldn't help it.

He drew something out of his pocket—a Swiss Army knife. He opened it to the largest of the blades, held it in the palm of his hand, eyebrows raised.

She leaped away from him, crying hoarsely, clutching her stomach. "It's not eleven yet!"

"It's ten after, honey."

She pressed herself against the false wall. "I know what's back there!"

He laughed—a high, crazy patter of sound. "And you're still hanging around in here?" He laughed again, sat down on the bench. "Okay, have it your way. Come here to me."

Before she could even think about it, she'd done it.

"I really thought you'd be harder."

"How?"

"Put your hands behind your back."

She was doing it when she noticed from the bulge appearing on his pants that he was getting an erection. This broke his power, at least for the moment, because it so outraged her. Her feet seemed to start going on their own as she propelled herself away from him.

She raced to the ladder. The door was closed, but she knew it wasn't locked, it couldn't be, not unless he was planning on spending the rest of his life down here.

He was right behind her, of course, yanking at the

robe, laughing nervously. He wasn't at all excited; he didn't even raise his voice when he told her to come back. With all the strength she could muster, she kicked at him instead.

He made a sound like the air escaping from a blown tire and dropped to the floor.

The door was locked! She looked down, and he was getting up, he was coming toward the ladder again, and the mask of the ordinary was gone from his face—for the first time completely and totally gone—and what she saw there was the reality of the man. His gaze was as empty as a lizard's, his lips fixed in a barren line; the expression was as bland as that of a dead body, as if it merely symbolized a man.

She butterfly kicked like a swimmer, gasping with the effort of it, clinging to the ladder and pulling herself up, up again, butting the trapdoor with her head again and again, until she saw stars and knew it was not going to move.

Somehow a foot connected with his forehead just right, somehow he flew backward toward the middle of the room and hit with the flop of limp weight. For a moment he was sitting, shaking his head.

She could drag a bench she couldn't lift. She jumped down, pulled it by its end, ramming it into the false wall as he got to his feet.

It didn't crack the wall, of course. That wasn't her purpose. She got up on it and from there grabbed the top edge. Her arms trembled, she scrabbled with her feet until they bled, but she got to the edge and rolled over into the dark without so much as glimpsing what might be below her.

She fell heavily enough to see flashes, lay for a moment stunned, staring up into the distant rafters. Every wound hurt, and her knees where she had hit hurt, too. Lifting herself up, she felt around for something to use as a weapon, but there was nothing. It was blank space.

She'd accomplished nothing.

Then she heard laughter, very soft, amid scraping and thudding sounds. He was coming over the wall. To her left, to her right, she looked. She fought the penlight out of her pocket and shone it around. She moaned, she hit her forehead, she growled. Nothing here, no exit!

When he dropped down it was soundless, it was balanced. She saw, also, that he had produced a gun. "Good," she shouted, "shoot me!"

He began taking aim, and she kept backing away. She could see bullets gleaming in the barrel as the chambers rolled.

She realized that she was under an overhang, also that her voice had echoed, and then that she was in the mouth of some sort of cave.

She threw herself down and there was blast of thunder and a flash, and heat rushing by an inch above her head. The pistol's noise amazed her. She'd never heard one except in the movies, and this thing was a great deal louder than that. It also sent sparks flying; it looked like some sort of firework going off.

Before her was darkness absolute. The penlight told her that the path led gently down.

"You won't come out of there, Cooie."

She started running.

"Cooie! *Cooie!*"

It was a cave, a big one. Or was it a mine? Maybe New Hampshire was full of old mines, who was to know? But if it was a mine, there were no pilings. No, it was a cave and it went deep, she could sense that from the dank exhalation that was coming out of it. It must be the source of the damp she'd sensed last night.

She'd never dreamed that this was here, never in a thousand, million years. She was exhilarated by it, and she cried out as she ran, cried high and wild, the scream of an animal set free, of a creature of the wild going back.

Then she stopped. The penlight would give out, she had to preserve it. How about behind her? Any sound? No. Yes. Yes, but not a sound of running feet, a slower, more deliberate sound. Thud . . . thud . . . no hurry in it at all.

There was no other opening. Of course not, and he knew it. All he had to do was wait her out. So he was strolling casually in, not venturing too close. He'd wait—and he could afford to wait. Hell, he liked to wait. Loved it.

What could she do? She had to choose between starvation back in this cold, dank hole or going to him and getting it over with.

"Co-o-oie? You've been a ba-a-ad girl, Cooie. You better come to papa, you better start being a good girl *right now!*"

Why would he sound so cheerful, when he might well

lose her? If she went back, it might be best. Words were still her best hope.

Come on, woman, *no!* In here you have a lousy, miserable little edge of a chance.

She didn't believe it and couldn't make herself. "You're going to die here," she told herself, "but you *will* die fighting."

The promise of the path before her had awakened enough hope to make her toss her head and go on.

He came casually along, his approach announced by the revealing eye of a powerful flashlight. " 'Okay,' " he sang to himself, " 'that's my baby. Okay, that's my baby . . .' "

Ahead there was a turning, and she took the smaller of the ways, and began to enter into a world where water had made wonderful curves in walls that gleamed crystalline blue in her fading light. Here she had to bend double and scurry along. Here she had to turn again and go deeper.

She stopped. With the light off she was in a darkness that had something to do with the absolute. It was darker than space, darker than the inside of the mind. Its silence must be connected to some final silence. There was a sense of incredible, amazing danger.

All of her life she'd felt safe—until these two days when she had known only extraordinary peril. She clutched at the cold, slick walls and devoured the darkness with her eyes. And heard, breaking the holy silence, the smooth breath of an unhurried man.

"I'm coming, honey," he whispered. "It's gonna be all right, lovey, you're gonna be all right."

She held her own breath, held it as if to expel it would be to empty herself of life.

"I hear you, sweetie. I hear you being quiet. I understand that, sure I do." He was no longer whispering. This was the gentle calling of a father to his frightened child. "I'm gonna get you and hold you in my arms and you aren't gonna have to worry about anything anymore."

She gasped; she couldn't avoid it. There was a shuffle somewhere back in the dark, and the flashlight came again, its glow turning the walls into a flickering crowd of eyes. Again she ran, moving deeper, not trying to remember her path or find her way, going mostly like a blind rat by feel, taking only an occasional reading with her light.

Always the corridor went downward, always curving this way or that like a crazy old trolley track. There had to be a branch somewhere, a hole to hide in, a turn to take where he would not follow. Down she went, down and around. More and more she used the penlight, trying to find some branch, anything but this obvious passage. He'd drag her out by her hair.

"Co-o-oie. Co-o-oie. Oh, you're down there. You're going deep, Cooie. That's okay, I guess. Cooie, I liked you, I really did. I was gonna do it so quick, just for you! Cooie, it would've been just—little! We would've kissed and it would've been over. Just like that. I had it all planned." She heard him sigh a ragged sigh of the sort a man used to cover a sob. "It's gonna be shitty now, Helen Myrer. Fucking doctor. Well, look what a good job you did, you cured me, fucking *doctor!*" In the ringing silence that followed, she heard the thuttering of quick, efficient feet that knew exactly where they were going.

She did not run, could not. She'd run away from him before and it had never worked, and it wasn't going to now.

She turned to face him. Now she could see the dancing glow of his light . . . and in that glow a shadow—the large shadow of a rocky outcropping.

She went to it. She pressed herself as hard as she could against the rock, hoping that she was hidden. He was coming fast now, real fast.

But why? A few moments ago he'd been strolling. Now, though, there was this definite urgency.

Could it be that there was a way out in this direction? She thought of caves as having only a single entrance, but why did that have to be true? Maybe she was closer to escape than she realized.

Now she could hear the thumping of his feet, now the grunts of effort as he ran. Oh, he sounded desperate all right, even frantic. There was a way out down here all right . . . and maybe, if she was careful, he would lead her there.

He was Cyclops with a burning eye of light, an eye she thought surely would see her, surely had the power to make the hidden visible, to turn the rocks that concealed her into clear air.

Closer he came, the light of his eye bouncing and swaying and shining along the stones. Here and there she could see marks where she had slipped, and she had

to bite her hands to keep from crying out for fear that
they would lead him to her hiding place.

He roared past. As he did she heard a deep inner
noise, not a moan, not a growl. His hate was hooked to
the dark in a way she was no longer prepared even to try
to understand. For the first time in her professional life
she was beginning to entertain the notion that evil could
exist in a state that might in some way be intractable to
science. But the moment he was gone she dismissed the
whole idea as a superstition of the cave.

He was gone, dear God in heaven. She blurted out a
laugh, stifled it instantly, cursed herself for a fool.
Clinging to the rock, she listened. Then she began to follow along, moving slowly, carefully. She even breathed
as lightly as she could, aware of how sound carried
along these reflecting chambers.

She used her nose, trying to see if she could smell
outside air. But she could not; she could smell only the
ever more distinct odor of animals.

Her lips curled. The place must be full of rats. God
only knew what they found to eat in this mineral-en-
crusted hole. Maybe they came for the salt in the water
that sweated down the walls.

When she used her light, she saw an increase of wonder. Here there were stalagmites and stalactites. This
was a real cave in every way, a huge cave. In her mind
she held a picture of the way back to Kevin McCallum's
basement. If she got lost, there was always that alternative. She touched the slits on her belly, and thought, No.

Either she was going to find her way out of this cave
or she was going to die here. Under absolutely no cir-

cumstances would she ever, ever go back to the hell she had come from.

So, then, where would she go? Ahead the space narrowed into a corridor. To her right was what looked like a steep-sloping pit. No telling where that led, though, and it was much too steep to climb. No, the pit was a trap. By contrast the corridor was negotiable, sloping off to the limit of her light and exhaling a cool, steady wind. Her choice was made for her: she went on.

My Diary "The Process"

It has made me feel very sad that I won.
When I was cooking the Last Breakfast, I was
crying. It made me mad at you, Doctor, because I have never cried before. Usually when
I am cooking the Last Breakfast, I am getting
toward the peak, I am getting really happy.

What I want to tell you is that this whole
thing is very relaxing and very nice-feeling. I
cannot write like the poets. My poetry is in
what I do. You have to understand that, if you
are going to understand me.

We only recognize arts that are nice. Painting and writing and such like. But what about
MY art? My art is what I am doing to you.
You may call it torture and murder, but it really does not have a name. Planned violence.
Getting my heart fixed up for a while. Being
in control. Seeing people really naked, when
they are suffering and while they die.

I edge life out of you, and get to see you suffer every inch of it. After you are dead, I know
you better probably than God does. Other arts
are also like what God does. The painter cre-

ates a landscape, the writer a person. But it's all just oil paint and paper. My art is the art of seeing you as you are, in your most intimate self.

So, why am I so unhappy now, Doctor, if I am getting to do my art once again?

Oh, this is all fucked up and don't make the kind of sense I want it to make. You were supposed to shrink my head, damn you. You did not do your job, here!

You got no idea what real pain is. You got no idea, Doctor.

CHAPTER FIFTEEN

The Depths

She moved along swiftly, using her light only in brief flashes. She would die with the batteries, and she knew it well.

This corridor was wide but low, forcing her to crouch and also lose touch with the walls, which created the distressing effect that she was scuttling along on a vast, sloping plateau. Then she would turn on her light and see the ceiling inches above, the walls a few feet away, the pools of absolute dark ahead and behind, and it was all she could do not to just fall down where she was and shut her eyes and scream until her voice died.

A rhythm came into her head, and she began moving forward like an edgy dancer.

For some unknown time she went down, went deeper and deeper. As the immediate tension dropped, the pain of her wounds began to reassert itself. There was the persistent sensation that she was leaking out through the red smile he had incised across her lower abdomen.

She stopped, went to all fours. After a moment's perfect stillness, she sucked air. She was trying to find a smell of dry grass, of air that had been warm, of flowers or the forest. But there was only the musty, dank odor of the cave with its hint of animal bodies.

From so far away that it seemed almost to be one with the walls and dark of the cave, there came a long, trailing howl. As it faded, it was replaced by another sound, more distinct and persistent, perhaps the deep rushing of water.

An underground river might well spill into the lake. She imagined Lake Glory in morning light, its water the clearest blue, wavelets hurrying along ahead of a light breeze, sailboats here and there just being touched by the sun.

Once again the howl echoed. She had to think that it was a human sound, for it bore within itself the indefinable quality of sentience. Did he howl?

Without any warning at all, a responding sound came out of her—a deep, growling thunder of a sob, followed by another, then by the convulsive jumping of the chest.

Her heart knew the meaning of the sound, but not her damned, science-stuck *mind!*

Oh, no, don't you dare abandon science. Science is what you have that will save you, science and intelligence, not your black emotions and your deadly fear.

Crablike, she scuttled along—and, quite suddenly, found that she could see without her light. She stopped.

She closed her eyes, opened them. Now it was dark again. She tried the light and found that the space just ahead looked much as it had during that strange, glowing moment.

What would do that? She went back on her haunches . . . and there it was again. This time the rough places in the floor all cast shadows, long and thin, that touched her, that crossed her, that made her shrink back.

She fought a wave of sick vertigo. The light was him coming back. He'd realized that he'd passed her. What had she been thinking—that she'd gotten away? How foolish was that?

She went down to all fours and crawled, speeding along like an infant. Her shadow raced out before her, darting against the long, low ceiling. He was so damn fast, he was like a force of nature in these miserable tunnels and arcades. Her mind cried out, Think, think, there has to be a way.

There was no way. What was going to happen was that he was going to run her down.

Up she went, struggling and slipping in her terror, reaching out with hands become claws, and then her shadow came again, and this time the light was bright enough to define her shape against the floor. Now she could also hear him back there, a soft, swift whisper of movement that even as she listened became more clear.

The thought of him getting closer brought his loathsome face to memory, and the sour odor of his skin. Never, ever did she want to smell that stink again, never to have those horrible, moist, soft hands caressing her.

Looking for some nook that would conceal her, she

used her light much more than she should. She saw a mass of minerals that looked like the melted heap of a huge candle and went down behind it. She watched his flickering glow come and go, come brighter and go again.

The dark caressed her shaking body, the coolness was made cold by her sweat. She fought her loud breathing, tried to quell it, tried to be as silent as was possible.

"Hi, Cooie."

His voice sent a steel spike right through her heart. She *would* be touched by him again, she would be bound and she would die the slow, humiliated death of nightmare. She couldn't move, she was beyond physical control. All that was left was to wait for the hands.

"Come outta there."

She couldn't move, not at all. As had happened at the cabin, she was frozen. No wonder people had to be carried to the gallows.

"Look, I know where you are. If I have to come over there and haul you out, I'm gonna have to be a little rough, I'm afraid."

She'd better get unfrozen because all that was left was to plead. But she couldn't move, she was like stone. She wanted to explain to him, but no words would come.

"Cooie, damn it!"

She fought to open her mouth, to make the words come out—take in breath, force yourself.

"Cooie!"

"Okay," she said, "you got me." She rose into the yellow eye of the light, shielded her eyes with a hand.

There was a low, satisfied sigh from the figure behind the light. He radiated competence and control. "I'm sorry, Kevin. I just couldn't help myself."

"It's okay. I was gonna just—I mean—we'd gotten almost to be friends, you and me. Like you said we should. I guess I feel a little hurt, Cooie."

"Don't feel hurt."

"Because when they hurt my feelings, they are really animals, is all, they are just there to do what I need, is all."

In this place that she found so strange, dark, and confusing, she suddenly understood that he was totally and completely at ease. The little hope that remained now slipped away. He knew this place perfectly, of course. He'd probably been coming here all his life. He shone his light straight into her face. "Open your eyes!"

"Yes!" She stared into the glare of it.

"I guess you people just can't come down to my level, you high-and-mighty doctors!"

"What did she do to you? What did she do wrong?"

"Is every fucking doctor I am ever gonna fucking see gonna be a woman? Why the fuck does it have to be a woman?"

"All women aren't your mother."

"Just fuck the little hairless asshole, laugh at him 'cause he's—" The light came closer, the light bored into her wide-open eyes. "What am I?"

"I don't know. Did you—with your mother?"

"What—am—I!"

"I don't know, I don't know! I can't analyze you, I can't even begin!"

"Then you must be a fucking moron!"

"It is rare for somebody so smart to be . . . like you."

"Like me how? What is so weird about me?"

"You kill people!"

"You kill people, you kill people! The bitches run. You bitch, you ran! *You ran!*"

The raw power of the wild captured her then, captured her and whirled her around, turning her away from the raging shadow behind the light, bidding her take her chances in the dark.

When she turned she saw how the glow of his flashlight ended abruptly at a sharp defined edge. It was the pit again, the one she'd seen coming in. She backed toward it.

"That's a mistake, hon."

Gravel dinged as it slipped away behind her heel. If only the fall was far enough, if only it would kill. But even dying down there of exposure, she had no doubt, would be better than what he had in mind.

"That's a mistake, I said!" He lunged at her. She hopped back, teetered.

"Oh, no, it's not!"

His hand came down on her shoulder. "Cooie—"

She flung herself out into the air, shrieking and kicking and clawing. Plummeting, she slammed against one wall, bounced against another, then hit a tumble of debris and began to slide in roaring, careening gravel.

Gradually it stopped. Gradually silence replaced its busy roar. She found herself in absolute dark, without any trace of light from above, not even a spark. Her back was shot through with pain where she'd hit the wall, her cheeks burned from scraping in the small stones, but her arms and legs still worked and she still had her light clutched in her hand.

She slid the switch back and forth. Nothing. She unscrewed the cylinder, felt the tine that pressed against the batteries. Was it flattened? Probably not, probably the batteries were simply dead or the bulb had been broken in the fall.

No, not that—the bulb felt fine. She played with the tine, prizing it up as best she could with the thumbnail she had broken back at the cabin, back when she was taking down the Polaroid of that poor woman.

Where was the stone floor she'd been lying on? Was it back in this cave somewhere? How perfect for him, a place of guaranteed privacy and no matter how much they screamed.

She shook her head, shaking off the thought. As she resealed the tube of the flashlight, the threads ground from dust and sand. She was almost unable to bear to look as she slid the switch to the on position. But she found that she had a very definite little bit of pale light. She could see that she was at the bottom of a long shaft, extremely steep. The lip of gravel where she had come to rest fell away into a deeper crack. There was no other way anywhere except back up, and the climb would have been impossible even if she had wanted to make it.

She crawled over to the crack, her hands and knees crunching in the soft material that covered this floor. Down here she could hear the water more clearly. Somewhere darkly flowing, there was certainly a river.

Drowning was a few minutes of pain, and rivers flowed out.

To get down the crack, she had to lie flat and draw the robe tightly around her, then slide sideways in the gravel. But she only went a foot, perhaps two, before the choked rubble stopped her. At first she thought that it was a dead end, but she heard some of the rubble bouncing off into what sounded like a very substantial distance. There was more cave down there, a lot more.

Quite without warning there was a pale flashlight eye watching her again, and a pudgy hand coming out from behind it, and a voice saying, "It's okay, Cooie, I got you, you're gonna be okay."

But it wasn't okay, and she pushed, she scrabbled clawing fingers against the ceiling . . . and went a few inches deeper.

"Come on," he breathed, "come on . . ."

Then his light was behind and above her, shining into the great scrape marks where her body had been. The arm that came in seemed able to stretch a long, long way, and the hand when it touched her naked thigh was strong. Its fingers closed her skin between them and pinched and pulled, but she pulled, too, she went farther into the crack, in and down.

Then the dark became total again. "Lights out," he muttered. "This is like digging out a clam, Cooie."

Dig away, bastard, dig away! She kept pushing, and the gravel kept giving beneath her, and the sound of its falling went on and on.

"Okay," he said at last, "do it your way."

She stopped, listened, her chest heaving, her own

breath blowing the ceiling's dank smell back against her face.

"Cooie, what I do takes an hour! It's gonna be days and days if you stay here."

She could not react to that; she did not know how.

He made a sound, a little, frustrated grunt. "Look, I need this, and I'm gonna get you and do it. I need it! For chrissakes, you think I want to do it? It's hard, it takes guts."

"Guts," she moaned.

"You think I want to put myself in danger like I do every fucking day of my fucking life? It's hard to hunt you people down. You could give me what I need to make it stop, to make it be quiet, Cooie. You could give it what it needs; it'd be a hell of a lot better than being buried alive! Because that's what you get if you don't come out. I am gonna just fill this in right behind you. I am gonna tamp it down hard. You'll suffocate and you'd do it slow, Cooie. Real slow!"

She saw the grotesque self-indulgence in what he said, and it made her focus on the fact that he *had* a choice all right, and it caused her hate to grow stronger than ever. It was already the structured, focused hate of a fully formed and normal human being, the hate of a rational woman for a vicious, intractable, cruel man. Now it became the hate of a soldier who knew that victory and survival were the same thing, who knew the secret of warfare, that you lived for yourself, died for the enemy.

She worked harder than ever, pushing against the ceiling and the gravel and jerking her hips, sidling along even as he filled in dirt from the far side, even as its coolness pressed against her.

Quite suddenly the gravel to her left stopped giving way and the wall he was building to her right became sealed.

She could hear him breathing on the other side, "okay she's my baby . . ." repeating, again and again as he tamped down his work and made sure the seal was properly tight.

Her breath was thick around her now, and inhaling didn't help. She gave it more effort but still didn't get the air she needed. Down in her throat, she screamed. It was hardly audible—the vague, lost gargle of someone in suffocation.

Her nostrils dilated and she breathed faster. Suffocation would be quick, suffocation was just a little bit of anguish and then release. She almost babbled her excitement, started breathing even harder. She squirmed, and her open hands slapped the ceiling beside her face.

Just as if she were on an elevator, she went down. It wasn't far, perhaps two feet. But fresh air poured in around her, causing a convulsive sneeze when she inhaled deep of the mildew and damp. Again she dropped. Muffled by the gravel and soil, she heard him make a sound.

Had that actually been laughter?

She slammed her hips from side to side, and as she did the gravel fell away more. Then she was going down fast. She hit a floor and was immediately covered by gravel.

Far away she heard a "hah" of surprise . . . and she

thought, also, more laughter . . . maybe a lot of laughter. She sat up, used her light. There was haze in the air, and she saw movement at the edge of the light, as if something large had instantly pulled back. She pointed her beam, but there was nothing.

She started to stand—and encountered the ceiling again. Basically she was still in the crack, just in a deeper section of it.

Again she sneezed, this time harder, and an odor came in afterward, one that made her stop and inhale more carefully. It was redolent of methane and ripe decay—fecal matter, perhaps . . . but not human, no.

Of course, the rats—if that's what they were—that she'd smelled earlier must be here. She was closer to the center of their lair.

She turned over on her stomach, came to a crawling position, then sat back on her haunches. She waved her arms over her head—and hit something that came clattering down, sounding very much like a board.

After switching on her light, she saw that's exactly what it was. But what was it doing here, down in this underground wilderness of nowheres? She picked it up . . . and found that it had wire wrapped around it, wire that went off into the rubble where there were more boards—boards that were worn from scraping. . . .

She lifted the wire, following it up the crack where she'd just been.

"Oh, God. Oh, no!"

It was a trap, it had been a trap from the beginning! He had *built* this, this was just another of his fucking mantraps!

She shook her head in disbelief, clutching the wire, yanking at it. And she heard that laughter again, echoing down from the galleries above.

Understanding hit her with the sheer, driving force of high-pressure water, hit her full in the face, blanking her vision, blanking her mind.

All this time, all this running and escaping—it had been planned. He had planned for her to get out of the basement, had planned for her to run just exactly as she had. Oh, he'd made it hard, he'd made it nearly impossible, but he had most certainly *made* it.

She realized the truth: the ones who went into the cave were the ones who gave him the most fun, that was all. And as for the others—well, he did them in the chamber, just exactly as he'd been preparing to do her. But there was this other level, this additional possibility waiting down here in the dank, intricate tunnels of his mind.

She touched the sliced lines on her stomach, remembered the same lines on the girl in the Polaroid.

Fumbling, she went for the light again, got it from where she'd dropped it, and turned it out. She shouldn't leave it on like that; she mustn't allow it to mark her position or go out.

He'd given her the light for the specific purpose of making it possible for her to play the game. Sure he had. The same thing went for the food and the robe and the slippers that had replaced her flip-flops—it was all so she could live a longer time, provide him with more fun.

She cursed herself, cursed bitterly. Because she'd come into the cave, she still had hours to suffer being hunted. And then there would be hours more with him. Maybe it would be days, it could easily be days. Not for one instant did she believe his claim that it would take only an hour. It would take a lot longer, as long as he could make it take.

She ought to surrender. So why didn't she? Back in the basement she'd been practically drunk with compliance. What had happened to change that?

Not only had she come to believe that there was definite, willful choice here, she had realized that the fact that he had this cave to hide his work and his bodies meant that his victim count must be very high.

She could well be battling the most terrible compulsive murderer who had ever been discovered. Her own individual death meant little—she recognized that. Life would close around the place she had occupied, no more stirred than a pond by the splash of a pebble. But she had to try anything to get this man, to bring him down on behalf of the concealed dead and so that others now living would not ever, ever suffer this.

And she wanted life. Sweet were the days.

She took her flashlight from the dark at her feet. Now, you will be methodical, you will be thoughtful. She turned it on and searched the space around her.

What he had done in here was to lay a subtle path. The whole thing—getting her to jump that wall, getting her to run, to hide in that first corridor—all of it was the product of thought and design. So what she had to do was get off that path.

He played like a cat played, slapping and pouncing, then allowing his prey to escape so that he could pounce

again. Maybe he'd watched the family's barn cats torturing mice when he was a boy, and maybe that's where
his fantasies had begun.

Because of the cave, Kevin McCallum's victims were
never found. So they weren't listed as homicides. Instead they would fall under the far less critical category
of missing persons. In most states their cases would be
abandoned to the files after a few months.

There were lots of missing persons—thousands upon
thousands—something like two new cases a minute in
the United States. Only the minors and the well-con-
nected people were sought with real energy. A person
living alone with no relatives to press for answers would
simply evaporate if a body wasn't found. Kevin McCallum could be a one-man murder epidemic, and because
he didn't leave bodies, he'd go on until he simply became too feeble.

"Okay," she muttered, "let's see how clever we are,
now that we understand the rules a little better."

Sure enough, there was another gallery beyond this
one, visible as a darkening between two high walls. She
went over to it, saw that it offered the promise of spa-
ciousness. Most of her predecessors must have run off
down here, hell-bent and blinded by terror.

For some moments she searched the walls. There
were shadows and cracks everywhere, and one in particular that looked as though it might be a hole. Her light
made it gleam: it was blanketed by spiderwebs. This
meant that insects must fly through it . . . so it had to
communicate with something, maybe even the outside.
She tossed a stone up, missed, tossed another, which

went in. It hit what sounded like dry rock, rolled a moment, then stopped.

She climbed the four feet necessary and put her head into the hole. The stench inside was overpoweringly awful . . . and the river's sound was louder, too—a lot louder.

She climbed in, discovering for the first time that a spiderweb was extremely sticky. There must be a big one in here, perhaps many big ones. Would they sting her?

For a few feet she sidled along. Then the ceiling lowered down and she had to crawl on her belly, dragging herself on her elbows. She noticed, as she moved, that she was wallowing in something thick and wet, something that stank dreadfully. Guano. She turned on her light, saw reflections in tiny eyes, and knew then that she had entered the lair of the rats.

My Diary "The Dumbest of the Dumb"

I want you to win. That is the fact. I know for sure that the State Police are looking for you. Now that I look back, I have known from the beginning that I couldn't take somebody from the Old Secret without causing trouble.

Only, there ain't gonna be a you to find. Dogs don't scent well in caves, so that isn't going to work. They will buy into that you went camping and got lost. So you will become another m.p. That isn't a big deal. The cave is full of them.

Am I tired, is that it? Tired and ready to call it a day? I am something great, as people like me go. I am a classic, one of a kind, the top of the heap. I have done a thing in here that is so incredible, it is like the ultimate fun house ride of all time, only the fun is real serious. What they have to go through is very serious.

She has no idea. She will be amazed to see what it will be, they all are. This is because I am a genius at what I do, and I would have been—oh, shit, what I would have been! Too bad that society does not approve. Why not feed me the condemned men. I could do men just as easy. I found out a couple times that they were men, the streeters I picked up. Did them anyway, working from my Gray's Anatomy. *You got to know where to cut, you don't want to just slash at them.*

I could be a surgeon, that's another thing about me that is wasted.

CHAPTER SIXTEEN

The Nests

In her frail light, their eyes were flickers of gold and red. She could just make out their bodies—they were big rats with gleaming coats and firm, strong tails. They watched her—they all seemed to be watching her—without rancor or lust or fear. They watched her with the assurance of things that were . . . tame.

What had he done here? She seemed to glimpse the suggestion of an even larger, even stranger design. If he had tamed all these rats, then what did that mean?

Her hands went to cover breasts and belly. She could see their interest—the sniffing, the rising on the haunches.

If she was going to use this tube, she would have to push herself up through their nests, a thought almost horrific enough to cause her to simply black out. Touching their black fur, being bitten by their filthy brown teeth—she was not able to do this, she was going to have to get out. Which was, of course, what they all did.

Maybe it wasn't nature that had brought them to nest here. They were tame, so maybe he had chosen this particular place, in some way inducing them to come. A man raised on a farm would know something about the habits of rats.

It would be a very clever way to conceal an exit, and Kevin was a very clever man.

She clamped her jaw shut, lowered her head, and butted her way up into the nest-choked tube. She could feel the giving softness of cloth and batting. Maybe he'd even brought it here for them.

She soon found that little ratlets were wiggling along her sides as she forced herself forward. The breaking of their nests made the rat mothers furious, and she began to hear their shrieking squeaks and feel them nipping at her scalp.

The farther she went, the narrower the passage became. She reached ahead and heaved, dragging herself another foot. Now the ceiling pressed against her head, forcing her to turn her face to one side and wriggle like an eel. At least the stinking guano was behind her, but here she was literally pushing through a mass of infant-filled nests, and the little things were scrabbling around her head and face in swarms.

Every time she pushed forward, she got more of them under her cheek, under her midriff. She fought not to hurt them as the mothers, following their young, squirmed down around her. Her abdomen stung from being scraped along the limestone floor. Even her temple hurt again, the scab having been torn off by the pressure of the ceiling. If she hit her thumb, she thought she might faint.

This thing had resolved itself at last to a simple issue: Did she have the strength to get to the end of this tunnel? If she did, she had a feeling she'd be at the surface.

Deep within, she knew that he wanted her to have the strength. He wanted to be back under his mother's hand, poor creature, because he was in hell and probably had been since the day she died.

That was the meaning of 1958—it had been his last year on the surface of the earth. He'd no doubt brought his first victim here shortly thereafter . . . an animal, then—perhaps a barn cat or a dog or some wild thing that he'd captured. Probably a rat, actually. What he'd done to that rat at the cabin had in all likelihood been his first call to her for help. Quite possibly he had announced himself to her by showing her the first thing he had ever done, which was to burn a rat to death.

This was so tight in here, Jesus, and that squirming! The poor creatures, this was the ruin of their world. The rapidly narrowing space had stopped her temporarily, and now she considered exactly how to keep going.

To reduce the sense of confinement, she kept her eyes shut. Another shove from her legs propelled her upper body forward about a foot, but into an even narrower space.

It was like being in some kind of a pipe, and she could no longer move ahead without shifting her posture. She stifled a mewling scream of frustration and drew back.

What she had to do was to get her hands over her head and turn her face to one side. Deep breaths caused her ribs to press the walls, her breasts to compress against the ceiling.

Carefully she moved baby rats off her face, extracted them from her hair, then forced her hands up into the nests. She couldn't feel anything except cloth bits and cool walls. It was an uncertain matter, but it felt as though the space might narrow even farther.

With her hands above her head, her side was stretched and the wound screamed. She refused to think about the dirt that was getting into her various cuts and scrapes. May she live long enough to get an infection.

The only way to move ahead was by lifting first one hip and then the other, feeling in the mess of nesting material for what little purchase she could find. In this way she went forward another inch, then another. Then she got a good push and progressed perhaps a foot. But now the tube compressed against her hips and she couldn't slide at all. To make any progress she had to lift them in sequence, like a dancer slowly gyrating.

This went on for such a long time that she became afraid she wasn't going anywhere. The sense of weight above her took her to the edge of panic. Jerking, clutching at the walls, she literally drummed her feet.

Panic finally made her try to sit up, to somehow break through the walls that enclosed her, and she kicked, she opened her mouth, started to scream—

No! Now, you take a deep breath, you let your muscles relax, starting with the jaw. All right. "Take it easy, Helen," she whispered. "Easy, now." She had to stop the deep breaths. They made her actually taste the rat-thick air.

She found that her hips were like a cork. So maybe this was over. Maybe she'd have to go back. She was preparing to slide out when she heard the wailing sound again. It was very definitely louder, and it sounded less human this time, more like the wind crossing some distant opening. It faded before she could be sure.

When she began backing up, the sense of relief was so acute that it actually made her heart beat harder. This was the most unpleasant place she had ever known, and getting out of it was going to feel awfully damn good. If she was lucky, Kevin had not realized that she had come in here and had lost track of her, at least for a little while. Maybe she could get back to the basement, maybe somehow open the trapdoor.

It wasn't much, but it was the only chance she had, and she felt that she must focus on it. But when she tried to create the propulsive thrust backward she needed to dislodge herself, she realized that she had a problem. With no leverage at all, how was she going to move?

Trying to stay calm, she felt the ceiling with her fingers, felt serrations in the stone. She jerked again, then again and again. For a moment after, she remained very still. Blood pulsing in her temples, breath coming short, she felt around her.

"Oh, no." She pushed, she pulled, she completely lost control. This was like being in a living coffin. She strove with her legs, her buttocks, trying to find some way to push backward without the use of arms that were extended above her head.

And she went cracking and crunching upward, upward like a corpse rising from the ground, upward into thick, sour-reeking roots and then matted grass, and then into a mass of nettles, of what proved to be a vast blue ocean of forget-me-nots!

She crawled, she waded, she came up and up into the sun and the loudness of bees and her own wild cries and wilder laughter. She was free, she had come free, she was out in the middle of the world, and the sky was high and blue, and there were swallows winging and white clouds flying and everywhere the easy hum of bees.

Something from the depths rushed across her foot, and she hopped out onto the surface. Suddenly vigilant, she raced her glance from place to place, an animal spotting for danger. But this was not Kevin's meadow; the flowers were different, and his house was nowhere to be seen.

She went toward the woods, her ragged, filthy robe fluttering around her, her penlight still clutched in her hand. The treeline was a dark, contemplative ridge not far away. As best she could, she hurried. The first thing she wanted was concealment. Then she would think about finding roads, finding help, finding the men with the dogs.

She'd made it. She was free. How wonderful, how incredibly uncomplicated it had been in the end. No wonder he'd nested the rats there; it wasn't just an exit, it was an easy one.

She thought about mantraps. She began to look down into the tangle of flowers, watching for the gleam of steel or the telltale tangle of nylon line.

She walked for what seemed a long time, then a very long time. This meadow was much wider than it appeared. But that was typical of meadows, wasn't it—especially to the unpracticed eyes of urban dwellers.

As she proceeded, her buttocks and thighs began to hurt more and more. Well, that was to be expected. She was all beaten up. To recover fully, she probably needed a couple of weeks in the hospital. At the very least she'd be admitted in guarded condition, and if infections developed, it could easily be changed to serious.

She stopped, confused. What was happening with that treeline didn't make sense. It wasn't that it was getting closer only slowly. It wasn't getting closer at all.

What's more, the meadow had become totally silent. No bees anymore. And the flowers were . . . vague . . . maybe forget-me-nots and maybe something else. Did they have seven blue petals or another number? And the sky, the clouds—they weren't moving, and she was lying down and looking up at them, wasn't she? She wasn't walking at all, she was still on her back!

The truth closed over her like dirt being poured into a grave. She was delivered back into reality then, into the dark and choking reality of her trap.

She felt her buttocks moving back and forth, back and forth, the muscles convulsing uselessly as her body, piloting itself, kept trying and trying and trying, where no effort mattered, to do something that could not be done.

When she fully understood that it had been nothing but a cruel hallucination, she broke down into blubbering, racking tears. She cried a long time . . . long enough, in fact, to cry herself out of tears. Then she heaved and sobbed, suffocating in her own breath. There wasn't nearly enough air in here to sustain the kind of effort that her panic had driven her to make.

Off in the distance the wailing rose and fell, rose and fell. Somewhere there was wind whistling past an opening, she thought, somewhere there were real meadows and real skies.

Or no—listen. Listen! That was a word, wasn't it? A long, despairing cry. . . .

Oh, God, what if she wasn't the only one in here alive?

It was then that she became aware of something touching her feet. She fluttered them and the sensation went away. But no sooner did she stop than it returned. "Kevin, if you're there, I give up. Please, I give up! Please get me out, get me out, oh, for the love of God, *get me out,*" and then her voice collapsed into miserable prelingual gabbling.

When the tickling began to sting, she realized it wasn't Kevin trying to grab her, but the rats. Rat mothers who had been shoved down along her sides were trying to tunnel through her back to their babies. Hadn't he given her shoes of some kind? Yeah, slippers. Well, they were long gone.

A furiously painful gnawing in the arch of her right foot caused ferocious jerking, almost a seizure. Like a liner grinding off a sandbar, with a dry noise and flaying scrapes on her poor thighs, she went forward.

"Oh, shit, oh, shit!" Was it another hallucination? Frantic fingers felt about for the floor, the ceiling, but felt only air. Was she at the end of the tube, could it be?

Oh, God. Oh, God, please let it be so. Let it be so, do not panic, stay calm, work the hips, lift a hip, lift the other, go up, up, yes, oh *yes!* Oh God, thank you, heavenly creature, thank you, O voiceless and silent God, who has somehow taken me through the very eye of the needle.

Amid an enormous rubble of nesting material and squirming infant rats, she came out, a stuck cork, a stubborn baby—and was born into a new blackness. When she realized that she was still in the depths of the cave, she slammed her fists against the hard earth floor. Then she calmed down. She drew herself to a hunched position, struggling against the pins and needles that began swarming up and down legs that had been deprived of circulation for a very long time.

Okay, it was no big deal. So she'd been wrong, this wasn't an exit. What did she know about caves? The thing was, do not let the part that wants to quit get the better of you. There was almost an inner tide of hope that waxed and waned. She needed it to get strong again, right now. "No exit," she whispered. The thing to do was to stay physical—first sit and listen for any useful sound.

The silence was interrupted only by the scrabbling of the rats.

All right, breathe deep, collect yourself. She needed to determine if there was any trace of him here, any trace at all. She didn't want to see a footprint, not anything.

She wanted to be so far away from him that she could

get no farther. Above all, she did not want him to come looming up out of the dark.

Where in hell was her light? Not in a pocket; there hadn't been room in that incredible squeeze. She'd had it in her hand, her left hand. Oh, God, no—not to get out of that hellish place only to find yourself rendered completely helpless by the loss of a two-dollar flashlight. With trembling fingers she scrabbled along the floor, searching.

It wasn't hard to find; it turned out to be under her leg. But when she tried to push the switch, she discovered that this was something else, this was not a flashlight. It felt like plastic, thick but oddly shaped. It could work as a nasty little club, actually. She stuck it in a pocket. Whatever it was, it was the first weapon she'd possessed since the poker.

It wouldn't matter much unless she had light. She crawled along, seeking the precious little tube along the soft, loamy surface, trying not to completely lose her orientation. She could easily end up dying here with the flashlight an inch from her hand.

She felt around, frantic now. Bitterly she groaned— and at the same moment her still-searching hand fell on the unmistakable tube. She snatched it off the floor and huddled with it, cradling it, touching the switch, sliding it—and was rewarded with a very slight but very real casting back of shadows.

"Jesus, thank you." It sounded just exactly like a psycho on a ward, just exactly that crazy. "But you are not crazy. You are not, absolutely not. You have your mind and your will, and it is strong."

She was surrounded by nesting material, which proved to be made of bits of cotton, torn wool, rayon, polyester, some of it printed and some colored . . . and all of it clearly from the clothing of women. There was even gnawed lace.

She took the implement out of her pocket. It was immediately clear that it was a section of bone. Whether human or not, she couldn't know, she was no expert. But it certainly looked as though it had once fitted into the socket of somebody's shoulder.

The light dimmed, and she cut it off. No sense in using it unless absolutely necessary, especially since she didn't know where Kevin was and must not assume that she was safe.

Jesus, Jesus . . . she had to stay alive, she had to do it for all these other poor women and for the ones he would get if he remained free. Never before had she wanted, consciously and carefully, to kill anybody, but she wanted to kill Kevin McCallum.

"No," she muttered. As bizarre as it seemed, she knew that the man was seeking to be controlled; otherwise she wouldn't be here. So he was looking for help. So the potential to get well was there.

But why do that? Even if he was curable, why bother? His only future would be behind bars. Unfortunately there was a powerful reason to capture and cure him. That was because compulsive murder was a disease, and it was spreading, and he offered an opportunity to help science understand it. She could conceive of a test that would predict the presence of this potential in the young, so that they could be helped before anybody suffered.

As to the larger social problems that had given rise to the disease in the first place, they would be more intractable to cure. The voice of the Commandments was old and faint now. To reinvest those words with their magic, we needed to find ourselves again.

Speaking of finding, what she needed to do was to find some part of this place that he didn't know about. But how could she expect to do that? He knew every shadow, every turn, for this was the interior of the man, his unconscious mind carved into the earth.

She sat down, being careful to shield her backside from the cold floor with her robe. No matter how useless or impossible it seemed, she had to try once more to find the key to Kevin's soul. She would still hold out the therapeutic promise to him, but no longer as an end in itself. No matter his specimen value, she could not care what happened to Kevin McCallum, not even professionally. The important thing was to end the carnage.

She listened, listened and thought. Here the sound of water was quite distinct, so much so that she thought there could be an open crevasse, even an underground canyon, with the river at the bottom. It was loud enough, certainly, to be right in the room with her.

Even if it led to the lake, though, it would be a dangerous escape route, given the dark and the rocks and the cold and the probability that it went long distances through water-filled chambers.

What the river most likely offered was a relatively easy death. If there was absolutely no other choice, that would be a way to go. However, she just could not drive from her mind the concept of the therapeutic promise or the notion that there was some way to reach him. Nothing so far had even started to work. Indeed, she had the impression that a big reason she was here was so that he could prove that he was stronger than a doctor. She spoke to herself, trying to put it all in perspective. "You can figure this man out. Without him around to throw you off balance, you can really think for the first time." But not ten seconds passed before she began to feel her throbbing side, her sore, skinned haunches, her head, her thumb. "Let the pain go. Just let it go so you can think." She had gotten herself into her present dire situation by a combination of his intelligence and her own—not stupidity, exactly. Better to call it failure of insight. But he made it hard to concentrate. Even if he didn't have the highest body count in history, he was going to be off the scale in terms of cruelty and imagination.

During her clinical years she'd dealt with many different problems—depression, sexual dysfunction, various neuroses. However, the patients almost all had one consistent presenting characteristic, and that was that they were deeply passive.

Kevin McCallum was the exact opposite, full of the energy and aggressive intelligence of the true predator. This was what had really thrown her off, she decided, this and the dreadful fear that had claimed so much of her attention. Nobody is good when terrified, nobody can think while in agony. The scared survive on luck, and he had made sure that she hadn't gotten any.

So, what to do? Should she wander farther or try to find the river or what? No, she had come here to this spot, and this was where she would stay.

She groaned, remembering her pitiful attempts to cope with him. Or maybe she wasn't giving herself enough credit; maybe she'd been closer than she thought. "Okay, Kevin," she said, "let's see what we can manage."

"What?" His light flashed in her face from a distance of two feet.

Instantly, without forethought, she lashed out with a foot and smashed it. She heard the pieces go clattering off against the walls.

"Shit," he said softly. "You've still got some fight, you have."

She slid to her feet, moving as if she were face-to-face with a cobra. Her heart was thundering. He'd been in here *waiting* for her, waiting while she struggled slowly through that little tube. Probably stood right beside the opening, listening to her suffer. She took a step back, fighting the feeling that he was going to grab her.

"I have a dozen flashlights."

Then why didn't he use one? "But not here."

He was silent.

She had to keep trying—not because she thought it would help, but because there wasn't anything else she could do. "You can be helped, Kevin."

"Sure, Doctor."

"I was just sitting here trying to figure out where I went wrong back at the house."

"I believe that."

He was to her right, sounding about three feet away. Moving with what she hoped was sufficient care, she drew her bit of bone out of her pocket.

"I know why you took the risk of abducting me from that cabin. Somewhere in there is a desperate man."

"Then why don't I feel it?"

He was closer, much closer! He must be stalking the sound of her voice.

"You do," she said, and took a long step to the right.

There was a sound, little more than the movement of air, and then nothing. When he spoke again he had returned to his former position. But he'd tried to grab her, she knew it, and barely missed.

"What I feel is very nice inside while I'm doing it."

She stepped back one step, then another. Now the wall was right behind her. She lifted the piece of bone. "You mean, while you're killing, or the whole time?"

An instant later he was in front of her; she could feel his presence, smell his fetid sweat. With all the might she possessed, she brought her piece of bone down. But her arm went in an empty arc, and she knew instantly that she'd missed. He was aware of the movement, though, for she heard an intake of breath. "You found a rock," he said in a mild, offhand tone of voice. "I thought I'd gotten rid of all the rocks."

She felt his fingers brush against her. He was casting about, trying to grab her . . . or perhaps stave her off. Then it got quiet. She listened, but there wasn't even the sound of breath.

She sidled along the wall, trying to put some space between them. She'd hardly glimpsed the inside of this chamber and had not the faintest idea of where she might step next. For all she knew, she could topple into that damned underground river at any step.

Then she became aware of a new sound and for an instant thought it might be hopeful. But he wasn't crying, not at all, not him. He was counting—but why?

My Diary "If You Read This"

You went up through the rats, and that, lady, showed for the first time that you have a lot of pure dee guts. Nobody has ever done that. Nobody!

But what is so funny is that I am writing this as you struggle and groan down in there, and I am right here. I can see the nests squooging (is that a word) out as you come up the tube.

I am feeling real funny, Dr. Myrer. I think I want to tell you about me. I was a real cute little kid, and I stayed like that until I was twenty. I got beat up a lot, but I also got sexed a lot. A surprising number of people wanted it with me. The thing that is so hard to write in these pages is that my mother, she did.

That is not a lie. But also, I have to tell you that I think I could control what I want to do which is to really FUCK UP women who are like her. At first, they had to talk like her, even, so it would feel like her. Now they just have to have light hair.

I am getting worse. In 1960 I did two. In 1980, I did eighteen. Last year, I did thirty-

four. How many in all I do not know. Dr. Myerer, this is a cave of bones. Truth. Cave of bones and dead people. Probably hundreds.

I look back, I see lots and lots of faces, all begging and crying and screaming. I got to think, all those women died because of Momma? What makes me so mad at her? I mean, she did a little nothing perverse thing that at the time I hardly noticed.

But I guess I am finished, and that is why I took you. There are State Police out in force right now. I think they're gonna miss me, though. I mean, they came across the meadow behind a dozen dogs and they did not pick up enough scent to find you!

I think I belong to God somehow, I am a force of nature, I am a special angel. That is why I can't get caught.

Help me you bitch or you shall be the slowest, hardest, worstest of all!

CHAPTER SEVENTEEN

The Land of the Dead

She had to hit him; that was the only chance she had. But if she connected, she was going to go on hitting and hitting until he was dead, like a roach. "I'm your doctor, remember," she said . . . and realized that she was reminding both of them.

An instant later fingers touched her face. "Okay, Cooie."

She took a long step to the left, then another.

"That's stupid."

She felt around her, trying to find the wall. Not only was there no wall, the sound of moving water was louder here. If only she'd had just one good look around this place, just one, it would be so much easier.

He knew every stone, of course, every turning. She

listened, she cupped her free hand to her ear and turned her head about. He made no sound.

She was aware of an actual, physical sensation of vulnerability. She could not define it—it wasn't a shivering, a feeling of coolness, a tightening of the skin—but she could certainly sense it. You'd feel like this if a snake was sliding up between your breasts.

"Cooie?"

She stifled the impulse to respond. She wouldn't speak again until she was ready. This was one game of his where she'd finally understood the rules. They were playing chess, and only he knew the layout of the board.

There was a new rule, though, that was in her favor, and it was amazingly important: he had no light.

He'd been about six feet away, just now, well to her right. She listened, heard nothing but the deep, busy surge of the water.

God, but it stank in here. It stank of the rats, she decided—their bodies, their offal, their food, whatever it was. But what was that other odor?

"Cooie, listen to me."

She tensed.

"There's a big river over near you. If you fall in, you'll drown."

He'd moved as he talked, then there had been an immediate swish of air. But where had he gone?

"You're right near it, Cooie."

She could hear him breathing, which meant that he was getting closer. But how?

Then she knew. She wasn't moving enough, which was enabling him to get steadily closer just by patrolling methodically. He could take risks, because he knew the ground. She, on the other hand, had to pick her way. She took a step back—and slipped easily two feet down. This must be the slope to the river. At least he hadn't been lying about that.

Instantly there was a scraping sound right beside her, and his hand came down on her forearm.

She screamed, she couldn't help it, emitted the high-pitched shriek of a scared girl. His grip tightened, but not before she had started rolling away. Her feet dug wildly, pushing to the lip of the drop-off. She came staggering up and ran straight ahead, her arms out in front of her.

"I can help you," she gasped. "I know you want it." Appeal to his need, use it against him.

There was no sound. He was moving, she knew, he must be. She wiped the air around her, trying not to panic at the thought of him touching her again.

"Let me tell you what I know about you." This was her move in the game. It was also a hell of a risk—but it was time for risks. "I know you can't resist and you don't know why. But I can help you stop."

Whoom, whoom—the sound of large steps being taken, charging right at her. She moved again, backing up, purposely gasping, then taking three quick steps to the right.

"All her life, you blamed her for something. What was it, Kevin?"

Silence and, in the silence, breathing.

"You blamed her and hated her. Why? She loathed

you, didn't she? Half a man—your failure to mature. Loathed you and loved you at the same time."

Air rushed out of his nostrils so hard that she heard it. He'd flared with rage. She went forward, went straight back. An instant later there was a rush of sound behind her, followed by a soft, angry grunt. He'd been right on her, right *on* her!

"And she wasn't alone. Nobody much liked you. Women feared you, both men and women were disgusted by you. Except for some. But the people who wanted *you* . . . well, they were all sick themselves, weren't they?" She could feel compassion for the little boy. She tried to use it—feel for the poor hurt little boy, Helen, put it in your voice. "You tried so hard, you did everything they wanted, you were perfect, but they just plain loathed you." She took three long steps straight ahead.

"Cesarean."

What did he mean, cesarean? Then she touched her belly. She recalled the Polaroid. Time to make a guess, take another risk. She was the expert, she was supposed to know. "Your head was too big, your body too heavy, Kevin."

Whoosh, whoosh.

What the hell was that sound? What was he doing?

"She had to have you by cesarean." She crouched down—and felt a burst of wind tickle her hair with another *whoosh*.

He had something, something that he was swinging.

"But it went wrong and—"

"And?"

"She blamed you, she blamed her baby."

"Shut up!"

"No! *Hell* no. Because I can help you."

"You're wrong, you babbling bitch! Lemme tell you, babes, you got more on your hands than you can possibly understand."

"I do understand and you know it, and that's why you hate me even more than the others. I'm Momma, but I'm also Doctor—what was her name?"

"Dr. Fuckhead."

She ran until she knocked against something—a thing that swayed. And what was this, now, a new sound? Yes, the swaying object was creaking. She backed away from it. "Nobody should have to suffer like you've suffered. Kevin, just answer me this. Just this: Has anybody at all ever touched you out of love?"

"I had loving parents and a normal childhood. My problem is, I also had this cave."

"No, it's not the cave, and you don't think it's the cave. The cave didn't cause your problem, the cave only serves it."

"It is the most incredible pleasure in the world!"

"It's hell!"

When he did not respond, she decided to venture on. "Okay, I'll tell you the truth." He was coming closer. But she didn't move, not now. "The truth is that nobody, not ever, has kissed you for the sake of you. Not your parents, not any woman. Oh, they've tried to fuck their way out of this death trip of yours. For sure. But that's not love, that just makes you feel madder, that just makes you go slower. Am I right?"

Not a word.

"I'm damn right. Kevin, listen. You can find—"

He was in front of her, he was snarling, his hands were coming around her neck.

She dropped down, rolled away, but he was on her again, his full weight slamming down on her, making her grunt. She pulled out, she crawled away, went scrambling to her feet. "You deserve love, Kevin."

More silence.

"You weren't an evil child, and nothing you did was all that wrong."

"I just fucking *do* this! You've got your 'Momma caused it' theory, but it's bullshit! Nobody caused it. The fucking devil." He made a long, deep sound, and she knew that it was a sound of despair.

Just as she moved, wind whistled past her face.

He'd lunged at her and now went crashing to the floor of the cave.

Then there was silence, but she knew that he was on his feet again. "You have your gun and your knife, Kevin, and I'm right here." She closed her eyes. "But if you do it, you have to do it knowing that every woman is not your mother. I am not your mother."

"You hate me!"

"The cesarean caused her a lot of trouble, didn't it?"

"She bled for fucking *years.*"

"Listen to me now, Kevin, and stop trying to sneak up on me. I've got ears, I can hear you over there perfectly well." She wished to God that it were true. "Listen to me, her bleeding had nothing to do with you. The cesarean was not your fault."

"I was the baby, you idiot!"

"You weren't the doctor, too, were you?"

"Dr. Halliwell was the best of the best." When he said it, she could literally hear his mother's voice. And she also heard another sound, a metallic click.

She froze, then took three fast steps back. That might have been the click of his gun—unlocking the safety, perhaps. It was only a guess, of course, but she was extremely vulnerable to a gun—all he had to do was fire at her voice. As long as he could forgo his torture session, she was dead.

"Kevin?" She dropped to the floor.

As she did, there was a more distinct sound, and she realized he sure did have the gun, because he had just pulled back the hammer.

Here was a chance to show him some real power. "Put the gun down. You think I can't see you? Your eyes are bad, Kevin, you don't eat properly."

There was a little chuckle. "You're the smartest one."

"And you really did put the gun down. Good. Just don't move and we can keep talking."

"Fuck you, dear."

"I've told you your whole life story so far, haven't I? I knew what really happened, didn't I, Kevin?"

This time the silence was eloquent—but what did it conceal? The gun was there as a last resort. What he wanted to do was come up right in her face and scare the hell out of her as he captured her.

"Nothing happened! I just ended up like this! That's what's wrong, and there's no answer. There is no cure! I just—you can't imagine—you cannot *possibly* imagine how delicious this is, because you come from the other side, where pleasure is pleasure and pain is pain. But I've crossed over—down here in the dark where nobody can see—I went across the border, lady. I live in an undiscovered country, babes."

What she had to do was survive at all costs, to stop him. Anything she could say that would serve that end was the right thing to say. She moved again—and her left foot slid along an abrupt slope. She drew back. Not that way, Dr. Myrer. "Kevin, let me tell you some more about yourself. Something that nobody in the world knows except you. Know what that would be?"

"No."

She now knew the reason for the mark on her belly and on the belly of the girl in the Polaroid . . . a mark that would almost certainly disfigure all of his victims. She touched her belly. "You're not a surgeon, Kevin."

There came, after a length of silence that was considerable, a sound like a crash of tumbling masonry. She knew that mad, inarticulate wail of agony, knew it from the psychotic wards.

Abruptly the sound was swallowed. Then silence.

"Kevin?"

"You fucking bitch!"

The shot was blinding—crazily, insanely, impossibly bright. It was loud beyond the final meaning of sound. She threw herself to the ground and rolled, blind to where she was going, blind to the crevasse.

She had seen him in the flash, though, seen that he was naked except for briefs. So this had sexual content for him—this truth telling? Here was a new wrinkle. He was more masochistic than she'd thought. But trying to make a dominating move on him would be foolhardy. Fantasies of being tortured by his victims would be a major driving force behind his rage.

Pain, however, was not all there was to the male fantasy of being dominated. The dominated man was relieved of his responsibility as an initiator and a controller. He came to rest as he had in his mother's care.

"You can't kill the truth, Kevin." She took three fast steps straight toward him and anticipated his thoughts neatly, because there were two shots, both wide. He'd reasoned that she'd move to one side or the other, because that's what she'd been doing so far. In the flash of the shots he'd doubtless seen her but had not been fast enough to change his strategy.

Now she dropped to the floor. But he wasn't stupid; he didn't risk another bullet. She crawled on all fours until she was well away. "That other shrink wasn't smart enough for you, Kevin. But I'm smart enough for you."

"Shut your filthy mouth!"

"I'll take care of you. I'll never abandon you. Let me, Kevin. Give me the gun and let me take care of you."

"Yeah, with a fucking bitch bullet."

"What would happen would be that we'd go to the police together and I'd put you in a facility and become your analyst. You'd get well, Kevin, under me. I'd take care of everything."

"I'd go to jail and get locked up for a thousand years."

"I'd tell them what to do with you from now on, until the end of your life."

"The death penalty."

"Doesn't apply to the criminally insane. You would get treated."

"And then I'm okay, I'm let go, I get out and open a hardware store in town. Come on."

"You never get out. No. But you do get well."

"Fuck that!"

"You spend your life under my care, and it would be good care, Kevin. You know what I'd teach you?"

She could sense the gun moving, aiming. She turned, took four short steps, turned again, took three more. She could still feel the gun.

"What?" came the sullen voice.

Quietly she exulted. She'd made it, she'd gotten through. "I'd teach you how to feel sorry for your victims—and for yourself."

"And to blame my mother and dad?"

"That's what the other one did, isn't it? Why were you taken to her—do a cesarean on the dog or something?"

"The fucking cat."

"She went down the wrong road. But I will not go down the wrong road, Kevin."

This silence spoke clearly: Helen was still riding the horse, she was still giving the right answers.

"I will teach you how to feel sex, Kevin. How to feel it the right way."

"You don't know nothing!"

"I think I know a lot. You'd like to feel a little pain yourself, wouldn't you? You've fantasized about it. Is it torture with a clothespin? It's been done to you, you know how much it hurts. What if I had you tied up? Would that be cool?"

There was an increase of breathing. Had he begun to masturbate? She was tempted to go closer. Either he would collapse in her arms or tear her to pieces, and she had no idea which it would be.

A hoarse voice, at last somewhat more calm: "You'd do it . . . in the treatment?"

The classic patient's fantasy. She played to it shamelessly. "Surrogation would be part of it."

"What's that?"

"A professional to help you learn normal sexuality."

"Doctor?"

"Yes, Kevin?"

"I've messed up real bad."

"Yeah."

"Doctor—" He stopped.

She forced back the revulsion that she felt for this sobbing, evil man. "Kevin, I'm going to take over, now. Can you let me do that?"

"Yeah."

She decided against moving toward him. She'd sooner put a black widow spider on her tongue than get within grabbing distance of this monster. "Okay," she said briskly. "You're naked."

"Yeah."

"Do you have a hard-on?"

"It went away."

She had to know his true emotional state. How close to the surface was his anger, right this second? "You have to tell me exactly when. Something we said made it go away. What?"

There were sobs now, very distinct, very small—and she could easily imagine Kevin the little boy right here in this chamber, weeping just like this.

He sniffled. "Well, when I think what I've done. Oh, Doctor, they begged me, but I couldn't stop!" He bawled, frankly and openly.

Now, that was the most genuine sound he'd made since the capture. Maybe this was the moment she'd been waiting for.

She made a decision. "I'm coming," she said so that he wouldn't be surprised. She reached him, had the impression that he was hunched up, lying on his side. Fetal. Not too surprising.

If she had any access to mercy for this terrible creature, it was through the realization that he could have feelings for his victims. She reached out, and her hand came into contact with his thigh. His hand came and clutched at hers, and she held it firmly.

It probably hadn't seemed like a very dysfunctional life to the people who had been living it: the bitter, injured mother, the father so withdrawn that he was now rarely even mentioned by his son, and the sweet-faced, big-eyed little boy with his interest in poetry and his strange, distant mind. He would have been a good child, of course, because he was trying to gain approval, to break down the wall that isolated him from their love.

But then there were these episodes with the mother. Had she come to him in the night? Was that where the sexual enactments had taken place? And the corporal punishments—inhuman in their ritualized intensity. And all of this against a background of bleeding and suffering and ceaseless blame.

"Okay, Kevin, you've got a doctor now. You've got a real doctor."

"She was a real doctor."

"You were in the state hospital, weren't you? How old were you? Twenty?"

"Seventeen."

"Tell me about it."

"I used to . . . go in the woods. I'd pretend I was hunting. Hunting them."

"Who?"

"Kids from school. They went out there for smokes."

"But not just for smokes."

He had come to a squatting position. There was a sound of shifting movement, and he was suddenly leaning against her.

"You know stuff about me I never told nobody."

She laid a hand on his forehead. "It's my job to know. You saw them having sex in the woods. You used to watch. Come up out of this cave and watch."

She felt the nod.

"But you got caught and beat up. But not right away. Later." She took a flyer, but she knew she was right, she had to be right. "The girl had seen you, not the boy. And she got you alone, and beat the shit out of you."

"She—"

"Humiliated you. You were littler than them, than all of them. Had you skipped a grade? Yes. Little Mister

Perfect, small to begin with. What did she do? Beat you with a belt?"

"She did it the old-fashioned way. She—"

"What?"

"Got me depantsed. In front of a whole bunch of girls. Half the class. They held me and she really laid it on. She laid it on!" Helen could feel the trembling, surging rage. The humiliation must have been hideous. Kids were brutal; they could be so cruel.

"And you were a laughingstock after that."

"There were pictures. Polaroids. They passed 'em around. People used to spit on me. If I even touched something, they acted like it had leprosy!"

"And nobody cared about what you knew. It turned out that spying on them hadn't given you a bit of power. Fucking wasn't a big thing for the other kids, they just needed a little privacy. You were the only one who cared, so they couldn't even be blackmailed."

"But other people don't end up like this."

"We're concentrating on you right now. Let's see what we can do for Kevin for once, and not worry about other people."

"Why not? Everybody in the world is more important than a lousy caretaker murderer pervert. I don't even deserve to live."

"You could help the whole world, do you know that? Make up a little for what you've done."

"You don't know what I've done."

"It's real bad, that I do know."

"Can't bring people back to life."

"If we could study you, test your hormones and come

to understand what makes you tick, we might make some strides toward preventing this in others. In that sense, you could help all of mankind."

She held his shoulder, his head, listened to his choking breaths. "The fucking bitches! They told all the guys!"

"And the guys kicked your ass even harder."

"I lost teeth."

"But the secret is, when you were kicked around, you felt something. You felt something inside. Especially that first time, when the girls did it. That's why they turned you over to the boys, isn't it? Because they knew you'd gotten off on it when they beat you up."

"Doctor, it was like living in the deepest part of hell, it was hell on earth. I went home with the best grades they had ever given and I put 'em on the kitchen table and Mother signed the report card and that was it, and then I went back to school and I had to—be there—and—"

"There were Polaroids of you being—what—thrashed with a belt? Naked, sexually excited?"

His silence was his agreement. That was how it had been. But it still didn't answer the question of how he had evolved. His rage had remained intact from the moment of humiliation until now. That was what was inexplicable about him. She could not address the mystery of the man, though, that would be a huge mistake. "You're not alone with it, Kev," she said smoothly. "I will show you—and you will discover—every single thing that led you to this."

"Doctor?"

"Yes?"

"I need you."

It was over. She wanted to laugh, to cry. She had actually done it, he was as docile as a sheep. "Kevin, I think it's time."

"Do I have to?"

She clasped his shoulder. "What you have to do is be my patient. But we can't exactly do that down here, can we? We need to get you into a clinical setting, first thing."

"What kind of a clinical setting?"

"Look, Kevin, let's think about that later. Right now, what we want to do is get out of here and both take showers and get cleaned up and get some food in us." She didn't add that he'd take his shower in the county jail, she in a hotel.

"We'll go to my place, we'll do it there."

She stood up. "Come on." She took his hand and drew him to his feet. He put his arms around her and embraced her, and she found that hideously difficult to bear. She did not allow herself to recoil, though. Instead she held his head against her chest. "You're trembling," he said.

"Kevin, I'm very tired."

"We could stay here a while. Stay in the cool. It's nice here."

She must not reveal the absolute loathing that he inspired in her, not if she expected to keep his fragile allegiance. Thank God he would be the responsibility of the New Hampshire Department of Prisons Division of Mental Health and not of Dr. Helen Myrer.

His hand now lay along her thigh. "What's it like—the real thing? I never knew."

"Well, it's what makes the world go round."

"You know what? I don't think we should fall in love. I mean, not if you're my doctor. I'm saving it. For when I get married. That magic moment, you know." He was trying to get her to approve of him to lessen his fear of himself. A less crazy man might have raped her right here and now, but all he did was chastely lift her hand and kiss it. She stroked his head with her other hand, encouraging the submissive impulse.

"You know what I'd like to do, Doctor?"

"What, Kev?"

"I've done a lot of work in here, and I'd like to show it to you before we go."

There was an odd sort of a note in this, she thought. "What kind of work?"

"Well, this room is very beautiful. It's like a cathedral. The walls are all cobalt blue, you wouldn't believe it."

"And you've done . . . carvings?"

"You could say that." He stepped back, disappearing instantly into the dark. "Look."

He had another flashlight, extremely powerful, and the sudden flood of light shocked her. But if he'd had a light all along—then why—

She saw first a skeleton. It was hanging on the wall, chained. The chest was there, part of one arm, and below it a heap of other bones. Then she saw others in the vaults of the room—the amazing blue vaults of some incredible mineral—was it blue quartz?

This place was a true glory of nature, easily the most beautiful underground space she had ever seen, a wonder of deep, iridescent blue soaring in arches to a distant ceiling. As he moved the light, he revealed more skeletons . . . many more. Some of them were still somewhat fleshed. Others were recent corpses. Those that were still intact all showed evidence of cesareans. But all were badly damaged, because this was where the cave rats fed.

He was watching her as he moved the light.

"Kevin, I don't need to see this."

"Sure you do."

Then he shone it on the closest of the figures, this one not ten feet away. She was tied, leaning up against the wall of the cave. She was covered with contusions just like Helen's.

It was the girl in the Polaroid. Kevin walked over to her and ripped away duct tape that covered her mouth. Her dry, cracked lips opened, and the long, sorrowful wail that Helen had heard before sounded again, again with the drama of wind in the night.

Slowly, as if she were coming back from some very long dream, her eyes moved . . . and rested on Helen. They were like darkness unveiled, those eyes, and they burned Helen's soul with black fire. "He makes us watch," the girl rumbled.

"Who are you?"

"I tried to warn you, sister. . . ." And again she wailed, softly, softly, as an animal mourned.

"Kevin, you've got to let this woman go!"

" 'S jus his bullshit . . . fulla . . ."

"I am an expert surgeon," he said.

Helen saw the gleam of a blade in his hand and understood that he'd kept this woman here for days, that the latest victim was made to observe the cesarean of the last.

She screamed, she couldn't help it—whereupon the light went out.

He was gasping with excitement, his breath shuddering.

She ran toward the woman, thinking to help her, to free her—but then she felt her hair grabbed and yanked, yanked so hard that bright green stars flashed in her eyes.

She'd failed; he was a million miles away, he was on another planet, the planet of eternal damnation, he was a dreadful, monstrous, implacable evil, completely beyond knowing.

She panicked, she lost it all, she was totally without thought, without logic, a creature in a desperate moment, absent hope, direction, sense, absent everything except her poor broken body, which dragged itself from his grasp and ran blindly off into the dark.

CHAPTER EIGHTEEN

The River

He had planned it all, even had the flashlight waiting for just the right moment. She hated and loathed him so much that it was hard to bear. Her most savage instincts were aroused, and bloody images of tearing him to pieces kept appearing. It was the most difficult thing in the world to face the humanity of the evil man.

He had been miles and miles ahead, always. All along, even at the last, intimate moment, he had been playing with her. The scale of the man's madness was larger than her concept of insanity, let alone her understanding of evil.

How could a human being enact this? Could there be such a thing as a demon? She muttered, "The Nazi doctors," and pushed away the temptation to reconceive him as something supernatural. The idea of Satan *was* Satan, as far as she was concerned, because it provided such a convenient means of justifying evil.

No, there was no demon, there was only Kevin McCallum.

"Cooie?"

"Kevin, let her go!"

His light promptly pinioned her. "The longer you wait, the longer she suffers."

"I can't watch that!"

"Yeah, you can."

Watch it and then be tied and left to wait while he hunts down another victim . . . oh, God, help me.

Then he held out something in the light. It reflected brightly, and it took her some time to understand what it was. He was coming closer, displaying the scalpel like a trophy. "It's sterilized."

To keep you alive longer. Once you were done, did you get antibiotics and perhaps a fluid drip?

"Fuck you!" It was the voice of the woman on the wall.

Kevin said, "Shaddup, meat."

"Kevin," Helen said hopelessly, "you can stop right now. Both of us can be saved if you stop right now."

He laughed a little—and it was soft, it was sweet. "Her name's Lenny. She's from Boston. Right, Lenny from Boston? She's been in here since Tuesday, and she's not getting watered anymore, so it'll be over by nightfall."

"God help you, Lenny, my sister, and all my sisters!"

"Fuckin' . . . fuck . . ."

Kevin chuckled comfortably. "Come on, Helen. Do your duty and end her suffering."

Helen had a vision of the Nazi doctors at work, removing the skulls of their victims to see how long people could last with their brains exposed to the air.

She saw also that she was *not* like them, because she had something that they did not have; she had the ability to see the other man as clearly as she did herself.

To bear a killer within, there must be careful work done: you could hypnotize yourself into becoming a monster like the Nazis, or you could indulge your rage, as Kevin had. She thought, in wonder and in terror, The truth is, he isn't crazy. *He damn well is not crazy!*

His light had shown her the way that she must go, for herself and for every woman in this terrible place. She stepped to the edge.

Instantly he was there, he was grabbing at her rags. "Cooie!"

She yanked herself away from him.

"Cooie, it's real deep!"

"Good!" She let herself fall backward, then heard the wind start screaming. It was a long fall into the water—but it was not lethal, just shocking from the fierce cold.

She was rushing downward in a maelstrom of bubbles, then hitting the bottom with enough force to snap her jaw and send the wind blasting from her lungs. Pure reflex caused her to gasp as water poured in. Gagging, she thrust upward, threw herself to the surface, then heard from above the most terrible noise she had ever heard or ever would hear. His ululating cry must have come from the very dawn of man or even before that,

penlight was still in the pocket, though, and she got it out.

She expected nothing and got just a little more. For five seconds after she turned it on, she saw a magnificently colorful little gallery of ocher and blue and green stalagmites, everything flecked with gold. She also saw, moving slowly, a light gray salamander-looking thing that revolted her. Its slow head turned toward her and it went into motion, and then the light died and stayed dead.

She had also seen that the water disappeared into a low crack, another of those damned slits, and that was the way she was going to have to go if she wanted to follow it.

This cave was a bastard at prolonging agony. It was so beautiful, but so totally and completely uncompromising. She hurt all over, her heart was going like some kind of crazy toy, she was sick to death of the whole thing and actually angry that she wasn't dead yet.

There came a time when you were just plain finished, and she was there now. She had tried every single possible thing with Kevin. She could not explain him. The therapeutic promise had no meaning in a case like his.

"You don't care about him anymore. You care about Lenny. You care about all the future Lennies. Come on, woman, keep moving!"

She'd actually put her arm around him. She'd seemed just inches away from a great and extraordinary victory. How she had been congratulating herself. She'd actually exulted.

But this was so much bigger than a single therapist.

The breakdown was moral as well as mental. That was why the crime had been so rare in the past. Even the most deranged human being was not *this* bad . . . as long as the ethical wall was intact. But once societies started killing en masse, individuals gained permission to do essentially anything they could imagine. All they needed to do was get away with it.

She crawled in the muck and as she did came into the most direct touch yet with the mission that had animated her efforts from the first. It was stronger now, clearer now than it had ever been. Because she *did* possess those ethics, she believed in the value, the beauty, and the extraordinary worth of her fellow man. She saw the human world as accessible to healing and the spirit of man as sure ground for renewal.

These thoughts brought her inevitably to Lenny. Untreated, how long did Lenny have? Unless he killed her right away, she might survive even a few more days, was Helen's guess.

Time to be saved.

Lenny's eyes were gentle, like the eyes of most women. She had narrow, arched brows. Lenny was pretty. Lenny had probably been walking down a quiet street in Boston, probably late at night, probably on her way home. Her mind had been full of the thoughts of the night, maybe her pimp or her boyfriend.

How much research did he do? Maybe Lenny was a loner, and maybe Kevin knew that. He did a lot of women; he must be careful about whom he took.

Or, maybe not. Maybe it was just the cave. The cave reduced Lenny to a missing person, and she'd always remain a missing person. The cave concealed everything, the cave gave him total and complete freedom.

No matter how small her chances, Helen was going to do everything she could to be reborn out of this damn womb of death and stop this man. Maybe she'd even have a thousand-to-one-odds chance to help Lenny.

"He's deficient," she said carefully. There, that sounded authoritative. Yeah, standing in front of an audience behind a lectern, telling all about it. "He is deficient in conscience." Okay, that was enough bullshit. Don't waste time preaching to the converted. "Lenny, I'm gonna try."

She went down to the end of the gallery, plunged her arm into the water. It was so cold that it hurt your bones. She yanked it out, held one hand with the other. One thing to fall into that, another to *get* in. Lenny couldn't wait, though.

You could smell the stink of evil, you could taste the darkness of the mystery. It was a hard one to live with, though. Look at Jeffrey Dahmer's mother, who'd wanted his brain to have it studied for defects. Helen might once have seen some validity in that, but not after observing this man as she had. She now doubted that any defect would be found.

There was no warning at all that the light would come, and she had not believed that he could have followed her. But then she saw a long gleam on the water, and she knew that, once again, he was here.

She had to admit that she was amazed. He had not come through the river—and, in fact, still seemed to be some distance back in a tumble of rocks—but he had certainly come.

She had to get in that deep freeze no matter how hard it was. Well, she would. She just wondered how long a person could live in forty- or fifty-degree water and would it cause her to become disoriented.

The light got brighter. Then his song, she could hear his song. That got her into the water fast. It felt as if her bones were exploding, as if the marrow itself were freezing into sharp, cruel crystals. She slid herself along, pushing up into the crack.

It was a little easier to negotiate because the water lubricated and slicked the stones, but it also came into her nose, and as soon as she shoved again, she knew that she would no longer have access to air.

The beauty of the ceiling immediately above her face shone down on her—there were long gold stripes worked into green rock—another wonder in a dark palace of them.

She also knew why she could suddenly see—his light was shining right down into the crack. Then she felt a hand come sliding up under her midriff.

He was going to scoop her out! She must not let him, she had to get down the crack, get farther, to prevent him from extracting her. She twisted, she threw herself deeper. For a moment the hand disappeared and she thought she was going to make it. But then it grabbed an ankle. She was face up and water was sluicing down her nostrils and she was helpless to prevent it going right to her lungs. She gave a heave, then another, then another—and she was suddenly in a very different place. She raised her head. She'd come through.

This was a pool, and to her amazement, it was glowing green. It was so incredibly beautiful that she gasped—an iridescent green jewel in a pale green grotto. The light glowed from down in the depths of the water, and she thought that it might be artificial.

He could easily have electricity in here. Probably did. She swam to the center of the pool, twisting around, seeking him. But he wasn't in here. It was easy to see under this clear water, and she thrust her head in and looked down. Maybe she could put out the light, and that ought to be done right away.

But she saw clearly that the light was coming from an opening, and there were tall water grasses waving there. This green, glowing, marvelous little grotto was lit from the outside! "Oh, my God. My God!"

Okay, get yourself together. Maybe there was time to save Lenny after all. She swam across the grotto, looking for some place she could get a handhold; but the walls were as slick as polished silver. She went back to the other side, but it was the same. Methodically she returned to the center of the water and went round and round, looking for even a small bit of purchase.

No. But what the hell did it matter, she could just swim out—of course, just swim toward the damned glow! She took a deep breath and headed down.

In the clear, pure water she could see perfectly. Down she went, stone naked and swimming as well as she could, down and down. The pressure rose, quickly filling her ears and nose and pressing against her eyes.

Then her chest started to hurt, and she understood that she was not going to make this, she had to return to the surface and get more air. She turned around and swam upward, fighting at the last, her body jerking from air hunger—and then her face broke the surface.

In three strokes she was at the nearest wall, pressing against it for the minimal purchase that it afforded. She was as cold as hell and dead tired, and she feared that she was still trapped. So close.

She was also running out of strength. It was beginning to look as if she were going to drown here—and how far away was Lake Glory? Fifty feet?

Way back she'd learned something about survival floating, but what was it? Lord, yes, the old YWCA in Manhattan—she'd taken the water safety course when she was twelve. "What," she said into the hollow, deadly silence, "what the hell was it?"

Take a deep breath, push back the panic. Put your head under, bend at the waist, float. Oh, yes, this was it. This wasn't impossible, this might work. She could get her strength back, saturate herself with oxygen, and go deeper—if the cold didn't cramp her muscles or kill her first. But what was she thinking; she was half-dead already and no damn athlete. She'd never do it. She raised her head, took a breath.

Damn, there was a rock over there by the edge! Why in hell hadn't she seen it before? It wasn't a very big rock, but it was definitely there. She could hang on to it, it was big enough for that. She took a stroke toward it, then another.

He leaped at her like a frenzied shark, blasting three-quarters of the way out of the water just from the sheer energy of it.

She took his full weight right in the face, and then his arms closed around her, his fingers clutching, finding her side and clawing at it, finding her wrist and grabbing it. Agony sent red flames across her vision.

She arched her back, she kicked, she growled underwater, her bubbles rising with his, and down they went in a wild tangle of battle. She had a hand free and with it went past the churning legs and found the parts of him that were most sensitive and crushed her fist around them.

That he felt. He felt it a good deal, because she could hear his scream even underwater and it was an ordinary, human scream this time—not some mythic bawling—but the plain shriek of a man crazy with agony.

Then she was loose and swimming straight up and gobbling air, in and out, in and out, hyperventilating, not caring how dizzy she got. Then down—straight down—straight toward the glow, nothing to stop her, let him drown—please, yes!

Down and down she went, heart clanking, head roaring, down and down—deep deep deep—and now the glow like the sun in the morning, powerful, huge—

Suddenly fronds were passing her, the light was spreading around her, light in long shafts all around her and her chest heaving and the air hunger about to do her in.

She went up past the softly clinging fronds and past a swift school of pale fish, up long shafts of light into blessedly warmer water, and her head came closer and closer to the dancing ceiling of the lake, and a breath started, but it was water, and she coughed, coughed harder, sank a few inches—sank a few feet—coughed much harder—and then with a kick, with a frail last paddle, came into the daylight. Even as she was filling her lungs, exulting in her escape, she thought: He's down there, he's like a shark, he's coming.

CHAPTER NINETEEN

The Fog Soldiers

Kicking as if he were already grabbing her from below, she looked for some way out of the water. About a quarter of a mile away was an anchored sailboat with a white hull and furled sails.

"Hello," she called. Then she cried out, "Help me! Help me!"

There was no response. Turning around in the water, she saw a dock with a rowboat tied to it. Swimming, her stroke sloppy and weak, she started toward it. The process was hideously slow, and she feared that she couldn't make it. "Help," she cried again. Her voice was so faint!

She arrived at the dock so exhausted that she was almost unable to pull herself from the water. Fortunately it was a floating dock and low, and she finally dragged herself up, rolling onto its surface.

She lay there in the morning light, staring straight up. There were long wisps of fog rising into the softest blue of skies and, beyond them, fragile little clouds, perfectly white.

This was real, wasn't it? She gasped, sat up. Once, twice, she hit the wood of the dock, hit it with the flat of her hand. This had to be real!

And it was real. Indisputably real. Her hand stung, the dock shuddered slightly, minnows even rushed past beneath it.

She looked around her more carefully. It was much earlier than he'd said. Before she'd even entered the cave, he'd told her that it was after eleven. But that hadn't been true. The light in the basement must have been from the predawn. She doubted that she'd been in the cave more than two or three hours.

It was about seven, no later than that. She took stock of her situation. The first order of business was to get the police. They had to go down in that cave and get Lenny out, and that needed to be done immediately.

At the end of the dock there was a long, steep stairway up the bluff. It was unlikely that she could manage that. Unless it was the only alternative, she didn't feel she should even consider the risk. She cupped her hands around her mouth and called with all the volume she could produce: "Hellooo the boat!"

At least it wasn't moving. She thought that they'd probably come in yesterday and were still asleep.

There were reeds choking the far side of the dock and,

immediately behind them, a stony bluff. She was too tired, she feared, even to walk the twenty feet along the dock to the shore.

The sun shone down on her, though, driving out the cold and death, and soon enough she began to consider those stairs.

That was when she saw that they went only three quarters of the way up. They were broken right off. Even if you had the strength, you couldn't get there from here.

She peered up toward the cabin. A deck, dark windows, that was all, not a sign of life. "Hello," she called. Boy, was that ever lame. You couldn't hear that from ten feet away.

She did not notice that the pattering of the water against the dock had increased slightly.

The sailboat remained motionless. What if there was nobody aboard? Maybe they'd taken a dinghy and gone somewhere around the point or down the shore where she couldn't see.

"Hello out there!" Why didn't they wake up? Or the cabin. It was just as still. Perhaps she could manage to throw something up against a window. It wasn't likely, but there was no reason not to try.

She was looking for a stone in the only shallow water, which was just beneath the pilings, when she realized that it must be the Old Secret up there. Of course it was. Kevin McCallum had broken those steps. She went over to the boat. It was green and looked very much like the one she'd seen. The caulking, she noticed, was fresh.

"Slim," she said on a sigh. Broken stairs or not, he'd managed to get down here.

She might have gotten out of the cave, but the fact she had to face was that she was still alone with Kevin Mc-Callum . . . still just as trapped as ever. Not only that, she was exactly where she'd started from. This only appeared to be an escape, and maybe he had designed even this horrible irony, that escaping from the cave only meant coming back to where you'd started.

It was making her increasingly uneasy to stay here, because she felt that it was only a question of time, and not much time, before Kevin arrived. He probably knew two or three other ways to get out of that grotto. She searched the water. There was no telling where he might pop up.

What she needed to do was get out into the lake, get well out, before he caught up with her. It was now fairly clear that he had not swum out behind her, because she had not seen his head break the surface. So he'd come another way. One thing she could be sure of: he had not given up.

She went to the rowboat and examined the new paint and caulking. She looked over the oarlocks and oars, trying to understand how to row it. She'd probably rowed a boat as a girl at summer camp, but she couldn't remember any specific instances. You sat facing the back and pulled the oars to make it go forward. That was the trick, not to try to push.

The thing to do was get in it and get out of here and to do that right now. Four or five good pulls and she'd be too far out for even a strong swimmer to reach her.

She found the oarlocks and set them in the proper holes. The oars themselves were at the land end of the dock, leaning up against the bluff.

She moved down the dock and got them. She was coming back when she noticed the reeds behind the dock moving slightly. She looked more closely . . . and at once saw why: in among them, as motionless as a snake, was the pale glow of a human body. He was no more than two feet away, so close he could lunge out and grab her at any moment.

She almost lost consciousness, it was so frightening. How could he possibly have done this? The only answer was that there must be another exit from the cave that opened up right under these reeds. He'd come the long way around. Because he'd been able to run through galleries while she swam, he probably hadn't even arrived much after she had.

Oh, he had indeed planned this, too, he had planned it down to the last, tiny detail. She was meant to be exactly where she was, there could be no mistaking it.

For her, he had lost his humanity. He was not a human being anymore, he was a brilliant predator, some kind of lizard-creature, a stubborn, clever, and implacable alien being that would not stop until it had broken not only her body, but her soul.

Not to scream, to remain silent, to continue to seem as if she had not seen him, was probably the most difficult thing she had ever done or would ever do. It was no easier than walking into machine-gun fire or jumping off a cliff. But she did it; she strode down the dock on her long legs, with the sun shining on her beautiful face and her ravaged, stringy hair, with all the nobility and courage that was in her, and it was enough—just—to stop her from plunging into a mad panic flight straight off the end of the dock.

But she told herself, and she knew that this was absolutely true: This was her last throw. After this, if he got her, he could do absolutely anything he pleased. Helen Myrer was at the final end of herself. Beyond this there was nothing.

He had, with his usual forethought, placed himself between her and the rowboat. As she'd had to pass him in the pantry, she now had to pass him as she returned along the dock with the oars. The one small possibility that she had was that he didn't yet think she'd seen him. Maybe. Very slowly, very *easily,* she had to walk those five steps.

She took the first of them, feeling the dock shift slightly in the water. Immediately beneath it there were shallows, but two feet from its edge the water plunged off into the dark green depths from which she had emerged.

She took another step, then another. Still no movement. Of course, with Kevin, he was probably just playing with her. He was going to come out of there and shoot her or grab her and haul her back. She knew nothing about guns. For example, would one work if it had been underwater?

A third and final step got her up to the rowboat. Was it really caulked, or was that something Kevin had done? What would happen when she got in—would the caulking give way and the boat simply sink? That would be like him, another of his killer pranks.

She looked at the knot that tethered it—and saw that it was too elaborately tied. How were you supposed to get that thing loose, anyway? She knelt, felt the hard rope.

She looked inside the boat itself—and found that all she had to do was unhook a metal hasp. It was so hard to get even small things right when you were this tired and scared.

She threw the line aside and jumped in the boat. The moment she did that, he came splashing and roaring up onto the dock. He had the gun, and it was pointed right at her. "Kevin, no!"

"Bitch!"

There were tears in his voice; she heard them, they were unmistakable. They meant that he was horribly dangerous now, this man who had previously been so calm. In his rage he would treat her with unparalleled savagery. He must not have really believed that anybody could get this far. She saw him glance up at the sailboat, then saw his face go deepest crimson.

No, nobody had ever gotten this far before. He was prepared for it, of course, but he didn't like it, not at all.

"Lenny is a human being, Kevin," she said as she shoved the rowboat off with her foot. "Please let me save her."

"Fuck her!"

The boat was drifting, and Helen struggled with the oars. She saw the gun coming up, saw him aiming. Cringing, she shut her eyes, waited for the blast.

There was a roar and a splash and a snarl of rage from him. The boat floated in a slow arc as she lifted the oars into the oarlocks. There was a click, then another, and then he hurled the pistol at her. It hit her knee and made her yell, and she knew that she would not swim again, not this day.

Off across the water she heard sudden, excited voices. Kevin had just made a mistake, and maybe it was one that mattered. "Helloooo the boat!" she howled. "Help us, we need help!" She dug with the oars, went off at a diagonal. The darn thing was so hard to control! She started to circle, dug again, and went ten or fifteen feet dead straight.

"You bitch, you're supposed to be my doctor!"

"You don't need a doctor, you need a—a—priest."

She feared that there was nobody to minister to him now, not in this fractured age.

He ran right off the end of the pier and started swimming like an Olympic champion, racing toward her. Frantically she dug the oars into the water, stood on them as best she could, given the new hurt. He'd been smart to go for the knee. Kevin never stopped thinking.

She dug again, had an oar get away from her, went in a half circle, grabbed the loose oar and dug again, went another few feet. His arms hitting the water sounded like a train churning down its tracks.

Then she suddenly couldn't see the shore. What? Where—oh, look. How beautiful. How amazing. Fog soldiers had drifted up with the rising of the sun, and she was suddenly hidden in among them. They passed her, tall gray sentinels that concealed everything they touched.

The splashes stopped. He had lost her, he had lost her in the fog! As quietly as she could, she began to row away.

The fogbank couldn't be deep, because she'd been able to see that sleeping sailboat a few minutes ago. No, it was just a passing thing, it wouldn't last. She hit the water with the oars, oblivious of the splashes.

Suddenly she could hear him swimming again, coming right toward her. She cursed herself; she should have been more quiet.

With a force that vibrated the whole boat, his hand came down on the stern. She saw the pudgy fingers, saw them close into a tight, firm grip. And for a moment there was just that hand, frozen there. Then his face appeared, teeth bared, eyes staring. Even though he used only the one arm to do it, he lifted himself right out of the water.

"No, Kevin!"

"Help me, Doctor."

What could she do for him? She didn't know, she no longer thought she could do anything at all. She brought an oar up, started to swing it. But she hesitated, horrified at herself. She was going to kill if she could. She was not going to be able to stop herself.

Deep within, in her racing blood, she could feel the animal that was her core. And the thought flashed, clear and strong: He's lost, but Lenny needs help now. She turned in the direction of the open lake. "Help us!" she screamed.

On the distance a voice replied. "Where are you?"

What in the world did they mean? "Here!"

"The fog's hidden you! Keep yelling!"

The voice was so young and strong and powerful. How she longed for him to come. "Over here, over by the shore!"

"Shut up, bitch." He brought up his other arm and could have come tumbling in but instead hung on the edge of the shaking boat.

She looked down at him. Why was he waiting? His eyes met hers. She could see his lips move and with stunning, overwhelming force realized that he was not asking her to help him get out of the water or even to be cured of the evil that he had allowed to consume him.

The lips moved again, and she knew, this time, the precise meaning of the plea. Almost on its own, the oar drew back, then drew back farther. But she did not have enough leverage, not sitting down. Carefully, spreading her legs as much as possible, she rose to her feet.

"Can you hear us?" came the voice calling again.

Lenny. They meant help for Lenny, help in time. "Over here!" she screamed. "For God's sake, hurry!"

She stood among the concealing, shifting fog soldiers, swaying with the boat. He was still looking up at her, and now he looked more like a child than ever before, as if all the years and crimes had fallen away, exposing the innocence within to plain view and question. His face held the same amazement that Mikey's had in infancy, when he'd looked upon his mother for the first time. In the maternity ward she had thought that people seeing heavenly apparitions must bear such expressions.

His eyes closed. "Cooie?"

How gentle he could sound . . . and how deceptive that was. "Don't move, Kevin." Her voice was strong. "Help is coming."

Two short, sharp shakes of his head, a sudden twisting back of the lips in obvious denial and anger. Then the face flushed again, and the complex eyes grew narrow with resolution. Kevin knew what he wanted, he knew exactly.

"Don't you move, Kevin!"

He lunged toward her.

"Hurry!" she bellowed toward the boat. But she also saw that she had no choice. His hand was going to grab her leg, and when it did, he was going to pull her down.

She could now hear a small motor out on the water. They'd launched their dinghy. "Over here, over here!"

"Okay!" The voices were closer now.

"Just calm down, we're gonna be okay, Kevin."

He snarled, he grabbed for her again—and this time got his hand around her left foot. She swung the paddle, hitting him in the head with the flat of it. He went sprawling and grunting away, ending up half in and half out of the boat.

"I said *don't!*"

From the dinghy: "We're coming!"

"Hurry, for God's sake!"

He hissed like a great reptile and came literally swarming at her, slithering right up over the side of the boat, his eyes fixed on her as surely as if there were some eternal connection between them. When she met them, she knew that it was true. They were tied in a bond for which the words had not yet been invented, and it was a terrible bond.

The fog soldiers surrounded them, marching like the memories of the dead. Now he made a choked sound, hesitating half in and half out of the boat. She thought perhaps that this had been the last of his fury and that the rising sound of the dinghy's motor had drawn him to surrender. "Kevin?"

"You can't cure me."

She didn't know how to answer.

"I'm incurable and you know it!"

"I—"

"Don't lie anymore! Please, just don't lie to me!"

She remained silent. In the face of all those dead women, of Lenny in her agony, what else could she do?

He seemed to go deep within, almost as if he were gathering himself for what was to come at the very last. His hands again started moving. She clutched her oar. He was right under her now, his back fully exposed. "I warned you, Kevin. I swear, I am going to really hurt you."

Just as his right arm went toward her feet, the fog soldiers marched into oblivion, and suddenly they were in clear sun. They were surrounded by dancing bright waves beneath the blue of the morning sky. She saw on the distance, like a ghost from a settled age, the sailboat with its pale sails blowing unkempt.

The dinghy was a hundred yards out. In it were three strong young men. And she thought: They've got to get to Lenny. Whatever happens, they've got to! "There's a woman trapped in a cave," she gasped. "Hurt bad!"

"Okay, lady. You're gonna be okay."

Kevin's hand snatched at her ankle, but she pulled away.

The dinghy was so close, didn't he realize that it was all over? "I can help you," she said, and actually heard the clinician coming back.

"Liar! Liar!" Again he grabbed at her, again pulled himself farther into the boat. This time, in avoiding him, she tripped and the boat lurched, the oar nearly flying from her grasp.

She recovered herself, but only just. She cried out—short, sharp—because his fingers had come around the ankle this time and gotten a grip that was as strong as an iron shackle. If he pulled her again, she would go over.

She looked down at the black hair, blood oozing out from where the oar had last struck, and then at the wide, naked back. The hand yanked. She cried out. The dinghy came closer, its motor whining.

"Lady?"

"He's a killer! He's vicious!"

His free hand closed around her other ankle.

"Under his house," she cried. "A cave. Get the state police, there's a woman inside—deep—way back—it's huge. Oh, God, Kevin, let me go!"

"The state police are already in the cave," Kevin said. "They've been in there for an hour."

"Lenny?"

He looked as hard as granite. "She's real deep, ain't she?"

She could feel his muscles tighten, knew that in another two seconds at most he would drag her under. She turned to the dinghy. "Hurry!"

"Let her go, mister!"

"Speed that thing up, for God's sake!"

"We're trying, ma'am."

It was still fifty yards out, humming along sedately.

Then he yanked and her legs shot out from under her and he snarled. She crashed down into the boat, hitting hard because she was clinging to her oar and would not let it fall from her grasp.

"Hey, lady!" The dinghy was loud now; she could hear it slapping the water, could see the young men pulling fishing knives out of sheaths.

Kevin began to drag her. She raised the oar high, higher yet, then shut her eyes and brought it down with all the strength left in her. She hit him with its edge, which broke his back with a sickening crack and caused him to utter an anguished, surprised roar. Then his clutching fingers jerked and went limp.

She could hardly believe the effect of the blow but understood from the sudden dead weight of him that she had shattered his spine. "Help us," she wailed. "Help us!"

"Hold on!"

But she could not hold on, he was slipping from her grasp. *"Please!"* she screamed.

She could hear the dinghy's motor drop in speed, knew that they were no more than fifty feet away. But he was slipping away from her, slipping as if something unseen were dragging him down. She struggled, she fought for his limp, helpless form, but she was too weak.

His eyes connected once again with hers—touched them, caressed them—and she saw there not only the monster, but also the boy who had gotten so terribly lost, the strange little boy who had never tasted of love. "I can't move," he whispered.

She tried to hold him, but his weight was mostly out of the boat, and she could not.

He slipped into the water and was gone.

CHAPTER TWENTY

Kevin's Prayer

Kevin McCallum sank into Lake Glory and was eventually declared dead. His body was lost in the deep, rocky maze that bottoms the lake beneath the bluff where the Old Secret stands.

The state police rescued Leonore Czerny, and she and Helen spent three weeks in the same hospital room, slowly recovering from injuries, shock, and exposure.

The remains of one hundred and sixteen identifiable individuals were found in Kevin's cave, a hundred and nine women and seven men. Where possible, bodies were returned to their families.

In some cases people had been sifting the threads of hope for twenty years. In others the identities will never be known. Kevin killed many more than could be numbered.

At first Helen and Lenny were in separate rooms. During the day Helen was her old self, strong and warm for her children, who came to visit often.

At night, however, the demons would come, and she would hear Kevin's voice say odd words—"It's time" or "Cooie"—and she would lie awake in the small hours. His hands would in some sense touch her forever, his rancid smell linger in her nose, his kiss force its way down her gullet. The nights were hard.

One day when her belly was healing to dried scabs and she was feeling distinctly stronger, a tall young woman came into her room. She had a curious, pinched face and strikingly gentle eyes.

"Hiya, Doc," she said, "how's it goin'?"

"Lenny."

Lenny smiled, and when she did the gentleness spread from her eyes to fill her whole face, and she was lovely. "Yeah. I come to see ya."

They talked together, about Boston and the Fenway, about the Red Sox and the Conservatory of Music, where Lenny had been a student.

"Look," she said at last, "I got to get past this thing."

Helen nodded. "Me too."

"How?"

"I don't know. I've been thinking about the camps. Maybe we get past this the same way they did."

"What camps? I don't get it."

"Auschwitz."

Lenny's blankness amazed Helen.

"I mean, Hitler's concentration camps. People survived them. They went on."

"Okay. But I gotta be frank, I'm having trouble. My boyfriend comes, and I can't even look at the guy. I just keep thinking of being tied up and I'm wanting to get away so bad and there is no way, and I am having to watch that other girl, Gloria Besor. I watched him open up Gloria."

Suddenly they were both in tears, and from then on they became roommates and, in the long run, the closest of friends. As night would fall, they would hold hands across the distance between their beds. They told Helen's kids that they were sisters, and in every sense except blood, this was true.

About three days after they had gone in together, a young man in a very neat uniform appeared at their door. He smiled into the floral wonder of their lair; they were counted as celebrities and had even had a visit of condolence and support from the governor.

The young man brought with him a plain manila envelope, which he laid on the table between them.

"What," Lenny said.

"Open it."

Helen took it, tore it open. "Oh, I can't believe it." She had asked for it a dozen times, but until now it had been languishing in an evidence room. "Lenny, look at this."

"What is it?"

"All during my . . . time . . . he was writing in this." She held it up. "This is the key to Kevin McCallum."

"Dr. Coxley wanted you to have it. He wondered if—"

Helen knew exactly what Sam Coxley wanted. It was what the entire profession wanted. "Tell Cox that I am going to write the damnedest paper that the *Journal of Abnormal Psychology* has published in years." As well as being chief of the New Hampshire Department of Psychiatry, Sam was editor of the *Journal.*

Now that she had this document, she felt that the paper would truly break new ground.

After the young sheriff's deputy left, Helen noticed that Lenny was, once again, crying softly. Helen knew that she would never again be entirely at ease with men, that both of them would suffer posttraumatic stress syndrome for years.

"You oughta burn that bastard's crap, Doc."

"It'd feel good, I agree."

"Tell me again about killing him."

"Lenny—"

"Tell me!"

"I hit him with the cut of the oar!" She'd said it a hundred times. "He went limp because his spine was shattered."

"His spine was shattered. . . ."

"He sank into the lake."

"And he got back in the cave!"

Helen went to her, leaned down, and embraced her. "He's dead, Lenny, *dead!*" Mother now also to this lost girl, she kissed Lenny's tears.

"Oh, Helen. Helen, man, I wish I could get right about that."

Helen threw open the diary—and there on the first page was an astonishment—a blessing from the hand of an evil man. She read it, read it again. The words blew through her mind like a gentle breeze of memory, and she glimpsed then the greatness that was in this, that was the greatness of human suffering.

"Len, I think you ought to hear this."

"I don't want to hear his crap."

"This isn't crap. This is the man. The mystery of the man."

"What mystery, Helen? I tell you and tell you—the guy was having fuckin' guy fun! That is *all!*"

Helen sat up on the side of her bed. Momentarily there was weakness, a little vertigo, but then she recovered. Day after tomorrow she would check out.

"Human suffering is always a mystery, Lenny."

"Yeah? Then the world's a mysterious place."

"It is mysterious. Listen to this." She read.

My Prayer
by
Kevin McCallum

My cave, O God, your gift thank you.

I remember each one you give me as a delicate meat.

I am become as Job my heart is so sore.

Lift my burden God.

This is My Prayer.

His voice was so clear, its pain so evident, and its deep indifference to the welfare of his victims so appalling that the two of them were rendered silent for a long time.

Evening fell, night came, and a sickle of moon climbed the purple sky beyond their window. They both felt, for the first time, that Kevin was truly gone, that all that remained of him was in their memories and in the sad green binder that stank of cigarettes.

Kevin was dead. But his spirit lives on.

ABOUT THE AUTHOR

Anne McLean Matthews has a master's degree in education with minors in psychology and English literature. She worked for many years as a freelance editor specializing in mysteries and thrillers. She is married, lives in Texas, and has one grown son.